Her Majesty's League of Remarkable Young Ladies

A MESSAGE FROM CHICKEN HOUSE

Winner of the *Times*/Chicken House and Institute of Engineering and Technology Prize, this exciting story is much more than a glorious adventure through a Victorian world of villains, plots and spies; it's full of spectacular gadgets and inventions sure to make the mind boggle! Our heroines must overcome deep prejudices to protect the realm from harm – using skill, science and bravery! Alison D. Stegert is a simply cracking storyteller who weaves real history into her daring tale.

BARRY CUNNINGHAM
Publisher
Chicken House

For Paul

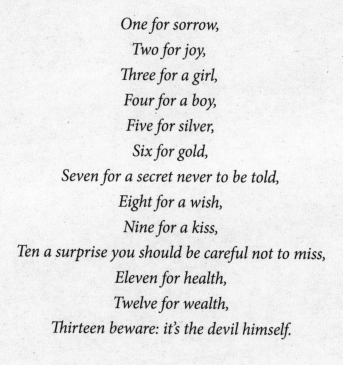

One for sorrow,
Two for joy,
Three for a girl,
Four for a boy,
Five for silver,
Six for gold,
Seven for a secret never to be told,
Eight for a wish,
Nine for a kiss,
Ten a surprise you should be careful not to miss,
Eleven for health,
Twelve for wealth,
Thirteen beware: it's the devil himself.

– TRADITIONAL RHYME ABOUT MAGPIES –

~Stafford House, St James's~

21 March 1889

Queen Victoria sat at the head of a dining table laden with rich food. To her right was her daughter-in-law, the elegant Alix Princess of Wales, and to her left was Bertie the Prince of Wales, her middle-aged son. The occasion was Bertie and Alix's twenty-sixth wedding anniversary – and the long table was filled with guests from the upper echelons of British society.

Prince Bertie sipped from his wine goblet before turning to flirt with the radiant actress seated to his left. The woman's peals of laughter rose above the din of chatter.

The Queen twitched at her son's casual behaviour.

But, as always, she had to endure. At least now there was dessert to look forward to. She readied her spoon.

As if on cue, a swarm of servants descended, bearing trays of sweets – puddings, ices, flans, sugared fruit and wobbling jelly towers. Two sweating footmen deposited an enormous platter covered with a swan-shaped silver dome in front of the Queen. The butler bowed. 'If it pleases Her Majesty, *Bavarois Surprise au Chocolat*.'

Her favourite!

The butler lifted the enormous silver lid with a flourish. His eyes boggled, and he let out a squeak of dismay. He fumbled the cloche, dropping it on the floor with a *BONG!* that echoed around the dining hall.

The chatter hushed, and thirty-nine faces turned towards the offending dessert.

The pudding was a glistening castle-shaped jelly, around which lay a circle of dead birds with open beaks and lifeless eyes. Their wings overlapped in a clever pattern of the black, blue and white feathers, three facing one direction, three the other, and in the middle the seventh bird lay on its back, feet sticking up and trussed with red floss. Perched on its tiny talons was a calling card. The Prince of Wales snatched it, setting the chocolate castle aquiver.

Compliments of
Mr Magpie

CHAPTER 1

~BEACON ACADEMY FOR POISED &
POLISHED YOUNG LADIES~

140 Gower Street, Bloomsbury, London
Early Friday afternoon, 22 March 1889

The door to the attic room flew open with a bang, sending Winifred's notes swirling in the draught. Miss Adelaide Culpepper slipped inside and closed the door. 'Winifred, we have a problem.'

Winnie held her focus on the tiny brass gear she was drilling. 'One moment, if you please. This is the smallest gear for my improved mechanical slingshot. After this final adjustment, I can assemble it and test it . . .'

'This is urgent.' Adelaide wrung her hands. 'We have a visitor – that is to say, *you* have a visitor.'

With a pointed sigh, Winnie looked up. Oh, no! Adelaide's lips were pressed together in a slight frown; her long neck strained inside the lace of her high collar. How odd to see such an outstanding older pupil of the Beacon Academy for Poised & Polished Young Ladies in an unseemly State of

Agitation. Although only seventeen, Adelaide had mastered the lady's art of Always Maintaining Calm.

More impressively (at least to Winnie, who was fourteen and rarely calm), Adelaide was brilliant at mathematics, logic and stenography, not to mention fencing, croquet, archery and tennis. (She also secretly rode a safety bicycle around London – in disguise, of course – a feat so daring Winnie was made to promise on her mother's grave she'd never mention it.)

Adelaide hissed, '*Sir Phillip* has paid a visit.'

'Sir who?'

Adelaide pulled at her collar. 'Sir Phillip Runcliffe-Bowen, the secretariat of the British World Fair Selection Committee. He wishes to speak with "Master Freddy".' Her eyes widened.

Winnie dropped her precious tools, a tiny brass gear pinging into the air. 'Good golly! It must be news about my Petit Prix application.'

Winning the Petit Prix for Young Inventors at the 1889 Paris World Fair was nothing less than Winnie's most ardent dream. And it was barely two months away. She tugged at her plaits nervously.

Adelaide twined her fingertips together. 'Even if it's good news, his timing is dreadful: Headmistress will return from her visits within the hour.'

Winnie stood, her full skirt knocking over her chair.

'I need a disguise – quickly! Help me transform from a Winifred into a Fred! Where are those boy's knicker-bockers and cap you wear while cycling?' Winnie pulled open the top drawer of Adelaide's dresser.

Adelaide shoved the drawer closed. 'If you don't mind, Winifred! That's my drawer of . . . *unmentionables*! And my knickerbockers are supposed to be a secret! Besides, there's no time to dress up. Sir Phillip is waiting in the parlour, hat in hand.'

Winnie smoothed the wrinkles in the sailor-style yoke of her Beacon Academy uniform. 'Whose brilliant idea was it to enter the Petit Prix as a boy?'

Adelaide let out a bitter snort. 'As if there's any other choice! And it was your idea, as you know full well. I merely forged your father's signature for you.'

Winnie growled. 'It's unfair and completely irrational that girls are not permitted to enter.'

'Save that familiar tune for another time. Right now, we need a plan.' Adelaide dabbed her brow with a lacy handkerchief.

'I know!' Winnie raced to the door. 'My darling brother Freddy is poorly with mumps – or dropsy. No, it must be a vile illness – like consumption!' She pushed Adelaide towards the door. 'Please inform Sir Phillip of Freddy's dire illness. Say he's in his sickbed, but his deeply devoted sister will leave his side to discuss the application on Master Freddy's behalf.' Winnie scooped up an armful of blueprints from the worktable. 'I'll show him my designs – er, *Freddy's* designs . . . Would you carry the prototype?'

'Cholera! Gracious heavens! Your poor dear brother!' Sir Phillip thundered. 'Miss Weatherby, perhaps it would be best to withdraw Master Freddy's entry until, er, next year – assuming he . . .' Sir Phillip, a wiry, upright man, grimaced and adjusted his cravat. His pale eye darted behind his tortoiseshell monocle.

Winnie batted her hand. 'Oh, please! Freddy is as tough as an India rubber ball! I've no doubt he'll be out of bed by week's end. Meanwhile, he begged me to demonstrate my – *his* – invention to you.'

Sir Phillip waved his hand dismissively. 'No need, my dear. I've read his entry. While the idea has a certain charm—'

'Thank you, sir!' Winnie beamed and rocked on her heels. 'I will be sure to pass on your compliment. The Boot-Button Butler will make buttonhooks a thing of the past! While an antiquated buttonhook fastens one button at a time, my – *his* – invention makes it possible to button up to ten boot buttons at once!' She strummed her fingers across the ten copper hooks inside her invention, which in its previous incarnation had been a humble kitchen whisk.

Sir Phillip blinked, stroking the left side of his forked beard. 'Despite its decidedly feminine application, it brings to mind a bear trap. And what if one's boot has more than ten buttons?'

'An excellent question! I toyed with increasing the number of hooks, but each one adds weight, making the device cumbersome. Ten hooks achieve the perfect ratio of efficiency and weight.' She cleared her throat. *Besides, a kitchen whisk consists of only so much wire . . .* 'I'd be delighted to demonstrate.'

Winnie wasn't wearing boots – so instead, she darted to the French doors. 'Adelaide, might I borrow your ankles?'

She gasped. 'Miss Weatherby! I couldn't – it wouldn't be proper.'

Winnie scowled at Adelaide, who was shaking her head violently. This was no time for extreme modesty. Was a stockinged ankle such an unseemly bit of anatomy?

The older pupil pointed to the clock in the hall. Five minutes to the hour. Adelaide made a hurry-up gesture and pushed the French doors shut.

'Er, Sir Phillip, seeing as I cannot find an available pair of feet, an inspection of . . . Freddy's mechanical drawings will have to do. They're here somewhere among these papers . . .' As Winnie flicked through the designs and drawings stacked on the tea table, the entire pile avalanched on to the floor.

Sir Phillip stooped to help her collect them, casting a glance over each blueprint. 'My heavens! Your brother's drawing skills are exceptional for one so young!' He adjusted his tortoiseshell-rimmed monocle.

Recovering from the unexpected compliment, Winnie located the correct blueprint. '*Voilà!* Sir Phillip, I present the—'

Adelaide pushed her head around the parlour door – behind Sir Phillip – and mouthed, 'She's back.'

Ah – the formidable Headmistress Thornton was in the building.

Winnie rolled up her drawing. 'Oh, dear, I believe I heard Freddy cry out! Well, Sir Phillip, it's been lovely meeting you – on Freddy's behalf. I hope you don't mind. I'll escort you out through the kitchen.' She turned him towards the servants' door at the side of the parlour.

Sir Phillip didn't budge. 'Egad! This design is phenomenal! Have you got a prototype of *this* invention?'

Winnie caught sight of the blueprints he'd picked up and gulped. Blast! Mixed up in her invention designs were Papa's top-secret plans for the A.A. Weatherby (& Daughter) Telautograph Machine. The previous Sunday while visiting her father, she'd decided boldness was required, so she'd smuggled the plans out of her father's laboratory to copy and add her *refinements* during the week.

To her horror, Sir Phillip had already spread the blue-print across the tea table and read the design description written in Winnie's neatest script:

The Weatherby Telautograph Machine –
WA-model sends facsimiles of signatures and
handwritten notes over telegraph wires.

'Why this is sheer genius! Can this also be your brother's work? How old did you say he is?'

'I'm sorry – this invention isn't ready for public scrutiny yet.' She snatched the design and hastily rolled it up.

'Miss Weatherby, I insist! Master Freddy must enter that invention. Forget boot buttons and the piddly Petit Prix for Young Inventors. The Telautograph could win the Grand Prix!'

Behind them, the French doors swung open. Head-mistress Thornton strode in.

'Miss Culpepper, fetch my shawl, if you'd be so kind. I'm chilled to the . . .' She stopped. 'Oh, I beg your pardon. I wasn't aware we had callers.'

'Madam,' Sir Phillip said, bowing. 'Allow me to intro-duce myself. I am Phillip Runcliffe-Bowen, the secretariat of the British World Fair Selection Committee.'

Headmistress cocked her head. 'Sir Phillip, I'm delighted. Lady Jenny and I are acquainted, but I've never had the pleasure of meeting you.' Her voice flattened. She narrowed her eyes at Winifred. 'I see you've met one of my more challenging pupils.'

'My sincere apologies, madam. I am most aggrieved you didn't receive the letter I'd sent ahead, informing you of today's visit. I've come on World Fair business to speak with young Master Fred—'

Winnie spluttered a cough and grabbed the gentleman's elbow. 'Sir Phillip was just leaving. Sir, your hat. If I may . . .'

'Winifred Weatherby, unhand my guest!' Headmistress Thornton smiled at Sir Phillip. 'You simply must tell me how Lady Jenny and your daughters are. I hope you have time for tea?' She gestured to the settee.

Sir Phillip bowed again. 'Why, thank you, madam. Unfortunately, I have another engagement; otherwise, I'd be delighted, for I am keen to examine the designs Miss Weatherby is coyly holding behind her back. Freddy Weatherby's invention is the most promising and lucrative I've seen in years! And I've seen plenty, as you can imagine.'

'*Freddy* Weatherby's?' Headmistress Thornton raised a thin eyebrow, and Winifred squirmed. 'Well, Sir Phillip, I'll see you out. And I'm sure Miss Weatherby will tell me all about her *brother's* ingenious designs in my office, where she can await my return . . .'

CHAPTER 2

Later that Friday afternoon

Alone in Adelaide's attic bedroom after a disastrous meeting in the Academy's office, Winnie shut the door and shook off the residue of Headmistress's fury. Of all her encounters with that woman, today's had been the worst. Accusations, insults and complaints rang in Winnie's ears. But there was no time to lose. At this very moment, Headmistress Thornton was seated at her desk, scratching out a scathing letter to Papa detailing all of Winnie's indiscretions and faults. Winnie had to act quickly if she was going to beat the evening post.

She grinned: the prize was in the bag, for she had a mechanical advantage Headmistress couldn't even imagine: an operational Weatherby Telautograph Machine.

She rubbed her palms together and dropped to her knees.

Late afternoon sunlight streamed

through the dormer window, stretching golden light across the built-in window seat and on to the polished floorboards. As she knelt in the warm parallelogram of sunlight, Winnie's hand fell to her waistband where a silver brooch was pinned. It was her mother's chatelaine, a traditional lady's accessory consisting of a fancy clasp from which hung sturdy chains and tools called equipages. She spread the chains over her lap; there was a silver bottle holding smelling salts, a coin purse, a tinder-box, a pair of scissors and a tiny silver notebook.

But Winnie (being Winnie) had tinkered with them, making several of the equipages more useful for her work. To the purse, she'd added secret compartments for holding bits of India rubber and tiny screws and bolts. She'd adapted the handle of the miniature magnifying glass into a pea whistle and added Stanhope lenses which held miniature images of her designs. The buttonhook doubled as a drawing compass and, when combined with the magnifying glass, converted into a slingshot. The silver notebook hid tweezers and a tiny key. She called it her Multi-Device Interchangeable Utility Chatelaine (patent pending).

She opened the notebook and picked out the key, no bigger than the hour hand on a pocket watch. '*Voilà!*' Winnie scooted forward to the base of the window seat. She poked the key into an almost invisible keyhole on the front wooden panel. The lock pinged, and she slid the front panel aside, revealing a secret cupboard she'd created.

Hidden in the low steamer-trunk-sized niche was a Weatherby Telautograph Machine – WA-model. WA were her initials, for *Winifred Alice*. It was similar to Papa's telautograph machine, but thanks to her unsanctioned tinkering, the WA-model combined both transmitter and receiver into one unit, effectively creating one superior device. And she'd made it lighter by replacing some heavy cast-iron parts with copper. (Jelly moulds borrowed from the larder made splendid covers for the wiring, even if their castle shapes were rather unconventional.)

The Telautograph – the handwriting transmitter detailed in the blueprints Sir Phillip had admired – was her father's most brilliant and important invention yet. It had the potential to transform not only the everyday interactions of people around the world but also to vastly improve the fortunes of Professor A.A. Weatherby & Daughter. The machine connected to telegraph wires, but rather than sending the basic Morse code of telegraphy, this beautiful invention sent electrical impulses that formed facsimiles – identical replicas – of the sender's handwriting, signature and even drawings. She could write a letter on the machine here in Bloomsbury, and at the other end of their private telegraph line that ran across London to Chelsea, the receiving machine in her father's laboratory would write an exact copy in the twinkle of an eye! No need for postage stamps or postmen or half a day's wait for delivery.

'Private, silent and quick as a wink,' as Professor Weatherby liked to inform potential investors.

A warm bubble of pride swelled in her chest. She'd helped her father develop the invention from concept to contrivance. And then she'd gone on to refine it further, so far unbeknown to Papa . . .

At her insistence, Professor Weatherby had covertly installed a seven-mile-long private telegraph wire between his laboratory and the Beacon Academy so she could continue to assist him. He'd used the WTM (Weatherby Telautograph Machine) to send Winifred odd jobs – small calculation work and estimates – when he was working on more important (and interesting) projects. However, she'd made the unfortunate mistake of using it to send him a twenty-three-point List of Complaints about the Beacon Academy for Poised & Polished Young Ladies. It raised many valid matters, including:

1. The Academy's frothy training, which resulted not in Poised Young Ladies but rather in silly girls who giggle and weep and mince about in high heels.

2. Dubious – TEDIOUS – subjects of study. Not logic, natural history and mathematics, but *alighting from a carriage with modesty and grace.*

3. The Academy's persistent odour of boiled meat.

4. Et cetera . . .

Why Papa had found this list so bothersome, Winnie could not understand. It was *truth*, plainly stated. Nevertheless, he had since forbidden her to use the Telautograph for 'petty, personal matters'.

Today's crisis *was* personal, but it was far from *petty*. Winifred rolled out the heavy machine on its casters and checked the connections were secure. She shifted the stiff function lever (formerly the bone handle of a butter knife) to 'transmit' and smoothed the paper on the writing surface. She activated the machine by removing the pencil that was wired to the device from its holder. She began writing in neat, smooth handwriting:

Friday afternoon

My dearest Papa,
I apologize at the outset for using the wire for personal matters; however, this is urgent. My explanation must reach you before Headmistress Thornton's letter, which is coming in this evening's post.
I beg you to disregard <u>her unfair accusations</u>. I am not incorrigible, nor am I wayward, and I am most certainly not impossible.

While there is an element of truth in Head-mistress's claim that I've been 'conducting business', I assure you it's not 'unladylike' in nature.

Headmistress has unjustly withdrawn my weekend leave, which means I shan't be able to join you for our customary Sunday dinner.

The inconvenience I know this will cause you is HER doing. I was looking forward to studying your revisions to the patent application.

Winnie stopped. Sunday was when she'd intended to return Papa's plans along with her improved plans for the WA-model, but now she'd have no opportunity. What a spot of bother.

Should she admit to removing Papa's plans from the laboratory? She twisted a braid nervously. No. He'd already be displeased with the prospect of another report of her 'unseemly conduct'. She lowered the pencil to the paper and continued writing.

I promise to apply my utmost to the business of becoming a Poised and Polished Young Lady.

Until that 'happy' day, I remain,

Your loving daughter,
Winifred

She pressed the pencil into its holster, ending the transmission. That was that – her words in her handwriting were pulsing down the wire towards her father's desk. In a matter of moments, the pen on his receiving machine would begin its ghostly dance across the page. A bell would ring twice, alerting Papa of the completed transmission.

He'd be irritated at the intrusion of 'feminine woes'. The timing was so poor! Papa would already be in a lather about completing his patent application, and this report would only reignite his worries about her 'ruining her future prospects', which to him only meant offloading her to a respectable husband.

Winnie scowled. There'd be no boring home and demanding husband for her! A sturdy drafting table, a well-equipped laboratory and an endless supply of exciting projects were all she needed for happiness.

But Papa wouldn't hear of her engineering dreams. 'Your mother, God rest her soul, wanted you to experience the supreme happiness she enjoyed as a homemaker, wife and mother. I owe it to my beloved Alice's memory to see you married and secure.' The mention of Mama's name always signalled the end of the discussion.

Winnie glanced above the desk Adelaide had graciously allowed her to use. Pinned to the wall were newspaper clippings. Next to the image of her hero, the

American inventor Mr Thomas Edison, was another:

Exposition Universelle, 5 May 1889, Paris.

It included an etching of Monsieur Eiffel's controversial new iron tower, a symbol of modernity, innovation and engineering, and she loved it.

If only she could enter the Petit Prix at the Paris World Fair! A win on an international stage would force Papa to see her potential as an inventress in her own right. But first, he would have to forgive her for today's *slight* misdemeanour . . .

She shifted the Telautograph's function lever to 'receive' and sat down in the shrinking patch of sunlight to wait for Papa's reply. 'Please don't be cross!'

CHAPTER 3

~The Beacon Academy~

The following week

Monday morning,
25 March 1889

My dearest Papa,
I hope you're well and not too sad about missing our customary Sunday dinner together. Did you receive Friday's telautogram? I trust your work on the patent application is coming together to your satisfaction. I look forward to seeing how you've progressed when next we meet.

With apologies for using the wire for personal matters,

Your loving daughter,
Winifred

Tuesday afternoon,
26 March 1889

My dearest Papa,
I do wish you would reply! Five long days have passed since my first telautogram. I expect you have received correspondence from the Hateful Hag by now! Please, do not listen to her. I can explain everything.

I'm sending this letter in the post in case there is a malfunction with the WTM or the telegraph wire.

I beg you – please reply; your silence is worse than a rebuke.

I remain,

Your loving, worried daughter,
Winifred

Wednesday morning,
27 March 1889

My dearest Papa,
My nerves are on edge! I'm sending this letter by post to comply with your wishes, but the urge to disobey is almost overwhelming! The wire, as you

know, is far more immediate and convenient.

I imagine by now you are frantically searching the house for the WTM plans. You mustn't worry.

Papa, I have a confession: I removed the WTM design plans from your laboratory. I now understand this was a terrible mistake, and I'm so very, very sorry to have disobeyed. I'd only wished to help you by finessing their presentation . . .

When we next meet, I can explain fully. For now, please be assured your plans are safe with me at the Academy. I would have brought them home with me on Sunday, but a certain headmistress prevented my visiting you.

I plan to beg her for permission to bring the plans to you later today so I can apologize in person, and you can complete your patent application.

Please, Papa, forgive your naughty daughter. I mean well, but it is as you rightly say: I am not only young and foolish; I am also a silly girl (who would be ever so grateful for a quick response from you by post or wire).

I remain,

Your tearfully remorseful, loving daughter,
Winifred

CHAPTER 4

Wednesday morning, 27 March 1889

Winnie tramped down the stairs, bracing herself for her next encounter with the headmistress. She had carefully avoided her since last Friday's incident with Sir Phillip, but there was no way around her today: Winnie had been summoned.

It was good timing: she needed permission to visit Papa, since he *still* hadn't responded to her letters. Near the foot of the stairs stood a sideboard with a looking glass over it. She checked her reflection, tucking stray hair behind her ears and tidying her plaits. She lifted her chin and tried on a genteel smile.

It didn't suit her impatient mood. She crossed her eyes. Behind her, a closet door swung open. Startled, Winnie sucked in a quick breath. How strange: an unfamiliar girl stepped out!

The girl squeaked, clutching her

chest. 'Oh! I beg your pardon. I was just . . .' She quickly closed the door, locked it, and pocketed the long key.

But Winnie had glimpsed inside. It wasn't a closet at all, but rather a staircase, narrow and winding. How odd that she'd never seen it before – and who was this girl? Perhaps she was one of the so-called Premier Pupils, mythological creatures who, according to Academy lore, inhabited the forbidden top floor of the building?

Winnie, realizing she was staring, dipped her head and averted her gaze. The girl's fashionable pale-blue-and-cream ensemble was striking. Marvelling at her delicate features, Winnie wondered if her parents were perhaps Chinese. Her silky, jet-black hair set the dress off to perfection. She gestured to the office across the foyer. 'Madam will see you now.' Her speech clearly revealed her as someone who'd attended London's finest schools from a very young age.

With another glance at the door to the mysterious staircase, Winnie nodded her thanks and entered the cheerless room. As always, no fire warmed the chill, no ornaments adorned the surfaces. Cold early spring light streamed through the windows.

Headmistress Thornton stood at the tall window, watching people on the street. Voices from classrooms filtered through the narrow building the Academy occupied, a neat, four-storey brick edifice with a black door, a polished brass knocker and gleaming bevelled windows. The sharp scents of beeswax and floor polish competed against the lingering odour of boiled cabbage.

Winnie coughed softly.

Headmistress Thornton stiffened without turning from the window. 'Have you not learnt a more ladylike way of announcing yourself while you've been at the Academy?'

When the headmistress turned, Winnie dipped her head. 'Beg your pardon, madam.'

She gave Winnie a cursory once-over. Disapproval trembled on her upper lip.

Winnie braced herself for the criticism du jour. Would it be the crookedness of her hair parting? Perhaps another reprimand for 'sloppy posture'? Or maybe Headmistress Thornton would return to her favourite nitpick: the pencil smudges that covered Winnie's fingers and often ended up on her brow. She tucked her hands behind her back, just in case. 'I wish to visit my father,' Winnie announced. 'I'm concerned for his welfare. You see, he hasn't replied to any of my letters, which is . . . troubling.'

Headmistress narrowed her gaze. 'Miss Weatherby—'

Oh, no – she couldn't refuse. Winnie stepped forward, twisting her hands. 'Madam, please. I know now I behaved unbecomingly on Friday, but I made a vow to do better.' Winnie raised her chin, smiled, and exuded charm and poise – anything to win this request. 'Please, I just sense that something's not right with Papa.' She gripped a plait for comfort.

Headmistress Thornton glided to her desk and sat magisterially on the chair. 'Miss Weatherby, all of this is beside the point. I've received an official letter that concerns you.' Her gaze dropped to an opened envelope. 'Unfortunate news, I'm afraid.'

Winnie's brow wrinkled. *Official? Unfortunate?* She drew in a breath through her nose.

'More accurately, it concerns your father. It appears you're quite right to worry: Professor Weatherby is missing. The housekeeper, Mrs Pugh, hasn't seen him since Saturday morning. She told London police the meals he ordered to take in his laboratory have not been eaten for the past three days.'

Winnie batted her hand. 'Oh, that's nothing out of the ordinary. When my father is preoccupied, he eats very little.'

Headmistress Thornton folded her hands. 'Professor Weatherby's bed was not slept in last night. Nor the previous two nights.'

Winnie opened her mouth. Then she closed it. Papa also had periods during which he slept very little, but they were when he was excited by a new project.

Headmistress Thornton smoothed the creases in the letter. 'There's more. According to this dossier and the newspapers, Professor Weatherby's disappearance is thought to be linked to various charges of financial misconduct. The police suspect he's avoiding questioning about patent violations, business malpractice and general skulduggery towards fellow inventors.'

Winnie frowned. So, Papa was in some kind of legal trouble – this was worrying, but at least he wasn't angry about her behaviour.

'I'll have to visit Papa's lawyer on his behalf. Thank you for passing on this news. If you'll excuse me, Head-mistress.' She turned towards the door.

'Miss Weatherby,' the headmistress said, 'I strongly advise against leaving the Academy.'

Winnie stopped in her tracks. 'My father is missing, and you expect me to do *nothing*?'

'I expect you to wait as you have been instructed.' Headmistress Thornton glared. 'This is more serious than you realize. A detective, a DI Jerome Walker, came here to interview you, which I forbade. I suspect the police will be on your tail as soon as you leave this building.'

The headmistress slapped a copy of the day's news-paper down in front of Winnie.

THE LONDON EVENING NEWS
'Mr Magpie' Strikes Again: HRH Prince of Wales's Anniversary Dinner Sabotaged

Winnie threw up her hands. 'I cannot imagine what the future monarch and a magpie have to do with my papa.'

Headmistress Thornton rolled her eyes. 'Not the headline, silly child! There.' She pointed at a small paragraph ending with 'cont'd on page 3' at the bottom of the page. 'This article lays out the whole sordid affair of how your father has cheated other inventors.'

Winnie sniffed at the halfpenny newspaper. Everyone knew the *Evening News* was filled with gossip and tripe. Papa would *never* cheat. She pushed the paper away. 'The gossip is unfortunate – and thank you for your advice – but my father is in trouble and requires my help. I bid you good day, Headmistress.' Winnie spun on her heel and strode towards the door.

Quick as a wink, the headmistress inserted herself between Winnie and door, laying her hand over Winnie's on the latch. 'Stop at once. I forbid you to leave the Academy.'

'I'd like to see you stop me.' Winnie shook her hand free.

'Never in all my years have I encountered such impudence in a girl.'

Winnie barked a laugh. 'You've seen nothing yet. Good day.'

'You cannot leave,' the headmistress said. Winnie

registered a surprising edge of desperation to her voice. 'E-everything you're wearing is property of the Beacon Academy.'

'I beg your pardon, madam!' Winnie said, outraged. Her father had bought the uniform!

'You may not wear the Beacon Academy uniform outside this building. I won't have you dragging its good reputation through the mud.'

'Are you serious? My father is missing, and you're concerned about the Academy's reputation?'

'Step out of that door with one thread of Beacon Academy property, and I shall immediately report the theft to the police!'

Winnie gasped. *The cold-hearted gall.*

Headmistress's voice softened slightly. 'Miss Weatherby, trust me. It's for your own good.'

Winnie's shoulders trembled with rage. 'Aarrgh!' She stormed out of the room, slamming the door and stomping up the stairs.

CHAPTER 5

Wednesday, mid-morning

W innie frowned at her frumpy reflection in Adelaide's looking glass. Her day gown from last year had become unfashionably short and uncomfortably tight across her chest, but she wouldn't let attire stop her departure. Headmistress could keep her silly Academy uniform, now strewn across Adelaide's bed. Winnie glanced at it wistfully.

Never mind. She had to find Papa.

No further telautograms had arrived. It had been silly to check now she knew he was missing. 'Where are you, Papa?' She rolled the hefty machine back into its hidey-hole and then carefully inserted the rolled-up scroll of papers and blueprints. It included all her designs and Papa's plans.

The door latch scratched behind her.

Winnie jumped to her feet and spun

around. As it creaked open, Winnie used her foot to close the door of her secret niche. Her hand fell instinctively to her chatelaine. She'd have to lock it later.

Adelaide, untying her bonnet, gave a start. 'Oh, goodness, Winifred! I wasn't expecting you. How different you appear without your uniform. Much younger! Why are you dressed like that?'

Bother, Winnie thought with a yank of one of her plaits. Seeming older would be much more expedient. 'I beg your pardon, Adelaide. I was just going. Actually, I'm *going*-going, and I'm not certain I'll see you again.' Winnie's throat constricted. Good golly – this was no time for tears!

Adelaide's brows shot up. 'What?' She grasped Winnie's hand and guided her to the bedside. 'Sit down. Tell me everything. What's happened?'

Winnie heaved a sigh. 'Father is missing! And the newspapers are spreading the most *dreadful* lies about him. I have to find him and clear his name, but Headmistress has forbidden me to leave the building in uniform, so I had to change. It's all ghastly and—' Words stopped. Winnie choked back sobs.

'Good heavens! This is most distressing!'

Winnie nodded mutely, dabbing at tears and hiccupping.

The older student patted Winnie's hands. 'Where will you go?'

Winnie breathed deeply, pulling herself together. 'I shall stay at home with the housekeeper. Together we'll figure out what's happened to my father.' What a relief it was to have some clarity – and all from the warm support of a friend. 'Thank you, Adelaide. Until you arrived, I feared I was making a mistake.'

She patted Winnie's knee. 'Not at all. Your mind is clearly made up – so go, and please keep me informed of any news.'

'You've been a good friend, first to allow me to use your room and desk for my inventing, and now this. I can never repay you for your kindness.'

Adelaide batted her hand. 'How you embarrass me! My dear Winnie, you are gifted and absolutely deserving of wonderful opportunities. It has been my pleasure to make room for your dreams to develop.' She squeezed Winnie's hands between hers.

Winnie returned the squeeze. 'In any event, I'm glad I got to see you. I was afraid you'd moved on. You see, there was a new girl assisting Headmistress today – and did you know that locked door in the foyer leads to a staircase?'

Adelaide's brows rose. She looked as if she were going to say something, but she only shrugged.

Winnie stood and put on her hat. How she hated her unfashionable dress and especially the shoes she'd outgrown. 'I'm sorry to rush off, but I'm ever so worried about Papa.'

'Of course.' Adelaide rose, slender and swanlike. 'Winifred, I'm grateful to you for not mentioning my part in the incident with Sir Phillip. If I'd lost my position here, I don't know where I'd go. Since my aunt's death, I've had so much financial strain—'

Winnie stopped her. 'Shh . . . No, please don't thank me. It was all my fault . . . as usual.' She walked to the door. 'Good day, Adelaide.'

Outside, a hansom cab pulled by an unusually smart-looking horse sat on the other side of the street. She hailed the driver. 'I say! Are you available?'

The driver nodded. As she stepped down to the pavement, she felt vulnerable and decidedly unpolished without the Academy's uniform. Well, never mind. She'd soon become accustomed. But the shoes! How they pinched.

The cabman opened the door panels and Winnie told him her address.

She slid on to the seat of the hansom cab, squeezing the skinny purse on her chatelaine. She hadn't required much in the way of money for the past year. She'd consult with the cab driver about the cost once the Academy was out of sight. A movement at the tall window on the left side of the building caught her eye. The curtains moved. There stood her nemesis, Headmistress Thornton, stony-hearted and prim, watching her departure.

Winnie raised her chin and attempted a carefree expression. She mustn't give the woman the satisfaction of witnessing her distress.

She ran her eye up to the dormer window on the top floor – Adelaide's garret bedroom where she'd hidden the official plans and Papa's invention. Leaving them behind was a precaution she'd probably regret, but she had a bad feeling about her father's current situation. Never mind – she'd have to slip back and collect them as soon as she found Papa.

When the Academy had disappeared behind them, Winnie let out her breath. It rasped around the edges, threatening to turn into a sob. Her stomach lurched. The cab rounded a corner so swiftly it threw her into the opposite side of the vehicle. 'Good golly, what's the rush?' Another sudden turn flung her in the opposite direction.

The rattling of the wheels quickened. Winnie braced herself with her free arm and both feet. 'I beg your pardon! Please slow down!' she yelled over the clatter. She made a feeble rap on the trapdoor to the driver in his post outside at the back. Another sharp left threw her to the right.

What on earth? Such speed was unnecessary. The driver must be a drunk, or mad, or – an escaped prisoner!

She swivelled to open the trapdoor. 'Sir, I beg you; pull over at once.'

It snapped shut.

'Well!' The nerve! She gave the trapdoor an unladylike clonk.

No response.

A surge of fear raced up her spine: she was being abducted.

The women of London had all been terrified since Jack the Ripper's murder spree a few months earlier. Those dark weeks had sparked the idea for an invention Winnie called the Ladies' Personal Security Device, a whistle which sounded like a woman's scream – only much louder.

Another sharp turn, through a gate, into a shaded courtyard, and on into a carriage house. The doors swung closed, enveloping the cab in darkness. The driver alighted, bouncing the carriage.

'Sir! I am appalled at your driving. I demand to know where you've taken me.' She waited for him to open the cab doors. Instead, his footsteps retreated. 'I say! You can't leave without an explanation!' Winnie fumbled in the dark, feeling along the doors of the cab, searching for the latch. She yanked it.

Locked! Her ears rang. Why? What on earth!

She kicked and pounded, heart thundering. 'Help me!

Someone!' She fumbled to find the pea whistle on her chatelaine. It wasn't as shrill as her Ladies' Personal Security Device, but it could make enough noise to draw the attention of a passer-by.

The driver's burly form emerged from the shadows. The cab's door panels squeaked open. 'My apologies for the bumpy ride, miss. If you'll come this way, Mrs Campbell will see you.' He held out a hand to her.

'I most certainly will not go with you, because you, sir, are exceedingly uncivilized. And furthermore, I know no one by the name of Campbell.'

The driver cleared his throat. 'No one here wishes to harm you, miss. If you please . . .' He bowed and stepped back.

Winnie's legs quaked. What if he was a cutthroat like—

'Miss Weatherby, I assure you, you are safe with me.' It was a woman's voice, crisp with a refinement that was far superior to the elocution of even Headmistress Thornton.

Winnie turned in the dim light of the carriage house, searching until she found its source. It came from inside an elegant clarence carriage that gleamed with polished brass fixtures and was pulled by a silver gelding. 'How do you know my name?'

'Please,' the woman entreated, leaning from within the carriage. Shadows and a mourning veil hid her face. 'Allow me to explain.'

A commotion outside the closed carriage house arose: a clattering of a cart, angry voices, the whinny of a horse and the barking of dogs. Finally, a strange horn blared.

'Oh, dear, it appears your pursuer has caught up. We must hurry.' Mrs Campbell snapped her fingers twice. 'Marcus, the girl!'

Before Winnie could protest, the driver bundled her up, tossed her head first into the carriage at Mrs Campbell's feet, and slammed the door.

Winnie landed in a heap, tangled in the yards of fabric of her skirt and petticoat. 'No! I demand— Oof!'

The carriage bounced, then rolled forward, out of the back gates of the carriage house. The sudden movement made it even harder to right herself. Finally freeing herself from the tangled fabric of her gown, she sat on the seat, arms folded and eyes glaring. Her hat was most certainly askew, but she left it as a protest.

Across from her, the veiled woman sat calmly on the plush seat of the carriage. 'I do apologize for my unorthodox methods, but circumstances require speed and absolute discretion, Miss Weatherby. Our discussion must remain a secret. For your safety, my identity must be disguised. You may refer to me by my pseudonym, Mrs Campbell.'

'My safety? You can start by releasing me this instant,' Winnie seethed. Pseudonym indeed. Only criminals needed to hide their identity with a false name.

Who was this mysterious Mrs Campbell? The quality of her clothing, a dark half-mourning dress of fine fabric accented with smart jet buttons, was obvious. Delicate, dark lace hid her face. A widow . . . The scent of violets and smoke wafted from the woman's gown. Tobacco?

'Miss Weatherby, allow me to allay your fears. The previous bumpy ride and our hasty departure were necessary. You see, Headmistress suspected you'd defy her, and, after the visit from that detective, she was on her guard. When she spotted someone loitering outside, presumably looking for you, she arranged for a hansom cab – with our driver – to be waiting outside. Marcus thought he'd lost the man, but unfortunately not. With luck, the change of vehicles will confound him and buy us time.'

Winnie's knees quivered with tension. She fingered the tools on her chatelaine for reassurance. Was someone really hunting for her? Why? She swallowed hard. Maybe this 'Mrs Campbell' was lying. Finally, she located the pea whistle. Thrusting it between her lips, she began blowing so hard her ears hurt.

'Good god, girl! Stop that at once.' Mrs Campbell leant forward and yanked the chain, dislodging it from Winnie's lips. She eyed the chatelaine. 'I only wish to make a proposition. After you've heard me out, you may take up my offer or you may alight wherever you wish, your father's home in Chelsea or your former Academy in Bloomsbury. I promise.'

How could this strange woman know her name, address and place of study? Winnie's heart hammered in her throat.

CHAPTER 6

Wednesday, noon

Mrs Campbell sat forward as the carriage clattered through the streets. 'Miss Weatherby, your special talents have brought you to the attention of my agency.'

Winnie stopped planning ways of escape. She ran her eyes over the woman again. Mrs Campbell was deranged, that was clear. But then, she had noticed Winnie's abilities, so she must have *some* insight . . . 'What agency?'

'The details will come in due course. Our top-secret work requires a remarkable young lady with extraordinary talent and few, shall we say, familial attachments. Being motherless – please pardon my frankness – and with your father's current state of affairs—'

'What do you know of Papa? I beg you, tell me everything you—' Winnie stopped. She cleared her throat. 'That you are aware of such private affairs alarms me further.'

'Private? I know little of your father's affairs – only what was printed in that disreputable rag that calls itself a newspaper. My more reliable sources inform me Professor Weatherby's debts were barely of consequence, yet your father's home has been ransacked, and a caveat has been assigned over his assets. Certain devious factions within the police force took the housekeeper into custody this morning, and if you return there, you will be the next one to end up detained.'

Winnie gasped. 'But why? Mrs Pugh has done nothing, and neither have I! My father is a quiet, scholarly man who loves reading and tinkering. He's just forgetful about timely payment of his accounts . . . He's harmless. Why, the horse pulling this carriage has more criminal intent than he does!'

'I've no doubt, Miss Weatherby. My agency cares not a whit for the disgrace surrounding your father. It's you and your unique inventing talents we're interested in.'

Winnie sat up straighter. Mrs Campbell's praise was most gratifying – practically dizzying.

'We will train you and put you into special top-secret service designing and building tools of espionage for our other female agents.'

Lady spies! Special tools? How positively intriguing. Winnie's eyes bulged despite her efforts to keep her expression neutral.

'In addition to a modest monthly wage, agents receive a generous bonus upon successful completion of a mission. All going well, you'll have more than enough money to hire someone to find your father.'

Golly, my own money . . . Winnie crossed her arms. As tempting as a monthly wage and bonuses sounded, Papa needed her now, not later. 'And if I refuse?'

'As I promised, you are free to go. However, you must know this: at least one person of nefarious intent is currently searching the streets of London for a fourteen-year-old young lady slowly making her way home in too-tight shoes.'

Winnie raised her chin, ignoring the pinch in her toes. 'I'll take my chances. Please tell the driver to stop. I wish to make my own way home. Finding my papa is my only concern.' She folded her arms and turned her gaze to the street before she could change her mind.

Why should she trust this mysterious, possibly villainous, veiled woman? The secrecy was ridiculous. Mrs Campbell indeed! *Agency! Pfft.* For all Winnie knew, Mrs Pugh was home at this very moment, beating the carpets with Papa's rug-dusting machine or boiling water for tea in Winnie's whistling kettle contraption.

'Very well, Miss Weatherby.' She thumped the roof, signalling to the driver to pull over. 'But I insist that Marcus accompany you home. It's for your safety. We've reached my destination. I shall take my leave.'

Once standing on the pavement, Mrs Campbell turned back to her and held out a fat purse of gold mesh. 'Miss Weatherby, I wish you to take this.'

Winnie tore her gaze away from the purse. She most certainly would *not* put herself in debt to a delusional woman.

Mrs Campbell sighed. 'Oh, for heaven's sake. Take it. Consider it payment for the inconvenience you've suffered.'

Winnie gripped the fabric of her skirt. Accepting it felt tawdry, but what if—

The purse arched towards her face. Winnie caught it as a reflex. The coins inside clinked between her fingers.

'I do hope we meet again, Miss Weatherby. Good day.' Mrs Campbell turned and disappeared into a nearby building. As the carriage pulled away, the sign came into view: Harrod's Stores.

Winnie blinked. *Lady spies and fashion shopping . . . How odd.* She sank back into the plush seat. A smile curled at the corner of her mouth. She had a reputation: not as an awkward pupil and troublesome daughter, but as a clever and talented *inventress*!

By the time the carriage reached Chelsea and turned into Tite Street, Winnie's tense shoulders had finally relaxed.

Still, her tummy tightened as the cab rolled towards number 34.

Winnie leant over to the carriage's side window, scanning the buildings along her street. It was eerily still. No residents walked the pavement; no nursemaids pushed perambulators towards the park. And there, at the home of Admiral Higson, her father's neighbour and dear friend, a sign.

Beneath the unicorn figurehead mounted on the front of his house, he had hoisted three signal pennants: a blue cross on white, a yellow and blue, and a white. The admiral, who had marvelled at the powers of Winnie's young mind, had taught her both Morse code and the nautical code when she was quite young and called her his little powder monkey. Flags 1-9-8 signalled danger!

Winnie tensed. Dear old Higsy might be old, but he was still cunning. She rapped on the front window. 'Mr Marcus, please take care.' She pointed to the signal.

The driver slowed and leant to speak over the clip-clopping of the horse. 'I see it. I was a sailor, miss.'

'Drive on, if you please. I was mistaken not to trust Mrs Campbell.'

The curtain in Reverend Wiggin's window twitched ... then, as if it had been a signal, the street was alive with shouts. The roar of carriage wheels and the thunder of hooves approached from behind.

'Yah!' Winnie's driver flicked the whip. The carriage lurched forward, slamming Winnie into the velvet-covered seat. She braced herself with hands and feet for another rough ride. Off they raced, down treed lanes, rounding corners at a precarious tilt and bumping over kerbs.

Winnie gripped the seat. So, the mysterious Mrs Campbell had spoken the truth: someone had been lying in wait. What did it mean? What could they possibly gain from detaining her, a mere young lady of fourteen years? And Papa had left bills unpaid before *and* been accused of copying other inventors' work – after all, he had a lot of rivals. Why all the fuss this time?

The clattering over cobbles rumbled through her bones. She swayed to the left, slid to the right. Voices shouted and blurred.

A sharp bang rang out. The driver slumped to the side and tumbled out of sight. The horse tossed his head and burst into a furious gallop. The carriage surged ahead, swerving madly, bouncing and jostling.

'Oh! Mr Marcus!' Winnie struggled to reach the front window. Surely it wasn't a gunshot! 'Sir, are you wounded?'

He was gone! The driver had fallen off the carriage!

'Oh, good golly!' Her throat squeezed. If only she'd taken Mrs Campbell's offer and not been so pig-headed.

The carriage raced driverless through the streets. Outside, people screamed and dived clear as the carriage thundered forward.

Inside, Winnie gathered her wits. She had to gain control of the carriage before someone died. She needed to reach the reins to stop the horse. Somehow, she had to crawl to the driver's box seat.

She gathered up the tendrils of her chatelaine and began assembling its various parts. She selected the compass, which she turned upside down to form a V. She inserted the stem into the whistle end of the magnifying glass. From inside the small silver purse, she removed a strip of India rubber with looped ends. She hooked it over the arms of the compass. '*Voilà!* A slingshot. Now for the missile.' The lead acorn-shaped plumb bob connected to the chatelaine chain with a tiny catch. Each bounce of the carriage made her fumble it. 'Blast! Oh, there!'

Winnie loaded the lead acorn into the sling and aimed at the front window. No, on second thought, an explosion of shattered glass was too dangerous. The resulting shower of shards would be pushed inwards by the various pressures straight on to her, causing serious injury. Perhaps she could squeeze through the door window and pull herself into the driver's box. Grimacing at the thought of pulling off such a daring exploit, she aimed for a side window, drew back the sling . . .

A mounted policeman galloped up alongside the carriage. He glanced through the window, his eyes widening at the loaded slingshot pointing at him.

Winnie lowered it. 'Beg pardon!' she yelled. Thank goodness for help. She hadn't relished the idea of climbing out to the dickey box while thundering down London streets – or footpaths, as that seemed to be where most of the carriage was situated now.

The constable reached towards the runaway horse, grasped the reins, and pulled it back. The wild-eyed grey horse resisted, twisting his head and snorting, but, at last, the clarence's pace slowed.

Winnie leant back. Safe.

The back of her neck prickled.

Or was she? In the distance, a bell clanged wildly. Were the police for her or against her? Mrs Campbell had mentioned 'certain devious factions within the police force'. How was Winnie to know who was devious and who was trustworthy?

'Bother!' When the carriage was nearly stopped, she unlatched the door and slid awkwardly to the street, just avoiding a fall in horse muck. She reloaded the plumb bob into the slingshot, aimed, and fired at the policeman's horse. The lead acorn pinged its haunches.

She winced. 'Pardon!'

With a wild snort and a leap, the horse took off again,

taking the startled policeman down the street.

Winnie's legs wobbled beneath her. How dreadful: Mr Marcus was nowhere to be seen. Ignoring the terror in her belly, she tried to look as if she didn't care and melted into the crowd of gawping onlookers.

CHAPTER 7

Wednesday, early afternoon

After trudging four blocks, Winnie's feet screamed from her too-tight shoes. She'd passed a tea room; perhaps she could rest there. She backtracked until she found it again and pushed open the door. Chatter stopped. A dozen ladies stared at her.

'Well, don't just stand there. You're letting the stink in. Come in and close the door,' a buxom woman said. Her apron and mop hat suggested she was the tea room owner. She scanned Winnie head to toe and back again. 'If I know anything, I know the look of a person in need of a cup of tea. This way, you poor dear.'

Winnie's shoulders sagged. So much for looking inconspicuous. She dropped into a chair, wincing at the blisters on her feet.

'You sit here until you're refreshed, deary. Everyone calls me Peggy; you may too. I'll bring you a nice pot of tea.'

Heat burnt in the corners of Winnie's eyes. She sank into her seat, allowing the din of feminine chatter to wash over her.

Peggy returned with a teapot and some hot buttered crumpets. She squinted at Winnie and lowered her voice. 'Are you in trouble, miss? If someone's bothering you, I can call for the police.'

'No!' Winnie blurted a little too emphatically. 'That is, no, thank you.'

The woman's brows rose. 'Never mind, deary. You catch your breath.' She poured a cup of tea for Winnie, then waddled off.

All the etiquette Winnie had acquired at the Academy evaporated. She stirred noisily, slurped her tea and inhaled her crumpets. While she was chewing her last bite, the door banged open, and a dirty, whippet-thin boy darted inside.

He ran to Peggy. 'Miss, there's a gang of those bothersome bobbies heading this way.'

Peggy took a threepence from her apron pocket. 'Well done, Clancy. Many thanks.' He took it with a grin and headed for the kitchen.

Women around the tea room began shuffling papers – which Winnie realized were pamphlets about suffrage – and stuffing them under their seats. Out came embroidery work and pocket bibles. Winnie gawped. These were the firebrand women Adelaide admired, the ones who wanted ladies to be given the right to vote.

Moments later, a policeman peered through the glass right at her. Winnie froze as the door creaked open. She ducked as if she'd dropped her napkin.

'Good day, ladies. Carry on . . .' The bobby tipped his tall hat, and the door creaked closed.

When Winnie sat up, Peggy was watching her, brow cocked. Winnie felt her cheeks redden.

Clancy bolted towards the front door, and Peggy snatched the back of his collar, stopping him. 'Ah-ah,' Peggy chided. 'What's your hurry?' She held out a hand.

Clancy huffed. He pulled two small apples from one pocket and a sweet bun from the other. 'They're for the lads. Little Miles is hungry.'

Peggy feigned a scowl. 'Very well, but you must do something for me. See this here young lady? I need you to see her home – without the police spotting her. Can you do it?'

'Depends. I haven't got all day for a walk—'

Peggy pretended to grab his ear for a good twist.

'Oi! Fine, fine. I'll take her.' He pulled down his cap to cover his ears. 'Where's home, miss?'

Winnie puffed her cheeks and stared at him blankly. Where could she go? Definitely not home, and not the

Beacon Academy . . . not yet, anyway. She needed to find Mrs Campbell. 'Harrod's Stores, please.' She downed the last drop of tea and stood.

Clancy guffawed. 'Crikey, that's fancy!' He tipped his sooty cap at Peggy before turning to Winnie. 'This way, miss. We'll take the scenic route.' He strode to the steep staircase that led upstairs and scurried to the top. He grinned down at Winnie. 'Hurry, miss.'

They climbed up another flight of stairs to the attic. Clancy threw open the window to the roof and leapt to the ledge as nimbly as a cat.

Winnie gasped. 'Where are you going?'

'We. We're going to Harrod's by the high road. This way. I call it cloudlarking, like mudlarking but with a better view and less stink.' He stepped on to the pitched roof.

Winnie poked her head out of the small window. The roof sloped steeply up. She hoisted her skirt and climbed up to the sill, huffing and puffing, tugging at her skirt and trying in vain to keep her ankles respectfully covered.

As soon as she was safely on the roof, he scampered away. 'This way. Mind your step.' He scaled the steeply pitched roof.

Winnie gazed around. Clancy wasn't joking. The incredible view stretched on and on. How on earth would she ever find Mrs Campbell in such a vast and grimy city?

Glimpses of the Thames, sunlight glistening off window-panes, swallows flitting about. Across the army of sooty chimney pots, St Paul's dome punched the sky in the distance. A flush of freedom burst in her chest, spreading down to her fingertips.

Carefully placing her feet, she made her way up the soot-covered roof. She'd lost sight of Clancy, but she could hear him talking on the other side.

'Good day, Mr Magpie! How is Mrs Magpie and the little magpie chicks?'

Winnie peered over the gable. Clancy, hat in hand, finished a bow to a solitary magpie, perched on a chimney pot. It cocked its head at Clancy and trilled.

Clancy smiled at Winnie. 'You'd better salute him too, miss. You don't want bad luck to befall you up here.'

'Superstitious nonsense. That bird has no idea what you said or why you're talking to him.'

'No, miss, you must greet him! A lone magpie is bad luck if you don't. You mustn't cross it! You know the old rhyme, "One for sorrow . . . and so on?"' He twisted his cap and threw her a pleading look. 'No more sorrow, please. I've had enough for a lifetime. Go on . . .'

Winnie rolled her eyes. 'Very well, but I'm doing this for you, not the bird. Scientifically, it's meaningless.'

Clancy shuddered before doffing his cap and apologizing to the magpie. 'I beg your pardon, sir. She doesn't mean it.' He scowled at Winnie. 'And you must bow.' He nodded a prompt to her.

Winnie's greeting completed, the bird flew off, leaving a slimy white dropping where it had sat.

CHAPTER 8

Wednesday afternoon

After the long, winding wander across rooftops, past pigeon coops and vermin-infested garbage heaps, they returned to street level. Winnie followed Clancy along a series of zigzagging backstreets. She was hopelessly disoriented and quietly alarmed, never having set foot in a dark alley before. Brown rats darted up walls. Painted women smoked pipes in doorways below the crisscrossed laundry lines. Drunks snored beside overflowing dustbins, and mangy dogs skulked like hungry wolves.

Winnie kept her head lowered as she hobbled along. Just as well she wasn't wearing the Beacon Academy dress here. It was no place for a poised and polished young lady. The environs made her feel seedy and vulnerable, a feeling made worse by the searing pain in her feet. She felt as if she'd stubbed her big toes on a serving fork.

Clancy paused to wait for her at a busy crossing.

'Surely it can't be much further. I feel as if I've crossed the Himalayas on foot.'

'There we are, miss: Harrod's.' He led her around a corner. 'Whoa!' He pushed her back. 'Two bobbies are there, and you can never tell . . . Wait here a moment.'

Winnie flattened herself against the wall, heart hammering in her chest. Being hunted was most unpleasant, but it would be awful if Clancy became embroiled. 'You've been so kind and helpful, Clancy, but I think we can part ways now.' She withdrew the golden purse that Mrs Campbell had given her. She hadn't wanted to accept it, but at least it enabled her to pay Clancy a little more than she could out of her own skinny coin purse. She fished out a coin. 'Here you go. I'm ever so grateful for your help and your company.'

Clancy studied the coin on his palm. 'Miss, have you got another? This one won't buy much.'

His words hit her like a slap. How rude to insinuate her tip was insufficient! Winnie's cheeks burnt.

Clancy held it up. 'Look here. This thing has a hole in the middle. It's not money. It's a token.'

Winnie looked. He was right. 'Oh, how embarrassing. I do apologize, Clancy. However, I hope you'll accept *these* coins.' She grabbed his hand and poured a small pile on to his palm.

He shook his head and let out a laugh. 'These are tokens too, to Madame Tussauds Wax Museum. See here?' He pointed to the words on the disk: *Tussaud & Sons 1889 Admit One.*

Winnie emptied the rest of the coins in Mrs Campbell's purse on to her hand. All tarnished copper tokens. 'Well!' Fancy Mrs Campbell, a woman who certainly carried herself as nobility, playing such a dirty trick on her! The nerve . . . Or was it?

Winnie stared at the purse. Engraved on its metal frame was the word *Loosy.* How odd, but the tokens were stranger still. Were they clues to lead Winnie back to Mrs Campbell?

She would have to find out. She opened her silver notebook hanging from her chatelaine and slid out a half-sized calling card. 'Keep this, Clancy, but show it to no one – especially not the police. It's my father's calling card.'

Clancy took the card and squinted at it. 'Professor A.A. Weatherby, Inventor of Extraordinary Contraptions.'

'When my father hears how gallant you've been today, guiding me across town, he'll see you're properly rewarded. You'll have to wait, though, as he's disappeared. That's why I'm going to Harrod's – in hopes of finding a mysterious lady who may help me until he's found.'

Clancy took off his cap and slid the card under the hatband. 'I hope you find your papa – and the lady.'

'I last saw her enter Harrod's, but I suspect by now she's elsewhere. Clancy, do you know how far away the wax museum is?'

Madame Tussauds Wax Museum towered over Winnie and Clancy. The enormous building spread to fill most of the block. Patrons were filing out of the door. A uniformed attendant nodded salutations to the departing patrons.

He grimaced when Winnie and Clancy stepped into the vestibule. After pointedly squinting at his pocket watch, he hissed, 'The museum is closing presently. I'm just about to lock the galleries for the night. Off you go, children.'

Winnie stiffened at the word *children*. Did she really look childish? She glanced at her reflection in a window, noting she was a whole head taller than Clancy. She stifled a gasp. Good golly! Her clothes were filthy, covered in streaks of dirt. Her plaits were untidy, her hat crooked, and soot smudged her cheeks and brow.

Clancy groaned his disappointment. 'Just a quick peek in the Chamber of Horrors, then. We have our tokens, sir.' He held out a palmful of museum tokens Winnie had given him.

The doorman sneered. 'Do you now? And *how* would you have tokens when I shut the box office quarter of an hour ago? Hmm? I'd remember such a grubby pair of street urchins.' He narrowed his eyes at them.

Clancy stepped back. 'I didn't nick 'em, if that's what you're implying.' He elbowed Winnie. 'She has a purse full of tokens. Show 'em to the man, miss.'

Winnie's cheeks flamed. How humiliating – first to be called a child, then a 'grubby urchin', and now to be accused of stealing tokens. Winnie pulled Mrs Campbell's purse from her pocket, fumbled it open, and took out a token.

The doorman's brows shot up. 'May I see that purse, miss?' When Winnie held it out, the man dipped his head. 'I beg your pardon, miss. This way.' He gestured to the inner door.

'Oi! What about me?' Clancy griped.

The doorman bristled. 'Have you got a personalized purse as well?'

Clancy blinked. 'No, just these tokens.'

'Well, then, I suggest you come back tomorrow. Earlier – and cleaner. Good day.' He used the broom to scoot Clancy towards the door before turning to Winnie. 'If miss would follow me.'

Clancy's shoulders sagged. 'Well, that's a rotten stroke of luck!'

Winnie hesitated. 'Oh, dear. I am sorry, Clancy. You've been ever so helpful, but I must bid you farewell now. You mustn't forget to visit my papa when he's . . .' Her voice trailed off. Just mentioning her father made her tummy burn with anxiety.

'I shall, miss.' Clancy added in an exaggerated whisper, 'Although I don't feel proper about leaving you with the likes of him. A bit haughty, if you ask me.' He nodded towards the doorman, who rolled his eyes. 'I hope you find your father.' With a tip of his cap, he slipped through the door on to the pavement. A second later, he reappeared, his face a mask of distress. 'It's the coppers, miss! They must've followed us! Run!'

A squeak of alarm escaped Winnie's throat. She turned to follow the doorman.

He had vanished.

Winnie jammed a token in the turnstile and rushed up the stairs to the lofty entrance hall, barely noticing the spectacle of the curved grand staircase, domed ceiling, tiers of balconies and ornate decoration.

Behind her, two male voices rang out. 'She's gone inside.'

'Hurry! We can't lose her this time.'

Winnie dashed up the grand marble staircase against a steady downwards stream of couples with children, pairs of spinsters, young men in stylish suits, all of whom were exiting the building. A movement, a flash of colour, above her caught Winnie's eye. On a balcony two floors up, a lone young lady dressed in pale blue and cream leant out to peer at her before disappearing again. Something about the colours tickled a memory . . .The door below her banged open. The voice echoed. 'There! I see her.'

Winnie glanced over her shoulder. One bobby pointed at her with his baton. Terror buzzed in her ears. She took the next flight two stairs at a time. According to the signage, she'd reached the Napoleon Gallery.

Winnie pushed open the tall doors and scanned the long hall. Bother – no crowd to hide among. Only an elderly woman in widow's weeds remained, viewing a tableau of Marie Antoinette's court in wax statues. Weaving past displays of battles and extravagant coronations, Winnie scanned the walls for a doorway. Finally, she spotted an unusual pattern of wear on the parquet floor. There must be a door concealed in the panelling. A passageway in the wall? *Oh, please let there be a way out!*

She felt along the surface until her fingertips discovered the catch. Thank heavens! Looking over her shoulder, she saw the elderly patron now accompanied by a second old woman walking towards the exit. One of the bobbies strode in, tipping his hat to the widows, who asked for directions. Winnie pulled open the door, revealing a spiral staircase of wrought iron in a dark, narrow shaft. She stepped on to the tread and pulled the door closed, enveloping herself in shadows.

Winnie's shoulders quaked in a shudder. Her terror of the dark trumped the relief of escaping the police.

The darkness seemed to throb with evil. 'Good golly.' She paused, heart thumping dizzily in her ears. Another abduction or runaway horse or even traipsing through London's seedy back alleys would be preferable to this shadowy passageway. She tried to swallow her fears, but her tongue was cotton wadding. She exhaled. 'There's nothing to fear in here,' she reminded herself.

Except spiders, rats and perhaps some bats . . .

Winnie gripped the banister and hauled herself up the spiral stairs.

Round and round, higher into the dizzying darkness she climbed until a distant noise stopped her. She waited, listening without the rustling of her skirt and ringing of her shoes on the iron treads.

Below in the Napoleon Gallery, footsteps clicked across the floor. A male voice muted by the distance called out, 'The girl came in here; I'm sure of it.'

'Check all those creepy statues. I'll look in the other gallery.'

The clack of footsteps intensified.

Winnie held her breath. Had the bobby noticed the same pattern of wear on the floor? She sucked in a gasp.

Had she closed the concealed door properly?

Light spilt into the stairwell as the door below opened.

Winnie dared not move. She gripped the banister.

'What have we here?' the bobby said, stepping on to the spiral staircase. 'Well, well, well.'

With each of his steps, vibrations trembled through Winnie's shoes up her legs.

Something thudded. The man grunted. There was a second clunk and a gong-like sound. The staircase shook violently.

Winnie glanced down to the pool of dim light below her. The policeman lay in a heap. She covered her mouth. Someone had bashed the bobby, knocking him unconscious. Who could have done it? Only Clancy knew about them, but surely he would call out to her.

A pair of hands grabbed the policeman and dragged him feet first back into the gallery. The door slammed shut, throwing her into utter darkness again.

Winnie clutched her chest. 'Ah!' Her foot caught in the fabric of her skirt and she stumbled, falling heavily against the metal steps.

CHAPTER 9

Four o'clock, Wednesday afternoon

Cursing the darkness, Winnie untangled the fabric twisted around her legs and sat down on the iron stair tread. Her palms and elbow ached where she'd whacked them, and her poor blistered feet throbbed. She held her hand close to her face, but the blackness erased it. She felt around, reaching for the central column of the spiral staircase and wrapped an arm around it, fearful of stumbling again, terrified of not finding her way out.

Her throat constricted, and her ears shrilled. She gulped air, but wooziness edged closer. Panting, Winnie twined her fingers through the chains of her chatelaine, feeling through the assortment of equipages for her mother's silver-and-crystal vinaigrette. Fumbling to uncork it, she gingerly waved the tiny bottle of smelling salts past her nostrils.

Blech! She recoiled from the burning vapours of ammonia, but her head was instantly clearer. With watering eyes, she recorked the vial and found the tinderbox equipage. Carefully flicking it open, she took out a match and struck it. Coloured light ignited, casting a glow on the rough brick walls of the narrow stairwell. She held the match aloft, looking to see how far she had to go.

Only two more turns of the spiral until she'd reach the next landing. She blew out the match, gathered up her skirts, and raced for the landing before the dark could disorient her. She burst through the door, shut it behind her, and sucked in a raspy breath. She'd escaped the police – for now.

Plush carpets, dark panelling and the mingled smells of tobacco smoke, mahogany and orange pekoe greeted her. She leant back against the closed door and lifted her gaze to savour the light. How strange . . . She'd stepped into a parlour where a table was set for afternoon tea, and around it sat three elegant ladies, all of whom watched her.

Between a young lady in yellow and another in pale blue sat Mrs Campbell, erect and sombre in her deep purple-black widow's weeds and veil. She nodded to the clock on the sideboard. 'Remarkable timing, Miss Weatherby! I hope you'll join us for afternoon tea. You must be famished after the eventful day you've had.'

Winnie's chin dropped. The table was set for four. A tiered stand displayed elegant morsels: crustless sandwiches, dainty iced petits fours, sugared fruit, jellies and more. Her tummy growled, and tears of exhaustion pricked in her eyes. Unable to speak, she sat down, sinking into the most comfortable embrace of her life. It took extreme effort to resist the urge to groan with relief. If only she could unbutton her boots!

Mrs Campbell poured steaming tea into each of the china cups. 'Allow me to introduce Miss Stella Davies,' she nodded at the young lady in yellow, 'and Miss Euphemia Lee.' Miss Lee was the young woman in blue. 'Ladies, I present Miss Winifred Weatherby.'

'How do you do,' they said in unison.

Although utterly spent and unable to make small talk, Winnie automatically smiled and dipped her head politely. As she did, she made two immediate observations:

The young lady dressed in luscious buttermilk yellow, Miss Stella Davies, was massaging her right hand, which appeared to be slightly swollen. She had dark skin and looked to be Winnie's age.

The other girl, Miss Euphemia Lee, Winnie had seen twice already that day, once on the balcony and the other time in Headmistress's office. It was the Chinese girl who'd surprised her in the Academy's foyer. She appeared to be slightly younger than the former.

Winnie's mind spun as furiously and pointlessly as a toddler's whirligig in a stiff breeze. How did these places and people fit together? And good golly, those sandwiches smelt heavenly. She interlaced her fingers on her lap to avoid the faux pas of grabbing food for herself.

Luckily, Mrs Campbell passed Winnie a plate laden with dainty sandwiches and sweet treats. 'Please, ladies, eat and drink while I fill you in. I'm sorry to say we're on a rather tight schedule.'

Winnie dived in. Never had a cucumber sandwich tasted so exquisitely perfect. Winnie chewed and swallowed and stuffed a second whole finger sandwich in her mouth while Miss Lee watched in wonder. (Or possibly dismay. Who cared?)

'She looks like a street urchin, eats like a street urchin . . .' Miss Davies raised her eyebrows at Mrs Campbell. 'Ma'am, are you quite sure we have the right girl?'

Winnie felt the heavy scrutiny of Miss Lee, who stopped nibbling her sandwich to frown at the grimy soot stains marring Winnie's cuffs. Her gaze locked on Winnie's Multi-Device Interchangeable Utility Chatelaine, and her eyes boggled. Miss Lee elbowed Miss Davies, gesturing towards Winnie's prized invention.

Mrs Campbell, who didn't reach for any food of her own, continued as if Miss Davies hadn't spoken. 'May I assume you're here because you wish to take up my offer,

Miss Weatherby?'

Winnie nodded, unable to speak due to her state of ecstasy over the cream bun she was devouring.

'Very good. Before I—'

Winnie held up a finger, swallowed, and dabbed confectioner's sugar from her lips with a napkin. 'I beg your pardon, Mrs Campbell. May I interject? I will take up your offer *only* if you promise to help me find my father. Surely an organization such as yours has . . . has *resources* to find a missing person.'

Miss Lee and Miss Davies barely stifled gasps.

Mrs Campbell sat back, tilted her head and appraised Winnie. She tapped her fingers on the arm of her chair. 'The League deals on a national and international stage, so yes, we have resources, but they are certainly not to be used for family affairs.'

'I understand . . . but who's to say my father's disappearance is not an act of international intrigue? He and his investors believe the Weatherby Telautograph Machine has the potential to change human interactions dramatically.'

This, of course, was a spontaneous and fantastical fabrication, somewhat of a speciality of Winnie's, but as soon as she'd said it, she concluded it was indeed a possibility worth considering. Why hadn't she considered it earlier? 'If you want my involvement, I shall require your assurance that you will help me find Papa.'

Miss Lee's teacup clattered on to its saucer. 'Mrs Campbell, surely you cannot agree! It wouldn't be fair! I wouldn't dream of demanding personal favours.'

Winnie felt heat rise in her cheeks. Why had the two other recruits taken such an instant dislike to her?

In the ensuing silence, the ticking of the clock seemed to intensify.

Mrs Campbell bristled. 'Unfortunately, Miss Lee, we have little choice – we need Miss Weatherby's unique skill set – and quickly.' She turned her attention to Winnie. 'I promise we will help with locating your father, as long as it is understood that official League duties must come first. In return, you will promise to do no investigations of your own. If I discover anything to the contrary, you will be ousted from the League. Do I make myself clear?'

Winnie blinked at the prospect of abandoning her search before she'd even begun. This promise was too restrictive – however, thinking logically, the official sources at the League would probably be more effective than whatever she could achieve herself. 'Very well.'

'Now, if we can return to the more important matters at hand, you are required to sign a contract.' She produced a small stack of paper, a pen and a pot of ink, and pointed at a dotted line at the end of the contract.

'Shouldn't I first carefully read each page and ask my

lawyer for advice?'

Miss Davies and Miss Lee exchanged scandalized glances.

Mrs Campbell pursed her lips. 'I'm afraid time is of the essence.' She pointedly handed the pen to Winnie.

Signing without due diligence was never wise, but Winnie didn't see that she had much choice. She dipped the nib in the inkwell and signed: Winifred A Weatherby.

As Mrs Campbell rolled the blotter over it, Winnie hugged her forearms against her belly. What if this was a terrible mistake? Finding Papa had to remain her first concern. Nor could she lose sight of her World Fair dream.

'Excellent. Welcome. My brother and I have been planning a team of young lady spies for several years now, and its time has come. Miss Lee and Miss Davies are two of four recently trained agents, and your appointment completes the quintet. Your somewhat condensed training commences tomorrow, and our league of young lady spies will be launched on its first official mission after you've all completed an additional induction course.'

Mrs Campbell tucked the documents into a brown envelope. 'We have a special role for you, Miss Weatherby. You see, Professor Dudley, who oversaw Research and Development and previously made tools of espionage for us, has retired prematurely due to illness, and this vital position must be filled as soon as possible.

'Would you like to see the facility? I think you'll find the laboratory quite sufficient.' Mrs Campbell stood.

A proper inventing laboratory for *her exclusive use*! Winnie stopped eyeing the last chocolate-covered maraschino cherry and shot to her feet. 'I'd be delighted!' The blisters on her toes and heels panged so brutally her knees buckled. 'But I hope it's not too far from here.'

'Miss Weatherby, it *is* here. The Tussaud Waxworks provides the League with . . . resources. We occupy its unused facilities and employ the Tussaud company's talent for our specialized needs. Which reminds me, before we view the laboratory, you have an urgent appointment with the wardrobe department, who not only dress our agents elegantly,' she gestured to Miss Lee's and Miss Davies's gowns, 'but also provide myriad disguises for their work.'

Bother. Winnie faked a smile to conceal her disappointment. Forget the fashion closet – the laboratory sounded far more intriguing.

Mrs Campbell looked Winnie up and down. 'Reclothing you, young lady, is our most dire priority. This way.'

Were Miss Davies and Miss Lee sniggering behind their hands? Winnie glowered at them. Well, one thing was clear: those two polished young ladies had not faced and overcome the challenges and dangers she had today!

Had they lost their father or jumped from a runaway carriage? Or scurried across London's rooftops and zigzagged through its seedy streets with pursuers hot on their heels? No, most certainly not. Their most strenuous activities were lifting teacups and casting aspersions at her. Winnie squared her dirty shoulders. Her current state of mess had been hard won!

Mrs Campbell led them to the stairwell door Winnie had come through earlier.

Winnie froze. The bashed bobby! What if he was still lying at the foot of the stairs – or worse, what if he'd come to and was waiting with his associate to nab her upon her return?

Mrs Campbell flipped a switch on the wall, and new-fangled electric fixtures buzzed alight, filling the stairwell with their stark brightness.

Winnie hesitated, peering down towards the foot of the staircase.

'Miss Weatherby,' said Mrs Campbell, 'if you're worried about encountering that fiend disguised as a member of the Metropolitan Police Force who followed you and the boy here, you needn't fear. Miss Davies surprised him with a well-placed uppercut. He is presently unconscious in an alley. You may remember the pair of elderly ladies in the Napoleon Room?'

Upper-what? Winnie nodded dumbly.

Mrs Campbell gestured to the two young ladies. 'They were these two young ladies in disguise.'

Miss Lee and Miss Davies bowed like magician's assistants after performing a successful illusion.

Winnie's chin dropped. *But how had they—* 'That's . . . remarkable!'

For the first time since she had arrived, the two girls offered Winnie genuine smiles. And with that, Mrs Campbell led the way downstairs.

CHAPTER 10

Late afternoon

Winnie frowned at the unfamiliar reflection in the wardrobe department's looking glass. She poked her tongue at the stranger, and the stranger dressed in eye-catching garnet poked hers back.

Mrs Campbell threw an impatient glance at Winnie. 'Are you quite finished? We really must keep moving, Miss Weatherby.'

Winnie sighed. 'Not recognizing oneself is most alarming! I feel as if I'm being mocked – by a very elegant lady.'

The Parisian wardrobe master stood behind Winnie. '*Et la pièce de résistance . . .*' On her head, he perched a feathery hat that included an entire bird's worth of plumage. His assistant, the coiffeuse, stabbed a hatpin into Winnie's new hairstyle, fixing the hat in place.

Mrs Campbell directed a dainty clap towards the wardrobe master. 'You've outdone yourself, monsieur.'

Monsieur Moineau bowed so deeply and dramatically, the tails of his coat flopped over his head. When he rose, he graciously gestured to his three clearly overworked assistants, a tailor with dark circles ringing his eyes, a bored-looking hair-and-wig coiffeuse, and a sour-faced dresser, who rubbed her lower back and muttered curses under her breath.

Mrs Campbell touched Winnie's sleeve. 'This lovely shade of garnet complements her complexion, and the cut of the dress is exquisite. She looks five years older and completely unrecognizable.'

Mrs Campbell was right: the dresser had laced Winnie into a fancy corset that was abundantly padded at the hips and bosom. The resulting curves were positively terrifying.

Winnie's hands instinctively reached to give her plaits a reassuring twist, but the braids were gone. Her hair had been curled and pinned up atop her head. At least they'd bandaged her blisters and given her a soft pair of flat, satin court slippers. The new, stylish boots had been packed in a trunk along with other articles of clothing, unmentionables, outerwear and accessories.

Winnie retrieved her mother's chatelaine from her soiled dress and pinned the brooch to her waistband.

There – much better. Instantly she felt more herself.

Monsieur Moineau squealed, his face twisted in *horreur*. '*Non, non, NON!*' He wagged a shaky finger at Winnie. 'Absolutely no. Not. Never!'

Winnie checked to make sure Mrs Campbell wasn't looking. She jutted her chin at the wardrobe master. 'Yes, yes, YES,' she hissed under her breath.

Wild-eyed, the wardrobe master lunged for the chatelaine.

Winnie spun away from him, sending the equipages flying on their chains. The crystal vinaigrette smacked him on the forehead.

'*Aïe!*' he cried, rubbing the red mark it left.

'Monsieur, the chatelaine stays,' Mrs Campbell ordered. 'Henceforth, it will be standard issue for our lady agents – as soon as Miss Weatherby has begun as our new quartermistress.'

Winnie beamed. The title of her position was most agreeable! And how novel for her inventions to be consider-ed desirable. She splayed the chains across her fingers. 'It's called the Multi-Device Interchangeable Utility Chate-laine, patent pending. Just wait until you've seen its hidden capabilities. There's a pea whistle for personal security, a slingshot for defence, a—'

Miss Lee interrupted with a *humph*, smoothing down her pretty blue skirt. 'But, Mrs Campbell, all those chains and dangly bits are noisy. I could hear them jangling when Miss Weatherby was several rooms away. It sounded as if she'd hidden a grandfather clock under her bustle.'

The demure Miss Davies blurted a hearty laugh, and Monsieur Moineau sneered.

But Winnie was too busy grabbing her silver notepad equipage and jotting down an idea: *Shorten the chains to reduce the clatter.* She'd always enjoyed the musicality of the equipages, a comforting sort of clunking and clinking that reminded her of her mother. But, of course, for lady spies, noiselessness was essential . . . 'A most astute observation,' she said. 'Thank you, Miss Lee.'

Miss Lee clearly hadn't expected this response and gawped at Winnie.

'Effie – you look like a fish!' Miss Davies said, giggling. Miss Lee blushed angrily and shut her mouth.

'Come now, ladies. The ordeal of outfitting Miss Weatherby took far too long.' Mrs Campbell herded them towards the door, calling over her shoulder to the wardrobe master, '*Merci, monsieur.*' She led the young ladies back to the stairwell, where she stopped to write a quick note. 'While I accompany Miss Weatherby to the Research and Development facility, Stella and Euphemia, you may wait in the parlour for Mr Marcus. When he comes for you, see that he gets this note.' She handed a folded piece of paper to Miss Davies. 'We shan't be long.'

Miss Lee scowled and stomped up the iron spiral staircase.

Miss Davies cast Winnie a slightly apologetic glance, then scurried after her. 'Effie, wait!'

'This way, Miss Weatherby. The Research and Development facility is top secret. You must swear never to divulge the wonders you see in it or speak of any of the work you carry out for the League. At stake is the future wealth and stability of the nation. More immediately, the personal safety of Her Majesty Queen Victoria is at risk.'

Winnie blinked. 'I beg your pardon? You're entrusting all that to a fourteen-year-old girl?'

'Precisely.' Mrs Campbell tilted her head. 'Well, actually, no. We're entrusting it to a small group of young ladies whose average age is 15.8.' Mrs Campbell began walking down a long corridor.

Although mathematics was usually comforting, a feeling of dread brewed in Winnie's belly. She hobbled along behind.

Mrs Campbell talked over her shoulder. 'Who would expect girls would be assigned to defend the Queen, stop potential threats and catch villains? No one will bat an eye at young girls. It's the element of surprise.' She stopped walking. 'It's brilliant, don't you think?'

Winnie's face twisted in disbelief. 'More like *irrespon-sible*! I don't know what I'm doing! I like to tinker: I build inventions from stolen kitchen utensils that I pray the cook won't miss. Are you aware I've been expelled from a long list of London's finest girls' schools? And my most recent and probably former headmistress declared me "wayward" and "incorrigible" and . . . something else . . .' Winnie tapped her temples.

'Impossible,' Mrs Campbell offered flatly.

'That's it. Thank you. I'm "impossible". What on earth are you thinking, entrusting the likes of *me* with anything?' She followed close on Mrs Campbell's heels. 'Wait,' she said. 'How did you know that?'

'Do you suppose I recruited you on a whim, Miss Weatherby? *Think.*'

Of course. Miss Lee had been at the Academy. Clearly the Beacon Academy itself had a role in her recruitment. But how, exactly?

The lady stopped in front of a door whose sign read: *Water Closet – Out of Service.*

Winnie swerved away. *How embarrassing!* 'Oh, I beg your pardon. I thought we were . . .'

Mrs Campbell opened the door, revealing an unusual sliding door made of articulating metal lattice. She opened it. 'After you.'

Winnie's mouth fell open. She stepped into the cubicle and gasped. 'Is this a von Siemens Electric Safety Lift?' She gazed around at its ornate interior of polished brass. She sniffed in the satisfying scents of machine grease, India rubber and metal. *Mmm.* A plaque near the door confirmed her suspicion. 'It *is*! Oh, how I've dreamt of riding in one and examining the mechanism! I had no idea a safety lift already exists in Great Britain. Herr von Siemen is exhibiting at the Paris Exposition Universelle, and Papa and I plan to—'

Papa! Oh, dear.

How could she have forgotten for even a moment about her own dear *missing* papa? All the intrigue and glamour of espionage had fascinated her, but it was the shimmering possibility of tinkering in her own inventing laboratory that had swept her away. What kind of daughter was she? What kind of human?

Mrs Campbell stepped into the lift, closed the door and shoved the control lever up. The elevator lurched upward.

A black-laced hand patted Winnie's forearm, and Mrs Campbell sighed. 'Fathers can be utterly aggravating and truly "impossible", but oh, how we love them.'

Winnie swallowed and nodded without looking at Mrs Campbell.

'Something you said earlier rang true, about the

possibility of your father's disappearance being an act of international intrigue. I shall require more information about this invention of his.'

'Of *ours*,' Winnie corrected under her breath. *Same old story*.

Mrs Campbell's brows rose. 'I see. So, you've made significant contributions to its development, but you've received next to no acknowledgement.'

Winnie sighed. 'Papa worries that my marriage prospects will be ruined if it's known I'm "mechanically inclined".'

Mrs Campbell shook her head. 'Or his importance might be diminished if it's known a young woman helped him.'

Winnie shifted from foot to foot. Papa only wanted the best for her . . . didn't he?

Mrs Campbell continued, 'I think as a matter of priority we may pursue this line of enquiry – the foreign interest in the Weatherby *and Daughter* invention. I've sent word to the Handler and Spymaster, that is, to Thornton and my elder brother.'

Winnie grasped Mrs Campbell's forearm. 'Oh, thank you. Papa is a good man – exasperating, yes, but good-hearted.'

Mrs Campbell shrugged. 'If foreign powers are seeking him, we have a problem.' She pushed the control lever down, and the lift rattled to a stop. The carriage overshot the floor level by six inches. She slid open the door. 'And the problem is *you*. Mind your step.' She stepped down out of the lift.

CHAPTER 11

Wednesday evening

'What do you mean, *I'm* the problem?' Winnie followed Mrs Campbell out of the cramped lift.

She found herself in a most impressive library. Floor-to-ceiling bookshelves lined the walls, and tables of various shapes dotted the room. She glanced at the book spines: mechanics, engineering, history, art, war, cryptology, mathematics, astronomy, chemistry . . . A research facility? What a luxury!

Mrs Campbell stopped near a massive marble fireplace that had clearly never had a fire in its grate. 'I mean you are an asset to the League – unless your father's business matters become . . . internationally *messy*, which would make you a liability. We shall see.' She ducked her head under the lintel and walked *into* the back hearth.

Winnie gasped.

'Do you see this groove in the

stonework? Push your fingers in, and *voilà* – the Quarter-mistress's Laboratory.'

The rear of the fireplace swung back to reveal a dark room.

'Good golly, that's ingenious!' The mechanism had to be extremely strong to bear the weight of all that stone. Whoever had invented it was clever indeed. She ducked her head and went through.

Mrs Campbell flipped a switch, and electric fixtures buzzed alight. 'Welcome to the Agency's Research and Development facility – *your* inventing room.'

Winnie gasped.

It was a long, windowless laboratory with a sprawling central workbench. Myriad tools and machines sat at regular intervals: a watchmaker's staking toolset, chemistry equipment, microscopes and bizarre contraptions Winnie couldn't identify.

'The skylight provides abundant natural light and ventilation in daytime.' Mrs Campbell checked the clock. 'Good heavens, it's late. Mr Marcus will be waiting to accompany all of you to the training facility.'

'I understand. Thank you for allowing this quick visit.' Winnie circled the long central workbench.

Papers, blueprints, notebooks and books lay jumbled up everywhere. The floor was littered with shavings of wood and filings of metal. The walls were lined with jars of bits and bobs and boxes of whatsits. Labels warned: *Volatile! Danger!* and *Explosive!* The poisons shelf included jars of hemlock, castor beans, henbane, belladonna and mandrake. There were sedatives, laxatives and paralytics. Intriguing half-finished projects stood everywhere.

At the far end of the room, she froze. How macabre! A floppy dummy dressed in a top hat and suit sat slumped in the corner. He was pockmarked with bullet holes and stuck with an assortment of swords, daggers, arrows, axes and darts, like a man-sized pincushion. The floor in front of him was marked with measurements back twenty feet, and various timing devices were set up nearby. On a tray lay an array of guns, including the most adorably frightening, fist-sized lady's pistol in shiny silver and mother-of-pearl. 'Is this a weapon testing facility?'

A space devoted to testing was the stuff of dreams. This weird and wonderful space held a lifetime of possibilities, discoveries and innovations . . .

Mrs Campbell ran a finger along a dusty shelf. 'It rather seems like the hideaway of a madman.'

Winnie grinned. 'Or a genius.' This space was hers. Never had she had so many tools or materials at her disposal. 'It's heavenly. I do wish there was time for a tinker and a proper poke around.'

Mrs Campbell returned to the entry. 'Alas, no.

Training and induction to the League will be your focus for the next four weeks. You'll be quite busy, catching up with your colleagues who've completed their foundational training. Come along. You and the others are expected at the Academy.'

Four weeks? Bother. Winnie took a final glance around at *her* laboratory and *her* equipment before exiting through the back hearth. Dark shadows stretched across the library, lit only by the faint glow of the gas lamps on streets outside. 'Mrs Campbell, which academy am I to attend now?'

Mrs Campbell closed the concealed door, ducked her head, and stopped beside Winnie. 'Why, the Beacon Academy.' She headed towards the electric safety lift.

'Surely not!' Winnie spluttered. She rushed to catch up. 'It's a posh finishing school for soft-headed girls. The most challenging subject on its curriculum is alighting from a carriage with modesty and grace!'

Just when she thought she'd escaped that den of daftness!

Mrs Campbell raised an elegant finger. 'Ah! But it's not the soft-headed girls we want.' She opened the lift door and entered. 'The Beacon Academy acts as the Agency's recruitment and training wing. Only London's most *impossible* girls will do.'

'Oh, that's very amusing,' Winnie retorted, not at all

amused. Surely, the woman was mocking her. Winnie squeezed into the small cubicle beside her. She fake-laughed, 'Now I suppose you'll tell me my nemesis, Headmistress Thornton, gave me a glowing recommendation, and my ally, Adelaide Culpepper, is a spy.'

The elevator lurched as it began its descent. Mrs Campbell cocked her head. 'Brava. Now you're catching on, Winifred. I knew you were a bright one.'

~BEACON ACADEMY~

Late Wednesday night

Winnie's new wardrobe trunk clonked heavily on to the floor of her new room at the Beacon Academy. 'Good evening, miss.' The porter dipped his head as he closed the door. The poor man had lugged that monstrosity through the mysterious locked door and up several narrow, winding flights of stairs to Winnie's new room.

No longer was Winnie sharing a room with five other girls; she and her new companions each had their own stylish room on the previously forbidden top floor where the mysterious Premier Pupils were housed – not that Winnie had ever seen such a creature. On the carriage ride from the Tussauds to the Beacon Academy, she'd learnt more interesting details about them. Miss Euphemia (or Effie) Lee was the daughter of a Chinese diplomat and scholar. She was adamant she was 'nearly fourteen years old' – and she made it quite plain she didn't like Winnie at all. Miss Stella Davies, who wore the yellow dress, was sixteen and came with a remarkable pedigree. Her mother, Sarah Forbes Bonetta, (may she rest in peace), had been an African princess and goddaughter of Her Majesty Queen Victoria. She had been a little warmer towards Winnie in the carriage.

Winnie pulled the hatpin from her hat, kicked off her shoes, and flopped on to her bed. What a day! The soft bed felt delicious against her stiff back. Everything hurt – from the soles of her blistered feet to the crown of her head, where hair pins scratched at her scalp and pinched her hair. None of her Academy classmates had witnessed her arrival with her new companions. What would they think when they saw her without plaits and with curves? They wouldn't recognize her – which was exactly the point. The mystery of the Premier Pupils was solved: they were recruits to Mrs Campbell's League.

Who was she any more? She rubbed her throbbing temples and closed her eyes.

They popped back open. She was still Winifred Weatherby, daughter of Professor Weatherby, who was missing. She sat bolt upright. Perhaps a letter from Papa had arrived in the post. She had to check immediately.

A moment later at Adelaide's door, she raised her hand

to knock, but there were voices – animated voices – on the other side. Perhaps it would be better to return later.

Just as she turned away, the door swung open. Adelaide gave a shout. 'Ahh! Winifred! You gave me a fright. I was just—'

'I beg your pardon, Adelaide.'

'Is that Miss Weatherby?' Headmistress Thornton appeared in the door frame. She grabbed Winnie's forearm and hauled her into the room. 'Adelaide, stay here and close the door.'

Adelaide's face was pale. Questions bottlenecked in Winnie's throat: how long had Adelaide been a spy, and why hadn't she ever said anything? How had she been recruited? But then she caught sight of something far more pressing.

Winnie's eyes widened in alarm. Mr Marcus knelt on the floor in front of the window seat with her secret cupboard open. Dash it all – she'd forgotten to lock it.

He'd rolled out the Weatherby Telautograph WA-model on its casters and was staring at the machine as if were a dog with a monkey's head. 'In all my years, I've never encountered such a thing, but I'd guess this is what was ringing. There's more in the crawl space, some papers and whatnot.' He pulled out Winnie's scrolls of designs and passed them to the headmistress.

Adelaide cleared her throat. 'While I was out, Helen

the new chambermaid was in here and heard a "ghostly bell ringing". She flashed an apologetic glance at Winnie.

Headmistress Thornton pointed to the brass plaque stamped *Weatherby Manufacturing Company*. 'Just as I'd suspected.' She turned to Winnie. 'Winifred, perhaps you'd care to enlighten us.'

'I, er . . .' Winnie couldn't take her eyes off the machine. If the bell had rung, it meant one thing: Papa had sent her a telautogram. 'Before I explain, may I please examine the machine?'

'Absolutely not,' Headmistress Thornton thundered. 'What is this machine, and why are there wires connected to it?'

Winnie blew out a breath. 'It's a Weatherby Telautograph Machine, a device that instantaneously transmits facsimiles of signatures and handwritten notes over telegraph wires. This is the WA-model, which features my . . . *improvements.*' Her cheeks burnt. Now that there were other people looking at it, she realized the makeshift covers of copper jelly moulds looked ridiculous, like a child's plaything at Brighton Beach.

Mr Marcus groaned. Headmistress sat heavily on the chair.

The man felt the wires at the back of the machine. 'How did a telegraph wire come into this building? Were you aware, Thornton?'

The headmistress's forehead creased. 'Of course not!'

'My father and I set up the wire.' Winnie gulped. 'I wanted to continue to help Papa with his work, so he installed a wire between his office and here. He sends me small jobs, calculations mostly, and I complete them and send them back.'

'There's a telegraph wire connected to the Beacon Academy. Good god!' Headmistress Thornton rubbed her temples. 'This could put the entire operation at risk. Marcus, you must report to the Spymaster straight away.'

Why did people always overreact to new technology? Winnie held up her hands to calm them. 'But – it's not a public wire. It's private, one of about fifty in London that my father's company sets up for wealthy clients. Only my father and I can use this wire. In fact, if the bell rang, it means Papa – and only Papa – has sent me a message, which I've been expecting for several days now, so if I may . . .'

She knelt beside Mr Marcus and rolled the machine's receiver paper backwards, so the most recent message scrolled on to the desk. It said:

What hath God wrought?

Winnie frowned. How bizarre. The handwriting was unfamiliar, most definitely *not* Papa's.

Mr Marcus stared at the writing. 'So, you're saying your father wrote these words from the other side of London, and it arrived here in his handwriting via a telegraph wire? Instantly? That's . . . extraordinary.'

Winnie nodded. It was indeed extraordinary.

Headmistress curled her lip. 'It's a strange message to send to one's daughter. Perhaps he wrote it after he'd read my scathing letter from last week detailing your misdeeds.'

Winnie continued staring at the words. 'No . . . I don't think so.' She trembled. Cold fear was climbing steadily up her spine. Something was wrong, very wrong.

'Well? Whatever does he mean by it?' Headmistress snapped her fingers. 'Miss Weatherby, this is no time for daydreaming.'

Winnie shook her head. She couldn't let on this wasn't Papa's handwriting now that she'd assured them the wire could only be used by him – that would get her into bigger trouble. Mrs Campbell had already hinted Papa's disappearance made her a problematic member of the League. Winnie tapped her fingertips together and chose her words carefully. 'Those words, "What hath God wrought?" were the words Mr Samuel Morse famously sent in 1844 in the world's first telegram between two cities.' That was true. She swallowed hard. 'So, I suspect Papa has made some minor adjustments to the machine and wished to test them. He wrote these words, which have become a common test phrase.' That part was untrue. She had no idea who wrote these words or why. But whoever it was, they knew enough about telegraphy to appreciate the wondrous advances of the Telautograph. Bother.

'Miss Weatherby.' Mr Marcus scratched his beard. 'This private wire, is it something a person could follow like Hansel and Gretel's breadcrumbs from one place to another, for example from your father's place to the Beacon Academy?'

Winnie swallowed again before nodding. 'Theoretically speaking, a person could follow it, but only if he knew what to look for and had experience and specific knowledge about telegraph wires. This knowledge is very technical and specialized . . .'

But then, so was using a telautograph – and someone had sent a telautogram from her father's transmitting machine. Anxiety churned in her belly. They undoubtedly knew enough to follow the wire straight to the machine. She had to keep it safe.

Headmistress shot to her feet. 'Egad! I don't like it. Marcus, have the staff check the perimeter, and once we're sure the operation isn't under immediate threat, you must go to the Spymaster to report this breach. It's the second one caused by Miss Weatherby's lack of attention to rules.' She stalked out of the room with Mr Marcus following close behind.

Winnie slumped.

Adelaide closed the door. 'Oh, Winifred, I am so sorry. I should have locked my door to keep the maid out. If I'd been here, I could have prevented her reporting the constant ringing to Headmistress . . . Winifred?'

Tears burnt in Winnie's eyes, and her face twisted. Where was Papa, and what was happening?

'Oh, dear! Please don't weep.' Adelaide passed her a handkerchief. 'Headmistress always overreacts. She enjoys the drama. You'll become accustomed to it.'

Winnie dabbed her eyes and drew a few deep breaths. Dissolving into mush would not help Papa. She must think . . . 'Adelaide, did she mention how many times it rang?'

She shrugged. 'All together, four? Five? She said it wasn't all at once. A few rings in the morning, and again in the afternoon.'

'It would be an even number. When a transmission finishes, the bell rings twice.' Winnie dropped to her knees. 'Four dings mean there were two messages!'

Adelaide knelt beside her. 'But where's the second message?'

'The last message on the roll is the most recent, then the previous, then the one before that.' Winnie carefully pulled the paper off the roll. There – before the odd message was an earlier message. Even as it unrolled, she recognized Papa's scratchy handwriting.

'I think your machine is malfunctioning.' Adelaide squinted at the squiggles.

Winnie shook her head and smiled at the reversed handwriting. Both he and Winnie were fluent mirror-writers.

When the full message lay flat, Adelaide's forehead creased. 'What is that?'

'Code,' Winnie answered. 'Papa sent me a cipher.'

Dearest W,

I've little time to explain, so I'll start with the most important facts.

You may remember Herr Peter Geier, that troublesome colleague from several years ago who was long badgered me to become business partners. Failing that, Geier & Co. made an offer for the rights to the machine. Of course I refused. He recently changed tack, becoming brutish and violent. I managed to escape, but I fear for my life.

You must take care. Do not talk to strangers. Take refuge in womanly ignorance if anyone asks about the WTM. Skerryvore is a refuge.

no doubt you will have seen the malicious news articles Rest assured, every word is false, designed by Geier to drive investors away from Weatherby Manufacturing Company and leave us destitute. His assault on my character appears to be working. Our biggest backers have pulled out.

DO NOT TRY TO CLEAR MY NAME. The slander is a ploy to draw us out. Credibility can be rebuilt later.

I still believe Mr Thomas is our best opportunity - more so now. I will make my way to him as we arranged. I will take R. Please bring T.

Franc is safe.

Be careful, my dear, and forgive my hasty style and seeming lack of affection. Until we meet again, I remain . . .

Your ever loving, ever affectionate

Papa

Papa's mirror-written letter deciphered:

Dearest W,

I've little time to explain, so I'll start with the most important facts.

You may remember Herr Peter Geier, that troublesome colleague from several years ago who has long badgered me to become business partners. Failing that, Geier & Co. made an offer for the rights to the machine. Of course I refused. He recently changed tack, becoming brutish and violent. I managed to escape, but I fear for my life.

You must take care. Do not talk to strangers. Take refuge in womanly ignorance if anyone asks about the WTM. Skerryvore is a refuge.

No doubt you will have seen the malicious news articles. Rest assured, every word is false, designed by Geier to drive investors away from Weatherby Manufacturing Company and leave us destitute. His assault on my character appears to be working. Our biggest backers have pulled out.

DO NOT TRY TO CLEAR MY NAME. The slander is a ploy to draw us out. Credibility can be rebuilt later.

I still believe Mr Thomas is our best opportunity – more so now. I will make my way to him as we arranged. I will take R. Please bring T.

<u>Franc is safe.</u>

Be careful, my dear, and forgive my hasty
style and seeming lack of affection. Until we
meet again, I remain . . .

Your ever loving, ever affectionate
Papa

Winnie tapped her chin. Papa had used some code
words in case the telautogram was intercepted. *Skerryvore*,
she recognized. It was a lighthouse, also known as a
beacon, so he was referring to the Beacon Academy,
where he believed the Weatherby Telautograph Machine
would be safe from Geier.

Mr Thomas. Winnie couldn't think of any associates by
that name. Unless – he meant Mr Thomas *Edison*, whom
he was hoping to meet with at the Exposition Universelle.
Of course.

And *Franc is safe* meant the francs or French money
was in the safe at their home.

Winnie hugged the paper to her chest. Papa was well
and taking care. They had a plan: All she had to do was
find a way to take *the T*, or transmitter of the Telautograph, to Paris by the fifth of May.

CHAPTER 12

Thursday morning, the wee hours

The curtains were drawn in Headmistress's office, and the last coals glowed pale orange on the grate. Winnie, Miss Davies, Miss Lee and Adelaide were sitting around in dressing gowns and nightcaps, yawning.

Spies.

Still in day clothes, Headmistress wound the phonograph to play the record cylinder. Opera music spilt out, soft and scratchy. 'This sound should muddle our voices in case anyone is listening.'

Winnie blinked. Eavesdroppers at this hour? It was well past midnight.

At this alarming possibility, the sleepy girls straightened up and glanced around the room. Miss Davies drew her dressing gown more modestly under her chin.

The faint glow from the fireplace threw strange shadows on Headmistress's face, making her appear hawkish. 'We hadn't anticipated that your first official briefing would be so soon. However, *unfortunate events* have transpired that require some immediate changes to maintain the integrity of the Agency's operations.'

Winnie shifted uncomfortably; the 'unfortunate events' were her doing. Mr Marcus had discovered signs that the Beacon Academy was indeed under surveillance. It remained unclear whether someone had followed the telegraph line from Papa's laboratory to the Beacon Academy or followed another lead. *Oh, Papa.*

Her father had been alive and well earlier today when he had sent the message, and he had taken the receiver unit, but someone else had used the transmitter hours after him. Was Papa safe, or had he been captured since he'd sent the telautogram? How would she ever know? And where had Papa been during the gap between her first telautogram and today? Had he put himself in danger by returning home in order to send the message? Perhaps he'd hoped to disconnect the wire between her home and the Academy but failed. Peter Geier's name was familiar, but she'd never met the man. Was he the orchestrator of the chase through London and the sender of the two men disguised as bobbies at the waxworks? What about that detective who had come to the Beacon Academy in the morning, DI Walker? She rubbed her belly, trying to erase the icy dread spreading from her core.

'Miss Weatherby, please!' Headmistress's voice penetrated Winnie's ruminations. 'I understand you're worried, but you must pay attention. As I was saying, we are concerned the entire espionage training facility may be compromised. Therefore, tomorrow, all of you will be relocated. Henceforth you will train and lodge at the waxworks.

'At dawn, you will rise, dress in your servant disguises, and take up your assigned positions downstairs. Miss Davies and Miss Lee, you will do the chambermaid duties. Miss Culpepper and Miss Weatherby, you will carry out scullery duties. The housekeeper will give each of you "errands". Take the prepared basket. While you are out of the Academy, please muddle your route by using backstreets and the underground rail.

'When you are certain no one is following you, make your way to the Tussauds Wax Museum. A discreet HML in chalk on the platform at the Baker Street Station marks a subterranean entrance to the waxworks. The tunnel is dark, so it's advisable to ensure the portable oil lamp packed in your basket is accessible. Please take care to arrive by noon at the very latest. Together, you will undertake an induction course into Her Majesty's service, while Winifred catches up on her foundational training in espionage—'

'Headmistress, excuse me,' Adelaide interrupted, 'but I would prefer to stay at the Beacon Academy. I cherish my role as your assistant . . . and I would like to continue.'

Winnie squirmed, reading between the lines. What Adelaide wasn't saying was she needed the salary. She'd hinted to Winnie that she was in some type of financial distress. And once Winnie had heard some unpleasant older girls call Adelaide 'the charity case'.

'Adelaide, this is not the time. For now, all of you must follow the Spymaster's orders, no deviations.' She arched a brow at Winnie.

Winnie had raised her hand. 'Are you saying we won't return to the Beacon Academy afterwards?'

'Correct.' Headmistress nodded. 'Least of all, you.'

Winnie frowned. 'I cannot and will not leave the Weatherby Telautograph Machine here, nor the designs. They are my responsibility – where I go, they go.'

Miss Davies snorted. 'You have some nerve, asking for *another* personal favour, Miss Weatherby.'

Miss Lee nodded. 'Especially since your blunder caused this problem. I don't wish to leave here either. I'm quite attached to my Premier Pupil room.'

'Shush, both of you!' Adelaide hissed. 'Miss Weatherby's father is missing, and you're being horrible.'

Headmistress Thornton stomped her foot. 'Ladies, please! That's enough.' She turned to Winnie. 'Absolutely no tele-whatsits are leaving this building. That contraption is a liability of the highest degree.'

'Then I will not continue with the League.' Winnie rose wearily to her feet. She had no choice – heavenly laboratory for her exclusive use or not. Papa was counting on her to look after his precious machine and take it to Paris by the fifth of May.

'Sit down, Miss Weatherby.' Headmistress closed her eyes and pinched the bridge of her nose. 'Very well. I will personally see to the transfer of that troublesome machine and your designs. But there'll be no wire connection – ever!'

'I will need to verify the transfer has happened – and I'll need direct access to the machine.' Winnie's eyes twitched from exhaustion.

Miss Lee pressed her lips together, and Miss Davies rolled her eyes. Winnie winced at their displeasure. How uncomfortable to be on such uneven footing with her colleagues.

'God grant me strength . . .' Headmistress prayed. With her lips pressed in a grim line, she nodded her agreement, and Winnie dropped on to her chair.

'Ladies, tomorrow morning when you wake, you are neither pupils nor spies; until you reach the waxworks, you are household servants, so think and behave like servants no matter whom you encounter. Consider this your first group spycraft exercise in subterfuge.' The recording on the gramophone droned to a scratchy stop. 'We'll take that as our cue to conclude. Now, off to bed.'

Thursday, fifteen minutes past noon

Disguised as a scullery maid, Winnie stepped through the door from the subterranean passage into the basement of the waxworks and clamped the wick on her portable oil lamp. She set her basket of eggs on the floor, untied her maid's bonnet, removed the wig of curly auburn hair, and gave her scalp a good scratch and her stiff neck a deep massage. What a relief to be Winifred again. She leant against the cool wall and closed her eyes for a moment.

'Ah, Miss Weatherby! Finally, you're here.'

Winnie opened her eyes. Standing in front of her was a strikingly beautiful young lady. Her dimpled face was so angelic, her eyes so bright and movements so graceful, Winnie didn't know how to speak to her. 'Er . . .'

'Let me take your basket. Would you like to put the lamp inside?' The pretty young lady picked up the basket of eggs. 'This way. I'll take you to our room where you can change out of your disguise.'

'Thank you.' The young lady's accent was unusual, hard to place – not quite North American. Winnie detected a glint of French, perhaps.

She led Winnie to an out-of-service water closet. 'Don't worry. It's not what you think!' She opened the door to reveal a safety lift, as Winnie expected.

Who is this young woman? A lovely scent of violets wafted from the folds of her green gown. She was both polished and poised. And amiable and helpful. Winnie resisted a strong urge to pinch her to see if she was real.

The young lady shoved the lever up, and the cubicle began its grinding rise. 'My name is Celeste Lemieux, the last of your colleagues but an early recruit to the League, although Adelaide likes to point out she was the first. I've just returned from a small mission on the continent – well, to be honest it was more of a shopping expedition.' She leant close and whispered, 'A spiffing new bespoke dagger from a master craftsman in the Italian Alps!'

Winnie's chin dropped. A fairy wand would be more suitable for this divine creature.

Celeste grinned, deepening her dimples. 'I've so been looking forward to meeting you. Mrs Campbell told us you're to be our quartermistress, which is fascinating. I so admire girls who understand mechanical things and excel at mathematics. I certainly do not possess those abilities.'

Winnie's brows shot up.

Smiling, she studied Winnie's face. 'You're far prettier than I expected. I supposed you'd look manly!' She giggled at herself. 'That's silly, of course. Why can't smart girls be attractive too?'

Winnie stifled a snort. No one had ever suggested she was pretty, least of all someone who was actually beautiful.

'Wait until you see our quarters. Isn't it exciting to be residing *in* the wax museum? Of all the places in London! The Beacon Academy was sufficient, of course, but this place . . . it has its own mystique.'

This delightful girl had also been at the Beacon Academy? How had she not crossed paths with her or any of them? Winnie found her voice. 'Yes, the museum is creepy and dignified at the same time.'

'Exactly!' Miss Lemieux nodded enthusiastically. 'As soon as you've changed out of your disguise, we have a briefing with Mrs Campbell and Headmistress to discuss our various roles. I've been recruited as weapons mistress for my sharpshooting and sword fighting skills.' She pushed the lever down, precisely lining up the lift carriage to the floor level. 'I've been told we have a lot of work ahead of us!' She exited the lift.

Winnie stayed put. 'Weapons, Miss Lemieux? As in guns?' *Egad.* No one had mentioned violence or weaponry!

Miss Lemieux nodded so vigorously her strawberry-blonde ringlets bounced. 'And knives. Et cetera. We'll have so much fun. Come along. I saved the bed next to mine for you. I hope you like it.'

Winnie followed the young lady down a long corridor. They were on the very top floor of the Tussauds building, and the jumbled stuff – broken furniture, huge paintings wrapped in calico, dusty marble busts – indicated it was the museum's storage area.

'Welcome to the Den of Spies.' Miss Lemieux giggled as she opened a creaking door to a spacious room with sloping ceilings and dormer windows. Light sliced through the shutters, marking the air and floor with golden stripes. Two walls were lined with built-in beds of dark wood panels, each with its own storage chest at the front.

Two young ladies sat at the central table, both scribbling in notebooks. Miss Lee looked up from her work and nodded a sheepish greeting to her.

'Good day,' Miss Davies said. 'Come in, come in.' Her smile was almost welcoming – a relief after yesterday's cold reception and last night's hostility.

'Look who's arrived! It's our clever inventress,' Miss Lemieux trilled. 'All of us are in this room together. Won't that be convivial?' She twirled around the room with the grace of a ballerina. 'And that reminds me. Since we are sharing a bedroom, we simply must dispense with the formality. I do hope you'll call me Celeste, not Miss Lemieux or anything stuffy.'

'Very well, but only if you'll use my first name too.' It was impossible not to feel at ease. Tension drained from Winnie's shoulders. 'I'm Winifred,' she said, 'but I prefer Winnie.'

Miss Lee and Miss Davies hunkered down into their work rather than offering a less formal stance. Winnie winced inwardly at their rebuff. At least they had the decency to wriggle at the awkwardness they'd created.

Celeste shook Winnie's hand warmly, then pointed to the chest attached to Winnie's bed where she'd placed her basket. 'This bed is yours, and the next one is mine, then Stella, Adelaide and Effie. In my part of Canada, these cosy beds are called *lits clos*. I'm not sure what they're called here.'

'Box-beds, I believe.' *Canadian. That explains the accent.* Winnie pulled back the bed's curtains and peered into the nook. *Cosy indeed.* She lifted the lid of her steamer trunk parked nearby. Her gowns and disguises were gone. Only her unmentionables remained with her chatelaine laid neatly on top.

Celeste pursed her lips. 'Ooh, I hope you don't mind. I took the liberty of hanging your things in the armoire. I thought you might object to someone handling your undergarments, so I left them for you to put away.'

Celeste's use of such a straightforward term made Winnie's cheeks burn. 'Thank you. That's very thoughtful.'

'I'm intrigued by your chatelaine. Mrs Campbell told us about all the things it can do. How very clever you are, Winnie.'

Winnie couldn't help grinning. 'Monsieur Moineau wasn't fond of it at all! "Absolutely no, not, NEVER!"' she said, exaggerating the wardrobe master's Parisian pronunciation.

Miss Lee covered her mouth, and Miss Davies snorted softly, but neither looked up from their booklets.

Celeste laughed. 'Monsieur excels at colour selection and choosing flattering cuts, but it would never occur to him to furnish a lady with anything useful like pockets or equipages.'

Winnie shook her head. 'Omitting pockets is a most dreadful sin and a grave design failure.'

'Indeed.' Celeste opened the armoire and selected Winnie's garnet day gown. She took it to the dressing screen in the corner. 'Would you like some help changing? I can't wait to see this dress on.'

Winnie stepped behind the screen to change.

She was nearly done when the door to their room creaked open. 'What's taking so long?' It was Adelaide's voice, pinched with irritation. 'The Spymistress and Handler are waiting in the library.'

'Oh, it's you,' Celeste replied flatly.

Papers rustled, and chairs scraped on the floor. 'We

were just finishing our decoding exercise,' Miss Lee said.

Winnie popped her head to the side of the screen. 'Good day, Adelaide. I'm almost ready . . . I got muddled at Piccadilly Circus and took the wrong train. On the upside, if anyone was following me, I'd say he's well on his way to Cardiff by now.' She stepped out from behind the screen, struggling to fasten the tiny buttons at her elbows.

'Let me help you.' Celeste took over. 'Oh, good gracious, you look so pretty, Winnie!'

Adelaide let out a strange sound, a tiny growl. 'I'll let Mrs Campbell know you're on your way. Come along, girls.' She tossed a small book on Winnie's trunk. 'Don't forget your training manual, Miss Weatherby.' Miss Lee and Miss Davies skipped out, and Adelaide followed. The door slammed behind her.

Winnie jumped at the bang.

'Someone got up on the wrong side of her box-bed,' Celeste muttered.

Winnie shook her head. 'I imagine she feels fatigued. Adelaide keeps late hours, rid— *working* into the wee hours of the night.' Oops, she'd almost let out Adelaide's secret about the safety bicycle. Oh, golly! Perhaps her night roving was League work . . . Once they were alone and could talk openly, Winnie would ask.

Celeste fastened the buttons on Winnie's other elbow and plumped the fabric over the bustle. 'Come – it's time to be serious spies. We must hurry, or Mrs Campbell will be cross as well.' She snatched the small, clothbound book from Winnie's trunk and passed it to her. 'Your all-important training manual.'

Winnie fingered the embossed green fabric of the cover: *The Birds of Great Britain: A Young Lady's Field Companion.*

Birds? 'Are you sure this is the right book?'

Celeste tilted her head, her dimples deepening. 'Time to find out! Would you like to operate the elevator this time, mademoiselle?' She darted out of the room, her feet pounding down the corridor.

'*Mais oui!*' Winnie shouted with a laugh. She hitched her skirt and raced after the cheerful Miss Lemieux. Perhaps this espionage adventure hadn't been a mistake after all.

THE BIRDS OF GREAT BRITAIN:

A Young Lady's Field Companion

Your training concludes with an examination.

HML

THE LONDON EVENING NEWS
A Mischief of Magpies Mar Royal Easter Monday Chapel — HM Cries 'Sacrilege'

The Queen's private prayers at St George's Chapel, Windsor, were invaded by an unwelcome mischief of magpies. Upon opening the door to the Queen's Closet, Her Majesty Queen Victoria was swarmed by a frantic flock of trapped birds. Their swooping exit gave the Queen 'a terrible fright'.

'It was incredibly lucky Her Majesty was not injured,' exclaimed her private secretary, Sir Henry Ponsonby.

It remains a mystery how the birds became entrapped inside the hallowed space; however, *who* set this dastardly trap is less mysterious. The calling card of the now infamous fiend 'Mr Magpie' was positioned squarely on Her Majesty's pew at the front of the Oriel Window.

The Queen was reportedly 'furious at the sacrilege' of a church on a Holy

Day by 'filthy birds with bad characters'. Accompanying the Queen to the Easter Monday service were HRH the Prince and Princess of Wales. Both were unscathed other than a white streak left by one of the birds on the shoulder of His Royal Highness's coat.

While the villain's motives remain unclear, the Palace is downplaying the danger of the 'pranks'. Sir Henry stated, 'The objective has not been to harm but merely to harass. None of the Royal Family is in danger.'

Increased security measures have been advised for the Queen and the Royal Family.

CHAPTER 13

~Madame Tussauds Wax Museum~

Four weeks later, Wednesday 24 April 1889

Winnie strode into one of the upstairs galleries of Madame Tussauds. She tipped her top hat to the doorman. 'Good day!' she said in a rather poor attempt at a burly voice.

The heavily moustached doorman bowed in reply. 'Good day, sir. Welcome to the William Shakespeare Gallery.'

What a lark! Winnie smiled inwardly. For her foundational espionage training examination, she'd disguised herself as a young gentleman artist, and it was working. Under her arm, she carried a thin board with drawing paper clipped to it for sketching likenesses of the wax figures. And below the sketching paper was her examination paper. She had to complete the five tasks in an allotted timeframe. She quickly glanced up to the mezzanine level, the spot from which her examiners would observe her. They hadn't taken up their positions yet.

She stuck her hand and half her forearm into the left trouser pocket, feeling for a stick of charcoal. She took a gold pocket watch from the pocket of her plaid waistcoat – four minutes until the start of the examination. Time to position herself for optimum observation. Winnie scratched behind her ears. The wig was so itchy!

She nodded cordial, manly greetings to the clusters of people she passed, taking in faces, personal effects and attire. All the details would help complete today's examination of her recently acquired espionage skills. Successful completion of the mission would mean Winnie would finally be encouraged to focus on her projects in the Quartermistress's Laboratory.

The bells of nearby St Marylebone Parish rang on the hour, and she moved to the tableau of *A Midsummer Night's Dream*. Using her stick of charcoal, she pretended to sketch the wax statue of Puck, but she read her examination paper instead.

Complete the following five tasks and describe them here.
    I) Identify the two targets.
    2) What gives them away?
    3) What is their signal of recognition?

4) Identify their item of exchange.

5) Are they avoiding another entity, and, if so, is that person in the vicinity?

Capital. She grinned. After four tough weeks of training and practice, this examination would be as easy as a stroll in the park. Winnie watched over the top of her board for the crowd's oddities to emerge.

Around the gallery visitors strolled, chatting and laughing. Children whined; heels clicked; men coughed; and Winnie's charcoal scratched across the page. Then, near the witches of *Macbeth*, a woman carrying a straw-and-silk reticule cleared her throat. She unfolded a yellow fan and held it near her face.

Odd. Nothing in her outfit warranted a yellow fan, and the temperature was quite cool in the gallery. The woman had a self-conscious stiffness to her manner. Winnie darkened the details of Puck's ears, and then shifted the page to fill in her examination paper.

A man across the room sneezed twice. The lady strode past him and dropped her folded fan in his pocket.

'And there it is.' Winnie jotted her answers down, slightly disappointed at the ease of the examination. Just as she was ready to signal her completion to Head-mistress, the moustached doorman raised his voice.

'No unaccompanied children are permitted in the galleries. Off with you!'

The rake-thin boy faked to the left and dashed to the right, slipping past the man.

Was this part of the examination? Winnie stood on tiptoes, stretching for a better view.

The doorman snatched the wiry boy by the shoulders and steered him back through the entrance.

'Oi! That's no way to treat a paying customer! Ow! Get your paws off me!'

That voice! Winnie moved closer. Good golly, it was Clancy. Oh, dear – what rotten timing!

Full steam ahead across the room Winnie chugged, head lowered.

People paused to gaze at her speedy progress.

Drat, she'd drawn attention to herself. She slowed her gait. By the time she reached the entry, the doorman was red-faced from the struggle to restrain a very wriggly Clancy.

'I say!' Winnie's voice came out both too high and too soft. She cleared her throat and lowered her voice. 'What are you doing with my assistant? We have drawings to complete. Look sharp about it!'

The doorman's brows shot up. He dropped Clancy in a heap. 'I beg your pardon, sir. I assumed the lad was unaccompanied.' When Clancy stood up, the doorman smoothed his coat.

'Hands off!' Clancy brushed the doorman's hands away. He cast a suspicious eye over Winnie – the young artist gentleman. 'Do I know—'

Winnie grabbed him by the elbow and yanked him away. 'Hush,' she said under her voice.

'Oi! That hurts.'

She guided him to the far end of the gallery, behind the creepy display featuring the witches of *Macbeth* and their huge iron cauldron. 'Just stand still, would you?'

'Oh, no. You bullies aren't nabbing me again. I've got a knife this time!' He made a break to escape her.

'Clancy, stop.' She used her normal voice.

'Wait a minute. How do you know me name?' He narrowed his eyes and studied Winnie's face. Recognition dawned, and his eyes and mouth popped open. 'Crikey, miss! What the blazes happened to you?'

Winnie covered his mouth. 'Shh. You must stop talking. I have only a moment. I'm in the middle of – that is, I'm . . . otherwise occupied.' She glanced over her shoulder to the mezzanine where Mrs Campbell stood. Fortunately, she was talking to Adelaide.

Winnie continued. 'I'm fine. Never mind this.' She gestured to the disguise. 'It's too hard to explain. Why have you come?'

Clancy's gaze circled her face, a look of shock twisting

his mouth. 'Why have I come? Well, it's not to find you, fank you very much. Ever since we parted ways, I've had nuffin' but trouble. This is me first outing since I escaped the band of wicked cutthroats who nabbed me. Thought I'd spend one of the tokens you gave me.'

Wait, what? Winnie held up her hands. 'Could we please return to wicked cutthroats and trouble? Whatever do you mean?'

'There's a gang of 'em, and they were waiting at your home for *you*. They nabbed me and did their best to see if I knew your whereabouts.' He pulled up his sleeve and presented his wrist. Rope burn, scabbed over and bruised. 'The other one's worse – all crusty and vile.'

Winnie gasped. 'Who did this to you? When?' Her innards clenched. The dear boy had been kidnapped – on her account?

He sneaked a peek around the *Macbeth* tableau. 'So, it happened like this. A week back, I went to call on your father, like you'd told me to.'

'Go on.' She clutched her stomach. What followed was sure to be unpleasant, but at least she'd have a recent account from her home. 'Tell me if you found him.'

'There was a man there, but he wasn't your pa, I'm sure of it now, though I didn't know it at the time. He was kind – at first. He let me sit by the fire and gave me some hot roasted chestnuts and a mug of warm milk with some strange scent in it. He promised a rich reward if I'd help him, even swung a fat sack of coins in front of me face. I thought he'd want help with the cleaning, on account of the wretched state of the home.'

Winnie gasped. 'No!'

'Strewth! Pardon my swearing, but I never seen such a mess inside a fine home. Furniture was smashed, glass was broken, and everywhere you looked, paper was strewn about as if the Jubilee had just happened. But that man wasn't concerned about cleaning the house, which made me suspicious that he wasn't who he said he was . . .'

Both hands covered Winnie's mouth. *Papa!* Later, she'd beg Mrs Campbell for an update from her intelligence network.

'He was concerned about "his daughter", Miss Winifred Weatherby. He asked all manner of questions about you, where you were going and when I saw you last and what you were carrying . . .' Clancy shivered and rubbed the back of his head. His face changed – hollowed – and he fell silent.

'What did you tell him?' Winnie's hands began to tremble.

'Nothing! I kept me mouth shut.' He looked away and gulped. 'At least I did until they started twistin' me ears and beatin' me . . .' He rubbed tears from his cheeks with the back of his hands. 'I only remembered the bit about your fine lady, the one who gave you the purse with the tokens. I didn't mean to say anything, miss, but they were hurting me.'

Winnie patted his arm. 'I had no idea things would turn so . . . dire. I'm sorry I involved you, Clancy.' She glanced down, and the sight of her trousered legs and men's footwear made her jump. Gracious! The examination. 'I beg your pardon, but I . . . I must, erm, finish a drawing.' She raised her drawing board and did a quick sketch of Clancy, including his too-short trousers. 'Are you safe now?' Two dots for dimples . . .

Clancy nodded. 'Peggy's letting me sleep in the attic of the tea room. That way, I can use the rooftops to get about in the daytime, until I feel comfortable again.'

Winnie sighed. 'I only wish I knew who this ruffian was.'

Clancy's eyes sparkled. 'I know his name, miss. One of those thugs called him Mr Geier. I remember the name because it rhymes with *liar*.'

Peter Geier from Papa's mirror-written telautogram! Winnie shuddered. 'He's a liar all right.'

Clancy nodded emphatically. 'Soon as I heard his real name, I knew for sure he was pretending to be your father. Turns out the milk had something in it to make me sleepy. When I was unconscious, those brutes bound me up, bagged me like a chicken for the slaughter, and tossed me in the Thames in the middle of the night. I came to when I hit the icy water. Half me luck, a waterman saw it happen and pulled me out.'

'Merciful heavens, Clancy! Promise me you'll take every care.'

He shrugged. 'I don't expect further trouble from Geier the Liar. He finks I'm dead. I *am* worried about the detective he's hired, though. DI Walker of the Metropolitan Police.'

A chill ran down her spine. *Walker was the name of the detective who'd gone to the Beacon Academy to interview me!* 'That makes no sense. Why would a police detective work for a criminal?' Her voice shook.

Clancy levelled a look at her as if she were daft. 'For the money. Geier told Walker, "You'll get full payment when you bring me the goods *and the girl.*" And he meant you, miss.' He paused to shake his head. 'Walker's the worst kind, playing both sides, cop and robber. You watch your step, miss.'

'I shall.' A sigh hissed from her chest. She rubbed her tight jaw. 'Goodness.'

Clancy nodded, and his brows shot up. 'DI Walker's easy to spot. He has a bushy moustache, and he carries a peculiar umbrella – the handle is a silver bat.' He shuddered. 'Its little glittery eyes gave me the creeps, miss.'

Winnie nodded slowly, committing the description to memory. 'Clancy, if anyone asks, you must never reveal that you've spoken with me or where. Promise?'

He nodded. 'I promise, miss, er, sir.' He winked cheekily.

She glanced up to the mezzanine. Her examiner had disappeared. 'If you need to get word to me, drop a note here in the witches' cauldron, but make sure no one sees you. No names, nothing to give it away. I'll do the same to you.' She put out her hand to seal the deal.

He chuckled. 'A handshake, how very manly!' He shook it, glanced at the sketch and cocked a crooked smile. 'Not a bad likeness. I'm off to see the Chamber of Horrors. Wish me luck!' He tipped his cap and scurried away, pausing only to poke his tongue out at the doorman.

Now, back to the task at hand: her examination. Up on the mezzanine overlooking the gallery, Adelaide tilted her head. She tugged her left earlobe twice, a hand signal. According to their field guide, it meant: *Abort. Return to Base.*

'Double drat.'

CHAPTER 14

~THE WAXWORKS LIBRARY~

Later

Still dressed as a male artist, Winnie trudged into the library where everyone waited. She placed the drawing board face down on the mantel, peeled off her itchy wig and seated herself at the oval table between Adelaide and Celeste. Her thoughts swirled with Clancy's news – her overturned home, her still-missing papa, an innocent boy being beaten by thugs and a brutal detective on her trail.

The four weeks of exhausting spy training within these walls had buffered her from the terror of being hunted, but the fear had just reignited, blazing stronger than ever. No longer a shadowy threat – her hunter now had a name, a description and a menacing history.

Had those villains caught Papa and hurt him like Clancy? She shook off the horrible image of a boy's body being tossed in the

Thames in the dead of night.

What would the Spymistress say about this development? Mrs Campbell had worried that Winnie's position could be 'messy'. Would they dismiss her? Strip her of her wondrous laboratory? Leave her to fend for herself?

Oh, bother! She'd been rash promising not to investigate and leaving it to the League's resources. Mrs Campbell had given her no news – only vague reassurances they were 'monitoring Professor Weatherby's whereabouts'. Promise or no promise, she had to do something with this information.

Headmistress Thornton paced in front of the towering bookcase holding the tomes on war history. Mrs Campbell sat alone at the far end of the room in a cloud of noxious tobacco smoke. No one spoke.

After stubbing out her cigarette, Mrs Campbell lowered her widow's veil and approached the group. 'I don't know where to begin.' She circled the table slowly.

'I too am lost for words,' Headmistress Thornton replied. 'Never have I seen such a bumbled mission. Winifred acted as if it were a promenade at Hyde Park!'

Mrs Campbell slid her hands under her black veil to massage her temples. 'What on earth were you doing, Winifred? While this was a *staged* mission, it was still important.'

Winnie puffed her cheeks. Of course she should have

focused on the task, but how could she have skipped an opportunity to speak with Clancy? Besides – she hadn't gone looking for this information. It came to her quite by chance.

How could she explain? No witty banter came to mind. No cheeky excuses. No sarcastic questions. She sighed. 'I'm sorry. I failed you, all of you. I don't know what else to say.' She stood. 'If I may, I wish to retire to bed with a bucket and a cold compress. I feel quite sick.'

Headmistress Thornton had taken the drawing board off the mantel. 'Miss Weatherby, is this the child with whom you were speaking?'

Winnie nodded.

Headmistress held up the likeness for Mrs Campbell. 'It must be that guttersnipe guide the doorman described to us.' Her pitch raised an octave. 'Why was this boy here? Did he know he'd find you here?'

'No! He said he wasn't looking for me.' A tired sigh heaved out of Winnie's chest. 'But he did have information about my father, and I had to know it. Interrogate him, be my guest. If you hurry, you'll find him somewhere in the Chamber of Horrors.'

The drawing board smacked the table in front of Winnie, making everyone jump. Headmistress's face purpled. 'Welcome to the wonderful world of espionage, ladies. This innocent-looking child may have been sent to find out if Miss Weatherby is here! Now he knows she is.'

She leant close to Winnie's face, pointing to the sketch. 'He knows you wear disguises, and he knows anything else you happened to disclose to him. He could tell anyone. I wager he'll disclose all his intelligence to the highest bidder.' Headmistress Thornton dropped on to a nearby armchair. 'We are ruined. This is a security breach we cannot remedy.'

Winnie's head swam with silver bats and rope-burnt wrists and broken furniture. Oh, to be in her box-bed with the curtains pulled shut . . . She folded her arms around herself.

Mrs Campbell growled, 'Thornton, enough. Miss Weatherby's father is missing. She had to choose between passing a relatively meaningless examination or discovering news about her beloved father. I daresay any of us would have made the same choice – the wrong choice.'

Headmistress laid her head against the chairback. 'I warned you! I told you she's hopelessly reckless.'

'Then count me reckless too.' Effie sat up straighter. 'I would have done the same thing if my father were missing.' She flashed a compassionate glance at Winnie. 'Except – apologies, Winnie – I would not have allowed the lad to leave.'

'An excellent point,' Stella said. 'Frankly, I'm awed that Winifred has been so faithful to her promise, especially when the Agency has done so little to help her.' She jutted her chin. Adelaide gave Winnie's shoulder a reassuring squeeze. Celeste slid her hand into the crook of Winnie's elbow and drew herself closer.

Winnie blinked back tears – the solidarity of the other League members lent her courage.

Mrs Campbell shrugged a shoulder. 'Very well. I accept I was remiss for holding back information, and I apologize. Winifred, we'll speak privately later.' The Spymistress drew in a breath. 'This . . . *misstep* provides an excellent moment of instruction. Ladies, you must remember Rule Number One: if there's any chance of being identified, abort the mission. The League must *never* be discovered. That is the most important thing. Winifred, think back. When you were in the runaway carriage, what did Mr Marcus do?'

Do? At the time, Winnie had thought he had been shot and fallen out of the carriage, but obviously he hadn't. Had he jumped from the carriage and fled?

Before she could answer, Mrs Campbell fired another question. 'When you and the boy arrived at the wax-works, and the so-called bobbies caught up with you, what did the doorman do?'

'He vanished.' Winnie frowned. Both events had felt like abandonment. She harrumphed. 'So, both "gentlemen" chose to leave the scene to protect the Agency?'

'Precisely. They've been trained to do so. It's what spies *must* do.'

'But that means they threw a young lady to the wolves! I could have been captured by fiends – both times.'

'But you weren't. You're a very resourceful young lady.'

'Perhaps, but I'm also a very loyal young lady, one who simply cannot abandon companions for the sake of some murky agency and its veiled leader.' She was referring to her companion Clancy, but Winnie glanced around the table at her colleagues. Despite their awkward start, the five young ladies had grown closer over her training period. And after their rallying for her today, she knew she'd never leave any of them in such danger.

'Miss Weatherby, watch your tone!' Headmistress Thornton shook a finger. 'That is no way to speak to your superiors. You must remember your place—'

A searing look from Mrs Campbell silenced the Handler's tirade. 'If loyalty is a fault, it's a good one to have. We'll discuss this later.'

Headmistress Thornton wrung her hands. 'We're running out of time. The ladies need to be ready – inducted and equipped – by Saturday.'

Winnie spluttered. Three days! How could she equip herself and the others with espionage tools in such a short timeframe? They must allow her ample time in the laboratory – after she'd had a sleep.

Adelaide cocked her head. 'Saturday? What happens then?'

Mrs Campbell hesitated. 'I'd hoped to hold a proper briefing later . . . Saturday is the night of the League's first official mission. Lady Holland is hosting a society soiree, and some members of the Royal Family will be in attendance.'

Good golly! Royalty on their first mission. Winnie glanced at the others. Stella's and Effie's mouths hung open. Celeste's eyes twinkled with excitement, while Adelaide's brow was pinched with alarm.

Mrs Campbell seated herself at the table. 'You mustn't fret. Your part of the mission will mirror Winifred's exercise today: identify the target from among a crowd and follow him without arousing suspicion. Once you've passed on the intelligence, you must get out of the way, melt back into the crowd. The police will apprehend him . . . or the sharpshooters will wing him—'

Winnie gasped. She'd signed up for a little intrigue and lots of tinkering – not bloodshed!

Mrs Campbell held up her palms to calm them. 'As I said, your mission is strictly reconnaissance – watch and report. You'll be equipped with customized spyware that Miss Weatherby will finalize. We've been planning Operation Bait-and-Snare for some time, waiting only for an opportune event to appear in the London society calendar. The guest list of Lady Holland's soiree is sure to draw out our notorious target.'

How intriguing! Winnie twitched with anticipation, and they all exchanged curious glances.

Adelaide held out her hands questioningly. 'Allow me to ask the question on all our lips. May we know who this notorious target is?'

Celeste rubbed her palms together. 'I do hope he's especially dastardly so we can bag the fiend and make a good name for the League. Tally ho!'

Winnie sniggered at Celeste's unbridled enthusiasm.

Stella shook her head. 'Your eagerness for the hunt is somewhat alarming, Celeste.'

However, even Mrs Campbell was amused. 'The target is indubitably dastardly, my dear ladies. Her Majesty the Queen strongly desires to see an end to his spree of troublemaking.' The Spymistress drummed her fingers on the table. 'I suppose it won't hurt to reveal the target of Operation Bait-and-Snare. All going well, that pesky fiend, Mr Magpie, will fly straight into our trap.'

CHAPTER 15

Wednesday afternoon

The spies' gasps of amazement filled the library, and excited chatter broke out until a clap settled them down.

'Ladies, you'll be fully briefed later. In the meantime, I'm sending you upstairs to the palaestra for self-defence drills with Colonel Monstery.' Mrs Campbell rubbed her temples.

No, not their hard-nosed fencing instructor . . . Winnie stifled a groan. Her cosy box-bed with its curtains beckoned from the attic. There would be no sleeping off the nervous headache she'd acquired, but she could use the solitude to plan.

Mrs Campbell gestured for them to stand. 'You'll all benefit from bodily exertion to work off the day's frustration. Thornton, you should join them.' She made a shooing gesture at the headmistress.

Headmistress Thornton gasped. 'I beg your pardon, Your Highness! That is an outrage!'

'Precisely.' Mrs Campbell fiddled with a silver cigarette case, turning it end over end in her hands. 'Off you go!'

Trying not to snigger at the older ladies' sarcastic banter, Winnie joined the end of the queue of four young ladies and one matron.

Mrs Campbell called over her shoulder, 'Winifred, wait there while I fetch a letter from my desk.'

When she came back, Mrs Campbell sat down across from Winnie and placed an envelope on the table. 'Today's debacle made me realize how very difficult it must be for you to focus on our work with the question of your father's safety hanging over you. You asked me to promise I would use my resources to obtain news of your father, and until today, you simply trusted my word. Thank you. And I apologize for withholding information.'

Winnie's gaze instinctively fell to the envelope. *Never mind the past, let me have the news now.* The envelope seemed to pulse with secrets.

'I had planned to have this discussion with you after completing Operation Bait-and-Snare. We do indeed have resources, top-secret resources, at Scotland Yard. However, I'm afraid they haven't uncovered much.'

Scotland Yard! Winnie's brows knitted. No wonder

there was little to report – if that rogue detective DI Walker was meddling.

'You can read it yourself, but in summary: your father is well, currently in hiding at an inn near Bedford. He has moved around to keep his adversary focused on him rather than you—'

'Me?' So Mrs Campbell already knew Winnie was quarry to a mysterious hunter. Winnie struggled to swallow. Somehow Mrs Campbell's knowledge of it made the reality more menacing.

Mrs Campbell nodded. 'My guess is your father's adversary threatened to harm you as a means of gaining what he wants.'

Pieces of the puzzle locked into place, forming a clear picture: Papa had fled to keep *her* – not his invention – safe. The coded message in his mirror-written telautogram made more sense. He'd hoped *she* would be safe at the Beacon Academy.

Mrs Campbell pushed the envelope closer. 'Your father's adversary is, as you suggested, a foreign entity from Prussia. His name is—'

'—Herr Peter Geier,' Winnie filled in the words. 'And he wants the credit for the invention of the Weatherby Telautograph Machine and the rights to produce it. But Papa has refused, and now Mr Geier is employing ungentlemanly tactics, such as defamation, extortion and intimidation.' *Not to mention breaking and entering, kidnapping and attempted murder of a child*. But how could she tell the Spymistress all that without risking her quartermistress role?

Mrs Campbell sat back and folded her arms. 'What *don't* you know?'

Winnie shrugged a shoulder. 'Why is Mr Geier bothering with me, an ordinary girl?'

'Aside from the fact that capturing you will draw your father out, I surmise he has discovered you are far from ordinary, that you are a girl with a remarkable mind, capable of understanding and recreating the machine for him.' Mrs Campbell drummed her fingers on the table. 'How would that fact be known to anyone when your father has gone to great lengths to hide your genius?'

Papa had poo-pooed so many of her inventions. He'd claimed they all lacked 'commercial promise', but the truth was he didn't want to be embarrassed by his mechanically minded daughter. Her one and only invention to be exposed to the public was—

She gasped. 'My entry into the World Fair's Petit Prix! Could the secretariat of the British World Fair Selection Committee have told Mr Geier about me? He saw my invention and my designs. He pushed to see the Telautograph. Now that I think of it, he was far too quick to understand the significance of the Weatherby Telauto-graph Machine by simply glancing at a schematic drawing.'

Mrs Campbell's brows rose behind her veil. 'And who is this secretariat?'

'Sir Phillip Runcliffe-Bowen. Headmistress Thornton had never met him, though she seemed to know his wife – Lady Jenny, I believe.'

'Yes, the name is familiar . . . I shall see that he's inves-tigated – when there's time. For now, our focus must be the successful execution of Operation Bait-and-Snare.'

Winnie wriggled, secrets and fears nipping at her conscience. A detective on her trail posed an enormous risk to the security of the Agency and its missions. 'Mrs Campbell?' Words backed up at the top of her throat. If she mentioned DI Walker, Mrs Campbell would have no choice but to drop Winnie from the league of young lady spies.

'Yes?' The tiny jet beads decorating Mrs Campbell's mourning dress click-clacked with her tiniest movements.

Winnie hesitated, anxiety burning through her belly. 'I fear what I'm about to tell you will jeopardize my position with the League, but I must let you know what Clancy told me.'

'Clancy? The boy from earlier?' Mrs Campbell's brows furrowed. 'Go on.'

'He had a rather nasty encounter with Mr Geier at my father's home, and it turns out that villain has employed a detective by the name of Walker. He's with the Metropolitan Police. He's the one who came to the Beacon Academy to interview me, but Headmistress forbade it.' Winnie grimaced. Expulsion from the League was now imminent . . .

'Oh. I see. That *is* rather inconvenient.' Mrs Campbell sniffed. 'Never mind. I have friends in high places in Scotland Yard who can deal with him. However, the implications for you are troubling . . .' She drummed her fingertips on the table. 'I shall discuss this with the Spymaster.'

Mrs Campbell nodded and slid the letter squarely in front of Winnie. 'That brings me to this. It is a telegram from your father to you via an old friend of your mother's. I don't believe you're acquainted with Lady Henrietta, but she's been affiliated with the Agency since it was only an idea.'

Winnie slid her finger under the seal of the envelope and withdrew a pale blue sheet of telegram paper.

```
DEAREST WAW. EVERYTHING IS TICKETY
BOO. RENDEZVOUS TERMINUS 5 MAY. YLF
```

'Does this mean anything to you? Mind you, it is a week old.'

Winnie's throat ached with emotion. 'It means I can sleep peacefully and dream happily for the first time in a month, because now I know Papa is alive and well enough to write and carry on with our plans. It also means you and I shall have to come to an agreement about an upcoming leave of absence so I can meet him at the Hotel Terminus in Paris for the Exposition Universelle.'

Mrs Campbell bristled. 'That is something we can discuss later. Winifred, Thornton and I had discussed making you redo your final examination, but instead I shall excuse you until a later date. Right now, the Agency needs you to focus on inventing. First, I want you to rest, and then when you're refreshed, you must apply your skills to custom-building tools for Operation Bait-and-Snare. Is that agreeable?'

Winnie stood, knees shaking. 'Most agreeable. So, you're not, erm . . . dismissing me from the League?'

'Dismiss? Now? Where would we ever find a replacement? The mission must go ahead – with precautions, of course. Off you go, then. Oh – one last thing. Before you start working in the laboratory, please note the logbook. Your predecessor left you a letter of introduction. Read it first.'

*

Dear Miss Weatherby, the new quartermistress,

As your predecessor, I wish to welcome you to the Research and Development facility. I regret that I am unable to assist you in person as you step into your new role.

No doubt you will be surprised to learn I knew your mother. Alice and I struck up a warm friendship several years ago at Bath when we were taking the waters, she for consumption and I for chronic digestive ailments. I left Bath recovered, eagerly anticipating a return to my work, while she left Bath unchanged, dreading having to say goodbye to her young daughter – you.

Miss Weatherby, I hope you are aware of how very proud your mother was of you. While Alice and I sat together in the spa's Pump Room, she delighted me with tales of your early tinkering. I was even privy to the drawings and designs you sent her. How endearing and clever they were!

In her final letter to me, Alice asked me to watch over you and to do what I could to open doors for you and your remarkable mind. Your father and I have corresponded as you've grown up, but his recent letters changed from cheerful vignettes of your inventing (mis)adventures to worries about your future marriage prospects.

His change of tone and direction caused me to step in. I recommended the Beacon Academy to him, knowing the door it would open for you. Your father is, of course, unaware of the Academy's connection to an espionage agency.

I invite you to finish my spyware inventions and make them your own. May I suggest you begin with the Vanishing Paper Project (nitrocellulose paper)? After reading this missive, hold it six inches from an open flame. (You'll find one of Herr Bunsen's burners at the far end of the workbench.) Prepare yourself for a rather spectacular (and slightly alarming) POOF! After the brilliant flash, all evidence will vanish, leaving not even a trace of ash.

My research notebooks are in the vault. Vol. 74 lists several applications of nitrocellulose for spy work. I know you will imagine even more!

Unfortunately, my digestive ailments have returned, which means I shan't have the pleasure of meeting you as a young lady. I wish you the most rewarding and full life, my dear Miss Winifred Alice.

Cordially and respectfully yours,
Henrietta Sophia Dudley
Engineer, Mathematician, Inventress & Spy

CHAPTER 16

~The Quartermistress's Laboratory~

Friday morning, 26 April 1889

Winnie woke with a start to the clatter of bottles. 'Wha—' She was in her wonderful laboratory. Bright morning light streamed down from the skylight directly above her. She pressed her fingertips into her knotted neck muscles.

'I beg your pardon. I didn't mean to startle you.' Adelaide stood on the other side of the laboratory near the cabinets of poisons and explosives. 'You missed supper last night, and when you didn't turn up for breakfast this morning, I thought I'd better make sure you hadn't worked yourself to death.' She nodded to a tray bearing a covered plate and a silver coffee pot.

Winnie rubbed her eyes and stretched. After letting out a most unladylike yawn, she smiled. 'You brought me breakfast. That's very kind.'

'Gracious, you've been busy!' Adelaide

peeked at the projects on either side of Winnie.

To her left sat the Telautograph WA-model, which she'd had to remove from the laboratory's vault to reach Professor Dudley's notebooks. The temptation for tinkering had trumped her yearning for bed. Overnight, she'd replaced its makeshift jelly-mould covers with more suitable polished tin surfaces.

To her right lay her first spy-trade invention, a weaponized lady's fan. She picked it up. 'What do you think of the Fan Fatale? It combines a communication tool, personal security and fashion accessory into one small item.' She frowned at the basic bamboo and rice paper prototype. It didn't look particularly clever. 'Monsieur Moineau will work his magic, making the fans more suitable for a formal event. I only hope it meets Mrs Campbell's expectations. Professor Dudley, the previous quartermistress, is a hard act to follow.'

'I'm sure Mrs Campbell will agree it's remarkable. Now, you, my clever inventress, must eat.' Adelaide lifted the silver cloche covering the plate, releasing a waft of deliciously savoury steam – spice and smoked fish.

'Mmm. I could eat kedgeree three times a day, seven days a week and be perfectly content.'

Adelaide chuckled. 'No, thank you. I'm far too fond of variety.' She passed the plate and cutlery across to her. 'There's cheese and dried pear for later. What else have you prepared for Operation Bait-and-Snare, Miss Q?'

Winnie shovelled in a forkful of spiced rice and flaked haddock. She chewed and swallowed. 'Everything is almost ready. I hope Celeste likes the concealed dagger sheath I made for her corset.'

Adelaide stiffened, her lips curling downward at the corner. 'It sounds suitably deadly.'

Winnie paused before taking another bite. 'I hope you don't think me forward for stating it, but I sense you dislike Celeste.'

'Who says I dislike her?'

'It's written all over you.' Winnie watched as Adelaide's reaction flared and subsided on her face. 'You've never been good at hiding your displeasure – if you'll pardon my frankness.'

Adelaide laughed. 'You know I prefer direct talk. And I don't *dislike* her; it's that I don't *trust* her. Miss Lemieux is too showy, too friendly, too wooing . . .'

'Too attractive?' Winnie wriggled her brows playfully.

'I hope you're not suggesting I envy her beauty. I don't. Beauty can open doors, but it's a curse in the long run. It turns women into prizes for men to bag, stuff, display and ultimately forget. I'll take strength over beauty any day.'

'Strength is good. Kindness is better,' Winnie teased.

Adelaide shook her head. 'Don't think me unkind, but Miss Lemieux reminds me of a spider. "Come in, come in!

Welcome to my web." Frankly, her abundant Canadian cordiality feels sticky – like a trap. I've known her longer than you have. You'll see soon enough: she doesn't like to get her hands dirty, which means those around her will.'

Winnie chewed thoughtfully. How different their opinions were! 'She is charming, there's no doubt. Mrs Campbell says Miss Lemieux's charisma is her greatest strength.'

Adelaide shrugged one shoulder. 'Beauty, charm and charisma are all excellent assets for a spy. But none is an advantage in a friend. My advice is to watch yourself, Winifred.'

Winnie frowned. She and all of them – Adelaide, Celeste, Effie and Stella – were in the League together. Surely, trust was the cement of their bond and was critical to their success. 'How am I to continue if I cannot trust someone I'm depending on for my safety?'

Adelaide let out a tiny snort. 'My childhood and upbringing were very different to yours. Through the various challenges I've faced and surmounted, I've learnt that one must not depend on others – especially not men.' Her expression had grown quite grave, making Winnie wriggle.

Adelaide waved off the unpleasant topic. 'Anyway, I've been thinking, Winnie . . . about this Mr Magpie terrorizing the Queen.'

Winnie swallowed her coffee, which was almost as bitter as Adelaide's lesson du jour.

'Whoever it is, he must be close to the Queen – mustn't he – to know her movements? A villain hiding behind a smiling face.'

Winnie frowned. Maybe Adelaide was right. Maybe she shouldn't be so trusting.

Adelaide shook her head and smiled. 'I nearly forgot: Headmistress has excused you from this morning's self-defence training. She wants you to focus on your work here.'

'Jolly good!' Those self-defence lessons always made her muscles sore. And Celeste and Stella delighted in taking advantage of her lack of physical skill. It was humiliating to lose *every* time.

Adelaide had walked back to Professor Dudley's shelves of explosives and poisons, and peered at the labels as if searching for something in particular. 'You must keep working. However, you are required to visit Monsieur Moineau for a final fitting of your evening gown for Lady Holland's soiree.'

Winnie rolled her eyes. 'Can't someone else go in my place? I've so much to finesse!'

'It's a *fitting*, silly. Only you will do. Don't you want to see your evening gown? It's a dream in crimson moiré! I wish it were mine.'

'You can have it.' Double drat. Winnie hadn't stopped wearing her practical men's trousers since Wednesday's bumbled examination. Saturday night, she'd be forced to dress in ladies' evening attire, which involved all manner of discomforts: bare shoulders, over-the-elbow gloves, hair pins, and jewels, and worst of all: heels.

Argh. Winnie rubbed her temples.

Adelaide appeared amused at Winnie's frustration. 'Most importantly, the final briefing for Operation Bait-and-Snare is at three o'clock, and your presence is required. Don't be late.'

Now that was something to look forward to!

CHAPTER 17

~THE GREAT LIBRARY~

Friday afternoon

Five young lady spies sat around the library table, each writing notes with disappearing ink on the blank pages of their field guide. Headmistress Thornton paced in the background, and Mrs Campbell stood in front of a slate board displaying a chalk drawing of Holland House and its surrounding gardens. Arrows swirled, and Xs marked various important locations.

Mrs Campbell's fingers were coated in a light dusting of chalk after an hour of explanation. 'Remember, ladies, you may converse with one another, but you will arrive separately, so no one suspects you are in league.' She put down the chalk, and Adelaide passed her a damp flannel to wipe her hands. 'Now, then. Thornton will test your recall of the critical points of Operation Bait-and-Snare.'

Headmistress nodded her head. 'Miss Lee, without consulting your notes, please tell us which royal guests will be in attendance and their order of arrival.'

Miss Lee stood. 'The royal guests arriving immediately prior to the beginning of the musical performance include His Royal Highness the Prince of Wales, who is called Prince Bertie by his family, and Her Highness Princess Louise, Duchess of Argyll. At the intermission, Her Majesty the Queen will arrive. The Queen's later arrival is intended to shorten the period of high risk and to give us time to identify the target.'

'*If* Mr Magpie is lured to this sparkly event with its dazzling guest list,' Mrs Campbell interjected, looking worried. 'All being well, he will make an appearance, and you will successfully identify him. We want him to be in custody and off the property well before the Queen's arrival.'

Headmistress gestured for Effie to take her seat. 'Well done. Next, Miss Davies, please tell us what you will do upon identifying the target.'

Miss Davies rose to her feet and dipped her head respectfully to Headmistress and Mrs Campbell. 'There will be four senior officials from Scotland Yard present, all of whom will be disguised as servants and waiting near the entries to the servants' passages. They will wear yellow carnations in the lapels. As soon as we identify the target, we must pass a message to one of them and clear the way, as they will move swiftly.'

Headmistress nodded. 'Well done. You may take your seat. Miss Lemieux, as our weapons mistress, would you kindly reiterate the steps in a worst-case scenario.'

'It would be my pleasure, ma'am.' Celeste rose. 'One highly trained sharpshooter from the Army will be strategically positioned outside on the grounds in the event the target should escape the building. If this happens, whichever of us witnesses the escape must follow him outside and blow her whistle to alert the sharpshooter. At the whistle blast, all lady spies are to take up position near the entry points marked with an X on the diagram.' She nodded to the map on the slate board. 'Scotland Yard has organized a special squadron of police officers to wait for a signal on nearby streets.'

Headmistress smiled. 'Excellent. Miss Culpepper, if you please, what are the overarching principles and directives of the operation?'

Adelaide stood. 'As we all know well, our primary task is to blend in as normal merrymaking guests, remaining inconspicuous so no one – target, guests and hosts alike – suspects we are spies. In a worst-case scenario, one must first and foremost protect the League. In the event of an aborted mission, we are to go to the Beacon Academy for the night.'

Headmistress raised a finger. 'Except Miss Weatherby,

who, after disguising as a dustman, must discreetly return to the waxworks via the hidden entrance in the Baker Street Underground Rail Station. We will debrief the operation here on Sunday at noon. Unless you have questions, that concludes the briefing of Operation Bait-and-Snare.' She erased the chalk diagram on the slate board.

Effie raised her hand. 'Ma'am, we know nothing about Mr Magpie's appearance. How will we identify him? The soiree will be a white-tie event, which means the men will all be dressed like penguins. Our task seems impossible.'

Winnie's head spun. Effie was right: Mr Magpie was an enigma. She and her colleagues were tasked with picking a single man out of a sea of finely dressed gentlemen. She raised her hand. 'We know from his actions – slipping in and out of buildings, perhaps fitting through windows, bypassing royal guards, getting away without arousing suspicion – that he must be stealthy and quick on his feet. An older, heavier man couldn't do that. Perhaps we can eliminate men of certain statures and ages?'

'An excellent observation, Winifred, but it's important to keep our minds open too.' Mrs Campbell cleared her throat. 'Quartermistress, are you ready to display your spywares?'

Winnie rose slowly. Bother! Her knees quaked. 'Yes, Mrs Campbell. Perhaps we could reconvene in the laboratory where I've set up my exhibit?' Winnie led the young lady spies through the back of the fireplace.

Winnie stood beside a retired wax figure of Marie Antoinette dressed in a turquoise ballgown. Magenta and white peonies and a feather adorned her tall wig. 'I shall begin by demonstrating the devices everyone will wear on the night. Monsieur Moineau has emphatically informed me chatelaines *must not* be worn with formal evening attire . . .' Winnie glanced questioningly at Headmistress Thornton, who nodded her agreement.

Double drat. '. . . So I've had to find other means to equip you with useful and protective tools of the trade.' She gestured to the waxen figure. 'Please note the . . . hair things.' Winnie winced. Who knew what milliners called these frills? 'Each lady will have at least one feather worked into her hairpiece.'

She pulled out Marie Antoinette's feather. 'You will find a pencil lead inserted into the feather's shaft so we each have a writing implement at our disposal. Seeing as our main task is to identify the target and surreptitiously pass on intelligence to the police, we may need a way to do so in writing.'

Effie raised her hand. 'The feather pencil is very clever and convenient, but what do we write on?'

Winnie nodded to her. 'An excellent question. A pencil is nothing without paper, which brings me to your second customized tool.' She unlooped the fan from Marie Antoinette's wrist. 'Behold, my latest invention, the Fan Fatale.' She flicked it open and fanned her neck. 'I've overlaid the silk design with translucent rice paper. If you have intelligence to pass on, you must find a discreet spot to hide while you write your note with your feather pencil. Then you simply tear off a segment of paper like this . . .' She ripped the outermost wedge of paper from the fan. 'But remember: write first, tear second, as it curls.

'For increased safety, I've inlaid a small mirror in the guard, that is, the outside edge of the fan. The mirror allows you to use candlelight and your hand to flash a distress signal.' She turned to Effie. 'Communications Mistress, what do you suggest we use?'

Effie beamed at Winnie appreciatively. 'I suggest we keep it simple. Let's use the "H" of Morse code, which is simply four dots or "dot dot dot dot" for "help", as you know.'

'Excellent, thank you. So far, Mr Magpie has not taken prisoners, so I expect this function to be superfluous.'

Celeste shrugged. 'It's hardly superfluous. It will be useful for adjusting one's coiffeur.' She bounced a ringlet of strawberry blonde near her ear.

Effie rolled her eyes. 'This is serious business, Celeste. Not a stroll in the park.'

'Oh, but I am serious,' Celeste sniffed playfully.

Winnie continued. 'The outermost guard of the fan has been reinforced and weighted with a lead rod. You can use the folded fan as a short baton, like so . . .' She gave Marie Antoinette a sharp strike to the skull. The fan sank half an inch into the figure's waxen head. 'Whoops.' She dislodged the fan with her fingernails.

Effie and Stella grimaced, while Celeste gleefully rubbed her palms together.

Winnie cringed. 'Perhaps our defensive mistress can later assist with its most efficient deployment.' She shot a hopeful glance at Stella, who nodded obligingly.

Winnie removed the model's flower hairpiece and displayed its base, a pea whistle. 'Your hair decor also includes a Ladies' Personal Safety Whistle to alert the sharpshooter, as explained earlier, to call for assistance from each other, or to draw attention if you are being kidnapped.'

Stella rubbed her right fist. 'Do I blow the whistle before or after I knock the kidnapper senseless?'

Celeste spluttered a giggle. 'Dispatch first, of course. You'd lose the element of surprise by starting with a whistle blast.'

Winnie cast an impatient glance at her punch-happy colleagues. 'My predecessor, Professor Dudley, left an unfinished project for me to complete, which I've incorporated into our hair decor. This device creates a diversion.' Winnie took the peony from Marie Antoinette's hair ornament. 'The wardrobe department created the flower from silk, with the exception of one petal, which I designed. It's made of a volatile material called nitrocellulose—'

'Otherwise known as guncotton!' Celeste supplied cheerfully. 'It makes guns go BANG.'

Winnie sniggered. 'Precisely. It can be used in paper or wad form. Allow me to demonstrate.' She lit a nearby candle. 'One must simply pluck the papery petal from her hair like so, and, when no one is looking, bring it close to the flame like this . . .'

A *POOF* and flash of bright light made everyone in the room jump. After a second of shock, laughter erupted.

'As you can imagine, this distraction would allow for an escape or similar. Stage magicians use the material for this purpose. Their stunned audience misses the sleight of hand.'

Adelaide gave Winnie an emphatic nod of approval.

'Brava, Winifred!' Celeste grinned at her.

Winnie blew out the candle. 'Oh – a word of warning. Take extreme care to keep your head far away from open flames, or else . . .' She pointed to the curl of black smoke rising from the candle's smouldering wick.

Her colleagues' nervous chatter gave Winnie a

moment to steel herself for the unsavoury task of mentioning unmentionables. 'Next . . .' Winnie gulped down a feeling of light-headedness.

Oh, good golly, how utterly mortifying.

'. . . the, erm, *corset* of our weapons mistress includes a concealed dagger.' She sliced a scalpel down the front of Marie Antoinette's ballgown, revealing her layers of frilly undergarments – petticoat, drawers, stockings, corset and chemise.

Effie squeaked and covered her eyes. 'Winifred, a little warning would be appreciated!'

Giddy with embarrassment, Winnie reached above the mannequin's left breast and pinched her fingers around the top of one of the corset's bone channels. She drew out a slender, wicked-looking knife.

Celeste gasped her appreciation.

'Celeste, it's advisable to practise withdrawing the dagger safely.' Winnie carefully slid the knife back in its concealed holder and gave Marie Antoinette a pat for being a good sport. 'And it's *essential* to practise re-sheathing to avoid injury.'

Celeste's smile withered. Her hands fluttered protectively to her bosom.

'On future missions, after we've all successfully concluded our weapons training, I shall incorporate similar sheaths into everyone's . . . unmentionables.' Winnie touched her burning cheeks. How red they must be! She flashed a sympathetic smile at Effie, who looked thoroughly scandalized.

Effie squeezed Winnie's hand. 'While the thought of weaponized unmentionables makes me woozy, I must say I am in awe of your talent. Brava!'

'Winnie, how is development of the armoured corset going?' Adelaide nodded across the laboratory to a headless mannequin dressed only in a chemise, drawers and a strange, stiff corset riddled with gunpowder blisters and pockmarks.

Winnie bit her lip. 'Unfortunately, I shall have to save it for a future mission. I'm almost certain it's bulletproof, but I cannot employ it without further testing.'

Stella grimaced. 'Oh, dear. Take all the time you need getting that right.'

'Indeed.' Winnie clasped her hands. 'Er . . . that's all. Thank you.'

Her four colleagues stared at her. Then they burst into applause.

Mrs Campbell glanced at Headmistress Thornton, who finally smiled.

CHAPTER 18

~HOLLAND HOUSE~

Nine thirty, Saturday 27 April 1889

The famous Gilt Chamber of Holland House was a frothy, churning sea of sparkling ladies and dapper gentlemen. Amid the roar, Winnie gulped for air, drowning in an ocean of golden opulence. Chatter and laughter swelled in her ears. Strong scents, heat, colours, light, brushes with strangers . . . all swept over and around her in a dizzying array.

Why are there no open windows? She flicked open her Fan Fatale and waved it at her neck. Had her chatelaine been permitted, she'd have smelling salts at the ready. She fanned herself harder and gazed about, looking for something to anchor herself to.

Celeste stood near the fireplace, surrounded by a flock of young gentlemen, poised like eager peacocks ready to show off for the prized peahen.

She was a Greek goddess in her

champagne-coloured silk surah gown with gold and black highlighting the gown's dramatic lines. Winnie shrank inside at the sight of Celeste's animated conversation and bold laughter. Oh, to possess such ease.

Effie, pink-cheeked and clearly overheated, had seated herself on a velvet pouffe in the centre of the room. She scratched behind the silk flowers festooning the neckline of her deep-blue damask gown. Adelaide brought Effie a cup of punch and briefly sat beside her. She wore a gown of dramatic violet velvet with matching court shoes. The gown's cut was elegant and minimal, for even Monsieur Moineau could not improve upon Adelaide's natural dark beauty. Winnie watched Adelaide rise from the pouffe, offer encouragement to Effie, and melt into the swirl of guests.

'She moves like a swan lifting from a lake,' Stella said, standing close enough for Winnie to hear over the din. She offered Winnie a cup of punch. 'You look lovely. That crimson perfectly complements your complexion.'

Winnie took the cup gratefully. 'And you are a queen in that sublime yellow.'

Stella smiled. 'It's a pity we must watch the men when the ladies' attire is so much more fascinating. Good evening, miss.' Stella disappeared into the crowd. Winnie watched her go. *Well done – focused without being obvious.*

It was a timely reminder. They had a villain to catch. Winnie edged through the clusters of people, dodging elbows, nodding greetings, and finally swerving around a wiry, short man who made sweeping gestures. His wrist connected with her bustle.

'Oh, I beg your pardon,' he said offhandedly. He squinted through his tortoiseshell-rimmed monocle, a question flashing in his gaze.

Winnie's smile froze. That forked beard – *oh, dear!* She nodded a brief greeting and trotted away as quickly as she could. The man was Sir Phillip Runcliffe-Bowen, the secretariat of the British Selection Committee – the very man she suspected had something to do with Papa's troubles and her pursuer.

Across the room, she spied a door to a balcony. She wove her way through the throng, pushed open the door, and let the cool night air envelope her. It tingled against her bare shoulders. She gulped in the freshness and savoured the spaces between people.

What should she do? Abort mission? She wasn't certain Sir Phillip had recognized her, though. He hadn't said anything, after all – and surely he'd be unable to place her face out of context. Five weeks ago, he'd met an awkward schoolgirl wearing a uniform and plaits. Tonight, she was an elegant young lady wearing an evening gown and coiffed hair. No, she'd continue. She strode back into the crowded ballroom, her gaze landing on Adelaide.

Adelaide caught her eye. She touched her forehead with two fingers – a hand signal meaning: *Possible Sighting*.

Winnie nodded. Her heart zinged. The thrill of the hunt was real. They were spying! A rush of excitement shot through her right to the tips of her gloved fingers. She returned to the business at hand. Now which fine gentleman was Mr Magpie?

An older lady seated nearby raised her lorgnette and gave Winnie the once-over. She added an approving nod. 'My dear, your gown is exquisite.'

'Why, thank you, madam.' *What would Celeste say?* Winnie mustered some charm. 'And you are a picture of elegance.'

The woman smiled approvingly. 'How pleasant you are, my dear. Might I trouble you to bring me a cup of punch?'

Drat – just when she needed to focus and follow up Adelaide's signal. She smiled obligingly. 'I'd be delighted. One moment.' Winnie found a waiter carrying a tray of crystal cups filled with pink liquid. An older man with bushy brows glanced past her. He was not their man – far too doddery. No, Mr Magpie had to be light on his feet to carry out his sneaky deeds. She took a cup of punch back to the lady.

'Bless you, dear. It's so lovely in here, but a tad hot.' She fanned her neck. 'Lady Holland hasn't opened this room for years, but I've always loved it best.' She patted the seat beside her on the gilded settee.

Winnie sat and grinned. The seat offered an excellent view of the room and was near a servant wearing a yellow carnation. When she identified the target, she only had to rise and turn to pass a note to the senior police official in disguise. 'So, you've visited many times, then?'

The lady sipped her punch and nodded. 'I play whist with Lady Holland, and we share an interest in growing dahlias.'

'How lovely!'

A bell ting-a-linged over the din of chatter.

A stout man strode majestically to the pianoforte and bowed deeply. 'Welcome, dear friends. Our soiree of song is about to begin. If you'd kindly be seated.'

'Oh, dear, I hope my husband doesn't miss the performance.' The lady stretched her thin neck to see over heads and around people who were making their way to seats. 'Sir Phillip stepped outside to attend to some last-minute matter. His work at the Kensington Museum keeps him busy. How remiss of me not to introduce myself. I'm Jenny Runcliffe-Bowen. And you are?'

Winnie's face froze in a shocked smile – this was Sir

Phillip's wife! 'Delighted to make your acquaintance, Lady Jenny. I'm ... I'm—'

The bell jingled again, sending people darting around, ducking to their seats.

Saved by the bell – for now. Sir Phillip had stepped out. Which was worse, that he'd left or that he would be returning? She had to escape this woman – but how? There was no polite way to retreat.

A tall, older gentleman with salt-and-pepper mutton chops sat down next to Lady Jenny with a grunt. His bear-sized proportions made the settee seem like dollhouse furniture.

Lady Jenny smiled at him. 'Ah, just in time!' She whispered to Winnie, 'My husband. I'll introduce you later.'

Winnie stared at the man. 'But that's not Sir Phillip.'

Lady Jenny tittered. 'Of course it is – I'd know after thirty-five years of marriage!'

Winnie gulped. This was not the man who'd visited her at the Beacon Academy. If *this* was Sir Phillip, then who was the man with the forked beard and monocle?

She gasped, earning a concerned glance from Lady Jenny. Whomever she had presented her Boot-Button Butler to had been an imposter – an imposter who had seemed very interested in her father's designs for the Telautograph Machine ...

She barely suppressed another gasp. Could the man

who'd come to the Beacon Academy have been Peter Geier in disguise?

Logically, there could be no other answer.

He was here.

The man who was hunting her and harassing Papa was somewhere in this crowded ballroom.

She frantically searched the room for a familiar face. Adelaide would know what to do. Celeste, with her entourage of male admirers, was easy to find but Winnie couldn't catch her eye. She spotted Stella and Effie, but they were focused on other parts of the room. Winnie twisted her fan in her hands.

Lady Jenny nodded towards the seats of honour. 'Oh, look there, my dear, near Lady Holland. It's His Royal Highness the Prince of Wales.'

Prince Bertie sat back with his leg crossed, a posture that reeked of power. Next to him sat his sister, Princess Louise, an upright and attractive woman in her middle years. She wore a lovely gown of Prussian blue set off with a tiara, earrings and choker of sapphires and diamonds. Winnie tried not to stare, but it was the closest she had ever come to royalty.

Beside Prince Bertie was an empty seat reserved for his mother. Winnie gave herself a discreet pinch. Before the night was over, she would be in the same room as HM the Queen.

The pianist, a thin, young man with floppy hair and dark, deep-set eyes, played an introductory progression of chords. The acclaimed vocalist, a Russian tenor by the name of Feodor Ivanovich, entered the room to warm applause.

Winnie gritted her teeth. Bother! It was too late to move now. If she spotted Mr Magpie, she'd have to stand, which would draw unwanted attention to herself. If only she'd stood when Sir Phillip – the real one – arrived, but she'd been too shocked.

The tenor lifted his chin. 'Your Royal Highness the Prince of Wales, Your Highness the Duchess of Argyll, lords and ladies, special guests, I thank you . . .'

She had to focus. Winnie let his words fade into a hum. She swept her gaze across the guests, focusing only on the black and white of men's attire and filtering out the glittering, colourful ladies in between. Where was the magpie in this sea of penguins? Winnie tapped her fingertips together. There was nothing like a puzzle to keep oneself amused.

She imagined Mr Magpie as short of stature and wiry of build, and most likely young and agile. Using that description, she eliminated every man with a paunchy belly, grey whiskers, and disturbing hairs sprouting from ears and elsewhere, which was three-quarters of the candidates.

The singing began, an aria from *Faust*. The words of the song pulled at her attention. *Drat.* Winnie strained to home in on the younger men who fit her list of characteristics. She studied their faces, their posture, their dress. One rose to the top of her list, an athletic-looking man whose meticulously neat attire included a sash of pale blue silk. *Black, white and blue* – only a scoundrel as brazen as Mr Magpie would wear the colours of his namesake. Thin moustaches and oiled dark hair accentuated the gentleman's proud air. And more tellingly, his left hand twitched and his eyes roved about the room restlessly.

Winnie fought down a smug smile. Now to inform the others. Effie was enraptured in the music, lips moving to the French words, her eyes glistening with tears. Adelaide? Winnie couldn't spot her, but Stella was looking straight at her.

Stella placed her hand under her chin, a signal meaning: *Spotted.* Winnie replied with a subtle nod and a fan movement to confirm the direction.

Stella signalled back with her fan. *Wait.* From her eye movements, Winnie knew Stella was looking for the others so they could carry out their orders to work together.

The target could leave, though – or do some terrible deed! The thought made Winnie wriggle with impatience.

This situation called for swiftness. Winnie used her fan to signal *Urgent!* to Stella. Stella's smile was strained as she signalled: *Wait.*

Winnie shook her head. There'd be no more waiting. She'd alert the nearest disguised police official. It would be disruptive, but at least they'd capture their man. She plucked the feather pencil from her hairpiece. How though could she write on the paper insert of her Fan Fatale while sitting so close to Lady Jenny? Bother.

She turned her head towards the disguised police official posted near the servants' door and stared at him until she caught his gaze. *Good.* She raised one eyebrow, then the other, to inform him she'd found the target. She winked her left eye twice to point left.

The official watched her with his brows knitted together, but he didn't move, and he didn't look left to the target.

Winnie redoubled her efforts at communicating. She winked faster, wriggled both her brows, and nodded towards the door behind him.

The official's brows shot up. He adjusted his cravat.

What was wrong with this man? She'd found the target; now he needed to do his part, which was apprehend Mr Magpie. Scotland Yard had clearly assigned dimwits to their senior-most positions.

Holding his gaze, she folded her arms and pointed

with the hidden hand.

The official's face turned red. He emphatically looked the other way.

Winnie huffed and rolled her eyes. She accidentally locked eyes with Prince Bertie, who was staring at her with an expression of bewildered alarm. *Oh, dear.* She squirmed.

Lady Jenny opened her fan and whispered behind it, 'Do sit still, my dear girl.'

Winnie cringed. Where were Adelaide and Celeste? She stretched her neck to peer around the Gilt Chamber.

Stella, wide-eyed, signalled: *Caution.*

Winnie replied by opening her fan in the direction of the target . . .

He was gone.

CHAPTER 19

Later Saturday night

Gone! Winnie nearly jumped to her feet but stopped herself, jerking back into the gilded settee like a bunny trapped in a hatbox.

Beside her, Lady Jenny gasped and began fanning Winnie as if she were swooning from music-induced hysteria.

The aria built to its famous dramatic climax with the tenor holding the high C note for an impossible moment. The song rolled to its conclusion, and thunderous applause broke out around the room. The tenor bowed deeply.

Lady Jenny furiously fanned Winnie's neck and cheeks. 'My dear, are you unwell? Shall I call for salts?'

'Thank you, no. I shall!' Winnie bolted to her feet while the applause continued and stepped towards the servant whose attention she'd tried to secure.

At her approach, his eyes popped. He backed up.

Winnie scowled. 'I say, I only—' She stopped. No yellow carnation festooned his lapel. He was a real servant, not a disguised police official! She gulped. 'I . . .'

Gunshots rang out in the adjacent parkland. *Bang-bang! BANG!* Women in the room shrieked. People dived away from the windows. In the pandemonium, two yellow-carnationed servants swooped in and pulled the Prince and Princess out of the room through a servants' door.

Winnie turned in a circle. Gunshots meant the target was outside. They were each to take position near a door on the ground floor.

Effie darted across the Gilt Chamber towards the door to the hall. Stella and Winnie followed.

Racing down the grand staircase was a line of four elegant young ladies. Adelaide came behind Winnie, and at the bottom in the fabulously ornate entry, Celeste herded them into a dark room that smelt damp and slightly horsey. It was a cloakroom.

Celeste left the door ajar, allowing a thin band of light in. 'The target must already be outside. Three shots suggest the sharpshooter missed on at least the first two. In case he's still alive out there, we're going after him. Here—' She handed an umbrella or a walking stick to each girl. 'As we learnt: never leave home unarmed. Adelaide, send the ladies around the gardens. I shall find our sharpshooter and warn him of your presence. Then I'll return indoors to ensure the Prince and Princess are safe.'

'But of course, *Captain*.' Adelaide snatched a cane with a growl. 'Come along, ladies – we've no time to worry with cloaks.' She stalked off.

After Celeste disappeared out of the door, Winnie jogged to catch up with Adelaide. 'I identified the target. At least I think I did – Stella saw him too. He's wearing a blue sash, and he has thin moustaches, but he disappeared . . .'

Adelaide stopped. 'Why didn't you make the signal to close in? He could be anywhere now.' She opened the doors, and they stepped outside. 'I'll take the front along the high street. You three split up at the side. Comb through the gardens at the back. Use your whistle if you find him. When you hear three blasts, meet on the terrace at the top of the garden stairs.' Winnie and the other two blinked. 'Go on. You will be fine.'

Stella shook her head. 'But, Adelaide, it's not safe for you to go off alone.' Effie nodded her agreement.

Winnie grabbed Adelaide's elbow. 'We must all take care. Upstairs in the Gilt Chamber, I think I saw the man who's been hunting me.'

She growled her aggravation. 'Just what we need. You three stay close together. Go!' Adelaide grasped a handful of violet velvet to lift her hem before running off towards the high street side of Holland House.

The night air bit at Winnie's bare shoulders. At least her gloves covered most of her arms, but there was no time for simpering. She had a scoundrel to catch.

Footmen, stablemen and gamekeepers huddled together in the circular drive. A police wagon had pulled up, and bobbies stood near the entrance talking with the steward and pointing at the various entry points. Winnie lowered her head. What if Geier's crooked detective was here? She shuddered at the thought.

At the corner of the grand home, they split up. She hurried, head down, to the Rotunda Garden as quickly as her full gown and high heels would allow and didn't slow until the grand house was a looming silhouette behind her. She paused to catch her breath, glad Holland House was well lit for the soiree. It cast its reassuring yellow gaze over the parklands, like a lion keeping watch on its territory.

Winnie strode through the darkness, senses keen, hoping she was heading in the right direction. She focused instead on movement – telltale signs of someone running away or hiding. Around her swirled a cacophony of womanly sounds: the lush swish of her silk moiré skirt brushing the tall umbrella, the clip of the heels of her court shoes against the paving stones, and even the faint tinkling of her paste 'jewels'. Ladies' clothing made it nigh on impossible to achieve stealth of movement.

She paused to stifle a sneeze. Beside her a garden bed had been cleared, and freshly turned dirt was being prepared for the next season's flowers. The gardener's wheelbarrow and tool wagon stood ready for the next day's work.

Dogs bayed in the distant mews, and men yelled to one another. Winnie swallowed hard. She squeezed the umbrella handle. What protection did this provide against a fiend like Mr Magpie? The man she'd identified had a cruel edge to his tidy appearance. Could he have hidden a weapon in his evening suit? A pistol or a knife? She gulped.

The path ahead forked, the left way leading into a tall stand of trimmed hedges, while the right way disappeared down a hill towards a fountain and wound back by way of the stables. She hesitated.

'Good evenin', miss!' A cheerful but gruff Londoner greeted her from behind.

'Ah!' Winnie clutched her chest and spun to face him.

There stood a man wearing a cheap suit and a bowler hat. His bushy moustaches hid his lips. 'And 'ere I was, tryin' to avoid givin' you a fright. I do beg yer pardon.

Now, you have nothin' to fear, miss. I'm with the Metropolitan Police, at yer service.' Before bowing, he tucked his umbrella under his arm.

An umbrella with a handle of a silver bat in flight.

CHAPTER 20

Saturday night, past eleven o'clock

Blood rushed to Winnie's head at the sight of the silver bat's glinting red-crystal eyes. DI Walker had found her.

'Judging by your very pretty gown, I'd say you were a lucky guest at Lady Holland's soiree. It certainly finished wif a bang! Or rather, a bang-bang-bang.' He laughed but stopped when Winnie gasped. 'Not that I had anything to do with the use of firearms, I assure you.' He cleared his throat. 'Might I know your name, miss?'

She had to stall him, lead him astray somehow. She nearly choked, trying to make her vocal cords work. 'Why do you wish to know?' Her fingers gripped the hook of her umbrella.

He cocked his head and squinted at her. 'As it happens, miss, I am investigating a crime and searching for a fugitive. A little birdie, as it were, called me here, to Holland House. You see, I've been looking high and low for a young woman who is more or less your age, and who might even fit your description, though it's hard to tell in this light.'

'Well, I doubt you'll find criminals or fugitives here. The guests of Holland House are only the finest sort.'

'Oh, I do beg your pardon. No offence was intended.' He lifted his bowler and bobbed his head apologetically. 'I wonder if you'd know the names of the other fine young ladies in attendance this evening. For instance, a certain Miss Weatherby, Winifred Weatherby, of Chelsea, London?'

Winnie resisted the urge to clutch her belly. Instead, she raised her chin, trying to look confident. 'There are many young ladies inside, but as far as I know there's not one Winifred among them, and I'm sure I've never encountered such a common surname as Weatherby.' Winnie tensed. Sweat prickled coolly on her brow.

Walker scratched his cheek and squinted at her.

Stella appeared, rushing stealthily up the rise on the path to the right. She stopped, eyes darting from Winnie to the man and back. She cocked her head questioningly. 'Is anything wrong, Winifred?' She covered her mouth at the slip. 'Oops.'

Winnie closed her eyes. *Oh, bother.*

DI Walker sniffed and fought down a triumphant

smile. 'We're just havin' a chat about the various guests at the soiree, weren't we, *Miss Weatherby*?'

Winnie regripped her umbrella to a defensive hold.

Stella's brows rose at the subtle motion.

'Now, then, Miss Weatherby. You're coming with me – to Scotland Yard.' He gripped Winnie's forearm. 'And you will come quietly, or I will make it most unpleasant for you.'

'Ow! You're hurting me!'

'This way, if you please.' He gripped more tightly and dragged her along.

'He has no intention of taking me to Scotland Yard. This is an abduction.'

'You know how to defend yourself. Ready . . . It's time to employ what we learnt from Colonel Monstery,' Stella called out. '*En garde!*'

Winnie rotated her hand left, right, then left again to break free. It worked! The colonel's gruelling lessons paid off. She took her fighting stance, bending her knees slightly and shifting her left heel at right angles to her adversary. Her head turned to the right as her body moved to the left.

'*Moulinet!*' Stella barked, mimicking the military intonation of their self-defence instructor in his drills for the ladies' use of the cane as a weapon.

Winnie windmilled the umbrella. (Rather awkwardly,

if she was totally honest. Stella, meanwhile, was a warrioress.)

DI Walker spluttered, grasping at her arm and missing. 'What the blazes! Now both of you must stop at once. That's an order.'

'*Espadon!*' Stella commanded, lifting her cane.

Winnie raised the umbrella and whacked, squeezing her eyes shut. 'Sorry! Oooh!'

Stella shouted the commands, 'Two! Three! Open your eyes, Winifred!'

DI Walker clutched his bowler and cowered. 'Stop that at once! Ow!'

'Ooh! My apologies!' Winnie cringed and whacked again.

'Three, four! Open your eyes and stop apologizing!' Stella bellowed.

Winnie blinked. Her teeth were clenched. It was no good. She might as well be bopping a naughty puppy with a rolled-up newspaper. The single-handed grip did not afford her enough strength. She grasped the umbrella with both hands and gave a grunting wallop towards the side of his head. It connected instead with his shoulder.

DI Walker staggered.

Winnie winced. 'Oh! I am so sorry! I . . . Ow!' *Whack!* 'I believe that was painful? I . . .'

Stella rolled her eyes. She drew back and bounded

forward with a growl, landing a side-handed chop to the left side of Walker's neck, then the right in a swift crisscross, then both sides again. She sprang back.

Walker's left knee buckled, but he remained more or less upright.

This was a job for the Fan Fatale! Winnie unwound it from her wrist and thwacked the man over the head, shattering the fitted mirror. *Oops – wrong side.* His bowler hat softened the blow, but still his eyes rolled. 'Oh, dear!' Winnie dropped the fan as if it were scalding her fingers.

Stella dived in again, landing the heel of her hand in an upper thrust on his chin.

His head snapped back, and his teeth clacked together. He dropped to the ground with a thud, his head landing firmly in the freshly turned dirt.

Winnie stared at his prone body lying half on the path, half in the garden bed. She covered her mouth. 'Oh, merciful heaven! I just assaulted a police detective, a crooked one but nonetheless. I used force! I broke the law! It's official: I'm . . . I'm a criminal!'

'Congratulations.' Stella stalked into the flower bed.

'Where are you going? We can't just *leave* him here!' Winnie recoiled at the sight of the umbrella still in her grip but now bent into a curve. She chucked the ruined weapon into a nearby stand of bushes and wiped her tainted hands on her gown.

Stella came back with the gardener's wheelbarrow and tools.

Winnie pointed a finger at the shovel. 'We can't possibly *bury* him!' Her breaths wheezed in and out.

The hedge behind them rustled and an opening parted in the branches. 'Hush! The two of you sound like a pair of alley cats fighting.' Effie peered through, her eyes popping at the sight of the man lying in the dirt. She rounded the hedge and toed DI Walker's ankle. '*This* is Mr Magpie?'

'No, unfortunately not,' Stella said blandly. 'Winnie was just explaining how he knows her name.' Stella stuck her hands on her hips and nailed Winnie with a bewildered look.

Winnie sighed. 'It has to do with my father's disappearance. Papa is hiding from a very bad man named Peter Geier, whom I believe I saw among tonight's guests. He hasn't succeeded in finding Papa, so he hired a crooked detective to track me down. This is him, DI Walker.'

'DI as in Detective Inspector? He's with the Metropolitan Police?' Effie grimaced. 'Please assure me he's not dead.'

'Dead? Of course he's not dead. He's . . . resting.' Winnie paced in a circle, driven by some unstoppable force of fear and excitement and horror.

'Well done, Winifred,' Effie said. 'You've thoroughly assaulted a public official.'

Stella cut her off. 'Yes, yes, she has, but we must stop faffing. Pull yourself together, Winifred. He's unconscious now, but it won't be for long. Help me lift him into the wheelbarrow. A shoulder for each of you, and I'll heave him by the belt.' She shuddered.

Winnie nodded at Stella. Panicking was a luxury. They had work to do.

'On three,' Stella said, counting down. They all leant over the stranger's body and heaved simultaneously. Despite their straining and grunting, he barely budged.

'Oof! We haven't got a chance,' Effie whined. 'We need the others. Where *are* Celeste and Adelaide?'

'Adelaide is of course doing things her way – that is to say, *alone*,' Stella said with a huff. 'And Celeste, true to form, gave herself the plummy task of guarding the royal guests.'

Effie chuckled. 'While we faced danger out here in the cold. I'm taking a leaf out of her book on our next mission.'

Winnie cracked her knuckles. 'Right – I've got a plan. While you two were whinging, I was assessing the situation. Every engineer knows, good planning at the start prevents repairing at the end. By applying basic physics here, we can reduce the effort and increase the efficiency.

First of all, the wheelbarrow won't do. We'll use the hand wagon instead – its four wheels are more stable than the barrow's one. Second, before we load him, we must first position the wagon on the path. Otherwise, his weight will make those narrow wheels embed in the loose dirt.'

Winnie studied the lay of the land, estimating slopes and heights. She moved the wagon to the edge of a rock wall. 'There. Even with three of us sharing his weight, we have little chance of lifting a man of his . . . girth on to the wagon. However, we can roll him to the ledge and tip him in with greater ease.'

Stella readied herself. 'I'll take his shoulders; you handle his . . . lower region.'

Winnie's face fell. She knelt beside his thighs. How perfectly awful to touch a strange man's legs. She closed her eyes, laid one hand on his hips and the other on his thigh and pushed in unison with Stella. 'Effie, turn his feet for us so his legs stay straight.'

The three young ladies pushed, all the while grunting and making unladylike noises and uttering unseemly words. Seams popped. Fabric ripped. Lace tore free from petticoats. They pivoted him at the edge of the garden bed to position him parallel to the side of the hand wagon.

'Ugh! I think moving a dead horse would be easier,' Stella muttered.

'It would be less awkward,' Winnie replied, vigilantly

avoiding certain unmentionable regions of the man's anatomy.

'Ooh, no! There's dirt in my silk shoe!' Effie cried.

'My flounce just fell off,' Winnie commiserated. Silk petals dropped from her hairpiece on to her shoulders, and strands of curls stuck to her sticky neck.

With one last push, they rolled DI Walker into the waiting wagon. His calves jutted out at strange angles and his head lolled back.

'Effie, please stop twisting your hands and fetch his hat,' Stella grunted.

Winnie staggered to her feet, panting and sweating despite the night's chilly air. There lay a crumpled DI Walker, her hunter and the would-be murderer of poor young Clancy. Jolts of rage and triumph shot down her limbs, erasing the residue of guilt or remorse.

Effie glanced around. 'Now what shall we do? Could we pull the wagon to the high street and leave him for the street sweepers to find?'

Stella wiped her brow with the back of her hand. 'When he comes to, he must be far away from Winnie – and me.' She frowned at her swollen knuckles. 'I know how we can send him on his way. While I was combing the park, I saw – well, first I smelt – the nightmen's wagon. It's parked outside the stable gates.'

Both Winnie and Effie curled their lips. 'Ew.'

Between midnight and five o'clock, nightmen carried out the necessary but disgusting work of collecting and carting off the human waste from the privies and cesspits.

The plan dawned slowly in Winnie's mind. It was effective and harmless – not to mention extremely fitting – vengeance for the abusive treatment he'd meted out to Clancy. 'Miss Davies! That suggestion is completely diabolical.' Winnie took the wagon handle. 'It's perfect.'

CHAPTER 21

Near midnight

At the back of the stables, Winnie and Stella rolled Walker to the middle of the nightsoil wagon tray while Effie kept watch for the return of the nightmen.

Winnie, reeling at the stench, repositioned the barrels, redistributed the straw, and double-checked that he was hidden.

'Ooh! Don't forget his hat.' Stella threw the bowler on to the heap.

'They're coming!' Effie whispered.

The three ladies scurried into the shadows between the shed and the stable.

A waft of fresh filth filled the air as the two nightmen edged their sloshing barrel of swill on to the tray. Joking and laughing, the pair completed their noxious task without so much as a splutter of complaint. A moment later the wagon rolled away, leaving a swirl of putrid gases in its wake.

The girls stepped out of the shadows, faces dirtied, dresses torn.

'That was the vilest experience of my life.' Stella held out her hands as if she couldn't move them far enough from her body. 'Look, my gloves are ruined.'

Effie yanked her filthy gloves off. 'Thank goodness we *had* gloves! That was revolting.'

Winnie watched the wagon disappear down the side alley, pitying both the nightmen and their poor old mare. She turned to her accomplices in crime. 'I cannot thank you enough for coming to my aid.'

Stella smiled at Winnie. 'It would be inexcusable to allow that vile man to drag off our clever quartermistress.'

'Indeed.' Effie entwined her filthy arm with Winnie's and led her back towards the grand house. 'After all, you haven't yet delivered our customized chatelaines and armoured unmentionables.'

Voices carried from the terrace above the north lawn. Winnie led the way up the stone stairs, steeling herself to take the full brunt of the blame. They rounded a bend in the stairs, and Winnie looked up. Silhouetted by the light of the house stood a woman. Although her face was completely obscured by shadow, Winnie recognized the trim figure and erect posture of Mrs Campbell. Winnie paused the climb to collect her thoughts.

Stella squeezed Winnie's arm.

Above them came their Spymistress's voice. 'Goodness, you ladies certainly took your time. Inside.'

Mrs Campbell turned. She squinted down the staircase as they approached. 'Good god! You look like you've been thrown to the lions. Monsieur Moineau's gowns are in tatters! Where are your gloves? As lost as our target, I assume.'

Winnie's heart raced like a locomotive, and nothing could stop it, not even squeezing her eyes shut. Seared behind her eyelids was the image of DI Walker unconscious and awkwardly stuffed in the garden wagon.

Mrs Campbell, still in silhouette, beckoned. 'The shooting was completely unrelated – the overzealous groundsman caught a poacher in the parkland and tried to . . .' She covered her nose. 'Gracious, girls! What is that odour?' She peered down the staircase to the dark landing where they stood.

'I can explain.' Winnie cleared her throat. 'DI Walker, that detective who's been on my tail, tracked me down. He tried to abduct me, so we – I – had to eliminate the threat.'

Mrs Campbell winced. 'Good heavens! But that doesn't explain—'

'The detective is now riding around west London on the back of a nightsoil wagon.' Winnie tugged at her earlobe distractedly. 'Hence the, er, stink. The problem was mine, but Stella and Euphemia were kind and loyal enough to assist me. Adelaide and Celeste were elsewhere, attending to the mission.'

They continued their climb up the stairs, finally reaching the terrace with its carved stone furniture and glowing lanterns. Winnie blinked. Seated on a marble settee was Celeste, cosily wrapped in a white fur stole, still radiant, clean and smelling of French parfum. *That clever vixen.*

Adelaide rushed from under the portico. 'Beg your pardon, ma'am. All clear on the high street side of the property!' Her hair was mussed, her cheeks pink from exertion and her gait uneven, but otherwise she was still a picture of unsullied elegance. Upon seeing her colleagues, she gasped. 'What on earth happened? Are you injured? Winifred, was it—'

'I'm safe – thanks to these two.'

The Spymistress huffed. 'Come along, ladies. We mustn't discuss this in the open.' When Mrs Campbell turned towards the house, golden light spilt across her features. She wasn't wearing her widow's weeds and veil, but rather a sumptuous gown of Prussian blue and sapphire-studded tiara and choker.

Winnie gasped and gripped Stella's forearm, and Effie covered her mouth.

Their 'Mrs Campbell' was in fact the Queen's sixth child, Her Highness Princess Louise!

She spoke over her shoulder. 'I'd hoped to introduce you to my brother, the Spymaster, at a moment of triumph rather than shame—'

The French doors from Holland House's Journal Room burst open, and a small, round dog skittered towards the girls.

Mrs Campbell, aka Princess Louise, moaned. 'Wonderful . . . Her timing couldn't be worse.'

Winnie's chin dropped.

Gingerly stepping through the door on to the terrace was a very short, very round woman dressed in black: Her Majesty Queen Victoria.

CHAPTER 22

After midnight

At the sight of Her Majesty the Queen, Winnie dropped into a deep curtsy along with Adelaide, Stella and Effie. Celeste rose and joined them.

The royal pug snuffled around the terrace excitedly. He paused at Winnie's feet, sniffed her gown, and backed away with a wary look.

The Queen turned directly to Mrs Campbell – or rather, *Princess Louise* – with absolute focus.

Princess Louise/Mrs Campbell held up a finger. 'Wait for it . . .'

'Louise, this fiasco is all your fault.'

'And there it is!' Princess Louise quipped. 'Of course it's my fault.' She moved towards the French doors.

'Mumsy, please. Let us move inside for the casting of blame and denunciations, out of the night air.' Mrs Campbell's cloying tone was completely unfamiliar.

Winnie elbowed Stella. *Unbelievable.*

The Queen wagged a finger at her daughter. 'Don't you "Mumsy" me, Loosy! I demand answers. My safety rests on the capture of this rascal, whom you allowed to slip through your fingers – *again*! I told you and Bertie your lady-spy idea was far-fetched.' The Queen appraised the five girls with her hawkish gaze. 'Operation Bait-and-Snare – ha!'

Winnie winced at the Queen's scathing disapproval.

'This is them?' The monarch, upper lip curled, nodded at Winnie and her ragtag bunch. She waved a hand in front of her nose. 'What a malodorous lot! They look as if they've clambered out of an horrific train wreck.' She pointed her walking stick squarely at Celeste. 'Except for that one. I rather like the look of her.'

Celeste curtsied again, deeper, her strawberry-blonde ringlets bouncing with delight.

'Mumsy, may I present the Most Honourable Lady Celeste Lemieux of Canada. She is an aspiring student of veterinary medicine and an outstanding equestrian. As a superb markswoman, she is an expert in handling weapons. She took responsibility for ensuring the safety of Bertie and me this evening.'

Winnie cocked her head quizzically at Celeste. *Princess* Louise – now *Lady* Celeste! Whatever next!

'To her left, the young lady in stunning violet is Miss Adelaide Culpepper. She's Thornton's secretary, having mastered both stenography and the typewriting machine I brought back from Canada. She's also a champion player of lawn tennis, among other garden amusements such as croquet and archery.'

Adelaide bowed her head. 'At your service, Your Majesty.'

'Ach,' she growled, waggling her cane at Adelaide. 'She's that young tennis instructor who took it upon herself to teach Princess Maud to ride a safety bicycle the summer before last. As We remember it, she was *dismissed*.' The Queen sniffed. 'We do not approve of young ladies riding bicycles in public.'

They knew about Adelaide's cycling? And she'd instructed a princess? Winnie threw a puzzled, hurt look at Adelaide, who offered a subtle, embarrassed shrug.

The colour rose slightly in Adelaide's cheeks as she twisted her hands and bit her lower lip. Her Majesty's eyes slid over Adelaide towards Effie. 'And this?'

Princess Louise gestured to Effie. 'Miss Euphemia Lee is the daughter of the former Chinese Vice-Ambassador to Great Britain. She excels at foreign languages, Morse code and cryptology. She ably fills the role of communications mistress.'

Effie bobbed and blushed.

Princess Louise continued the introductions. 'I don't believe you have met Miss Stella Davies, although you were quite fond of her mother, Sarah. May she rest in peace.'

The queen's brows rose. 'Not my goddaughter from West Africa? Are you Sally's daughter? You are every bit as lovely. I do hope you'll pass on my regards to your sister. And what skill do you contribute?'

Stella curtsied. 'Strength and speed, ma'am. And I enjoy hand-to-hand combat.'

'She can wrestle grown men to the ground without breaking a sweat,' Princess Louise added. 'Like her mother, she's musically gifted, and you should see her waltz, Mumsy. Pity this evening's soiree wasn't a ball or a ballet. It's as if Miss Davies has wings.'

Winnie wrung her hands, wishing for a comforting plait to twist. Who was she, but a misfit daughter of a muddle-headed, nearly bankrupt and recently disgraced inventor? Compared to her sparkling company – a royal goddaughter's daughter, an ambassador's daughter, a baron's daughter – she was plain as porridge. She shifted from one foot to the other. At least Adelaide wasn't from noble stock, as far as Winnie knew. She glanced at her ally, who appeared to be trembling with . . . what? Fear? Regret? Jealousy?

'And finally, taking up Lady Henrietta Dudley's

position is Miss Winifred Weatherby, our new quarter-mistress. She's directing her remarkable inventing skills towards the creation of customized instruments of espionage. She's a genius.'

Winnie flinched at the glowing description. 'I just tinker, really.' Winnie bowed, her face aflame. *Oh, bother.* Why had she said that?

The Queen arched a brow at Winnie before turning to her daughter. 'Loosy, as capable as they all sound, you must admit your experiment in feminine espionage has failed spectacularly. Just look at them! They're as subtle as a herd of stampeding hyenas.'

Winnie puffed her cheeks. The Queen certainly didn't mince words. She watched her colleagues' reactions to the criticism. Adelaide stiffened. Stella raised her chin. Effie's head drooped. Celeste didn't appear in the slightest bit fazed.

Princess Louise let out an exasperated sigh. 'Really, Mumsy, that's not fair. How can it have been a failure when Mr Magpie didn't make an appearance? The shooting was an unrelated matter, purely incidental. Meanwhile, the ladies' skills have exceeded our expectations, and we have yet to trial Miss Weatherby's cleverest inventions.'

'For the record, We are not convinced.' The Queen wriggled her fingers at the five spies. 'What are you calling them, Loosy?'

Mrs Campbell smiled. 'Her Majesty's League of Remarkable Young Ladies.'

Queen Victoria cast a doubtful glance at them, her gaze lingering uncomfortably on Winnie and her dishevelled hair. 'You know, when my darling Albert was alive, the two of us set up our own Operation Bait-and-Snare, but *we* nabbed our man. A weaselly criminal had aimed a gun at me while we were riding out, so we set a trap! The very next day, we followed the same route to tempt him to try again. That rascal did, and the police captured him; John Francis was his name. The whole adventure was *most* exhilarating!'

Princess Louise softly cleared her throat. 'But that was reckless. We can't risk your life in that way again, Mumsy.'

'And what of the Foreign Intelligence Committee? Shouldn't we leave these matters to qualified . . . gentlemen?' The Queen said the final word with a curl of her lip.

'The whole point of the League is to create an espionage team you can call on when you *don't* want to involve the Admiralty,' Princess Louise said. 'I know it's a work in progress. But give us time: these young agents will prove to you just how remarkable ladies can be.'

The Queen offered a curt nod, then glanced around, as if sniffing out goodies. 'In any event, I didn't come for this dismal parade. Rather, a little birdie told me there's a present waiting here for me. From Russia!' She rubbed her hands together.

Her little dog yapped and spun in circles.

'Enough, Bosco!' Princess Louise snapped, scowling at the pug. 'Yes, there's a gift from the Tsar, brought by tonight's tenor directly from St Petersburg.'

The Queen's grumpy expression softened. 'A lovely present will lift my spirits after the disappointments I've suffered tonight.'

'Then let's retreat inside,' Princess Louise muttered. 'Come along, ladies. Just . . . stand over there in the corner.' Celeste and Adelaide followed Princess Louise. Winnie and the others waited, then slipped inside the grand house's Journal Room and pressed themselves against a bookcase.

Across the room on a comfortable-looking armchair sat Prince Bertie. He looked up from his newspaper, sniffed the air and grimaced. He quickly lit a fat cigar and puffed rapidly, swirling a cloud of smoke around himself.

The Queen stood at an oval table in the Journal Room. Upon the table sat a tall purple velvet box embossed with gold lettering. 'Ooh, it's from the House of Fabergé! It must be one of their famous jewelled eggs!'

Prince Bertie harumphed into his billowing cloud of cigar smoke. He folded his newspaper and grunted to his feet to have a look.

'Stop right where you are, Bertie. Why are you smoking in my presence?' the Queen bellowed. 'You know I don't permit it, and frankly, right now, I cannot abide another stink.' Her eyes darted to Winnie and the other two reeking spies huddled in the corner. Prince Bertie made a mocking face at his irascible mother before snuffing his cigar in an empty whisky glass.

Oh, the shame. Winnie fiddled with a strip of lace hanging from her tattered gown.

The Queen lifted off the lid. Inside the box was a swath of white silk. She passed her walking stick to an attendant – who appeared from the shadows of the room as if from nowhere – and eagerly unwound the fabric. She peered into the box, then stepped back, frowning.

Prince Bertie peeked into the box. 'Well, that's rather disappointing.' He reached in and pulled out a small, pale green egg speckled with brown. 'A nest with eggs?'

Princess Louise leant in to have a look.

The Queen's face collapsed into a scowl. 'A twist of sticks and three ugly eggs? Where's my Fabergé?'

'Perhaps it's beneath the nest. Let's see . . .' Prince Bertie lifted the nest out.

The Queen sniffed. 'Why would Minnie and Tsar Alexander send this all the way from St Petersburg? It's an insult!'

The little pug whimpered at her feet.

Princess Louise reached in the box and groaned, 'Argh, no.'

In her hand was a small white calling card, edged in blue.

Greetings from
Mr Magpie

THE LONDON MORNING NEWS
Thieving Magpie Steals Imperial Jewels!
HM Cries Foul

Notorious pest 'Mr Magpie' swooped again at last night's society soiree at Holland House, pulling off a stunning heist. The brazen thief took flight with a haul of shiny treasure, namely an early birthday gift to Her Majesty Queen Victoria from the Russian Tsar and Tsarina.

The Queen was not injured or endangered during the robbery, despite reports of earlier gunshots at Holland Park and the presence of the Metropolitan Police. A mysterious figure was spotted in the grounds of the park and gunshots were heard, but the figure disappeared without a trace.

The stolen gift is reported to be a Russian Imperial jewelled egg created by the House of Fabergé in St Petersburg.

To add further insult, Mr Magpie swapped the priceless, jewel-encrusted golden egg with three magpie eggs in a common bird's nest made of muck-encrusted twigs. HM the Queen was reportedly 'not amused' at the thief's sense of humour.

One of Mr Magpie's now famous calling cards was found with the nest. How the sly criminal accessed Her Majesty's unopened birthday gift remains a mystery. Scotland Yard is investigating.

Scotland Yard Follows Its Nose to Magpie Gang

Two nightmen were arrested early this morning for assault, abduction and interference with a police matter. Scotland Yard has declined to comment if break and enter and burglary will be added to their charges.

West End publican Mr Harold Wilcox, proprietor of the Leek & Dagger Gin Den, claims to have heard strange noises 'like the moaning of a ghost' coming from the nightsoil wagon parked behind his disreputable establishment. Upon investigating, he found a man bound and gagged and wedged between the gong barrels. 'I couldn't shift the wretch on me own. The fumes nearly bowled me over, so I called for expert assistance from the ever-helpful London Constabulary.'

The victim, Detective Inspector Jerome Walker of the CID, was barely conscious and bruised. He claims he has no recollection of the assault and can only remember his final call was to the grounds of Holland House to investigate reports of gunfire.

Nightmen Liam Bottomley and Roger Humblebum of Southwark were apprehended at the Leek & Dagger and taken into custody for questioning in relation to the assault and kidnapping of the detective. The cesspits at Holland Park were reportedly the first stop on their rounds.

Amid rampant speculation that the pair of nightmen may be acting as or in collusion with 'Mr Magpie', the publican stated, 'Those reeking barrels are the perfect hiding space for stolen treasure — especially the Queen's golden egg. No one's game to look inside!'

There has been no comment from Buckingham Palace on the matter.

CHAPTER 23

Sunday morning

Breakfast congealed on Winnie's plate. The mingled smells of eggs and coffee only made her nausea worse after a sleepless, fitful night. Even with the curtain of her box-bed closed and tucked in, she'd been haunted by visions of DI Walker's rolled-back eyes and Queen Victoria's displeased scowl.

The other ladies arrived one by one, all silent with exhaustion and dread. Forks were not lifted. Cups remained on saucers.

The storm was about to break.

At the end of the hallway, the electric lift's door mashed open. The heels of ladies' boots ticky-tacked along the hall. Five young ladies sank lower in their chairs.

Headmistress Thornton burst into the breakfast room and slapped a newspaper on the table. 'Did *anything* go according to plan last night?'

Glances crisscrossed the table, but no one spoke. Adelaide puffed her cheeks.

Celeste raised her hand. 'If I may. Her Majesty the Queen was not injured, nor was any member of the Royal Family – despite the gunfire.'

'It's a blessing no one was harmed. Nevertheless, a fortune was stolen right beneath your noses. This does not bode well for your future, ladies. Her Majesty is rattled. She's convinced you're hopeless, and is a hair's breadth from closing down the League.'

The newspaper lay on the table in front of her but facing Adelaide, who sat opposite. Winnie read the second news article upside down, and her nausea trebled. The nightmen, those jovial fellows innocently going about their foul business, had been locked up and interrogated.

She pointed to the article that blamed them for her handiwork. 'Headmistress, can anything be done to help these two nightmen? It's wrong that innocent people should be caught up in this.'

'Wrong? That, my dear, is the only bright spot in this whole fiasco. Scapegoats are unsavoury, but they satisfy the public's hunger for "justice". You needn't worry yourself. Once it's died down, they'll be let off, and they can return to their normal existence. I should imagine a month in remand would be a holiday compared to emptying London's cesspits every night.'

'But it might be more than a month. In the meantime, they and their families are suffering needlessly.'

Headmistress levelled a glare at Winnie. 'Better them than us.'

Winnie's mouth dropped open. Had she heard what she thought she heard? 'I'm sorry, ma'am. I disagree. This isn't a game of chess with pawns to sacrifice strategically.'

Effie looked up from her lap. Admiration for Winnie shone from her face.

Headmistress shook her head slowly. 'That's what you think, Miss Weatherby.' She served herself some eggs and bacon from the bain-maries. 'And furthermore, as a group, you failed at the most important task of blending in and leaving no trace. When Marcus cleaned up after you last night, he found the following: one bent umbrella in the garden along with one lady's weaponized fan and shards of mirror, various pieces of lace and flower petals, including one made from nitrocellulose; the velvet-covered heel of a shoe was left in the Journal Room; and in the Gilt Chamber, he found a triangle of notepaper and feather pencil.

'Think for a moment what would have happened if Metropolitan Police detectives had found those peculiar items first? Or newspaper reporters? Today's headlines would read very differently. *Spies* – not nightmen – would be the suspects!' She threw up her hands. 'And women, not men!'

Winnie sank lower in her chair. Most of the debris was hers. Except the velvet-covered heel. How did that end up in the Journal Room, a room where no struggle had occurred?

Down the hall the lift rattled open again.

Headmistress shook her napkin open. 'That will be the Spymistress. Heaven help you.'

Princess Louise entered the room, dressed in a day gown of olive green rather than Mrs Campbell's usual widow's weeds. Replacing her veil was a pretty hat featuring a pouf of net and a single exotic feather that bobbed as she moved.

Winnie, Stella and Effie respectfully rose to their feet.

The Princess wagged her hand at them. 'There's no need for the formality. I prefer to be addressed as Mrs Campbell while carrying out League business. The simplicity is refreshing. However, in the presence of the Queen, please use the royal protocols, as Mother wouldn't approve of such informality.'

Refreshing, indeed. Winnie smiled at the avant-garde Spymistress.

Mrs Campbell removed her hat and gloves, served herself from the sideboard and sat. 'Let us quickly dispense with the unpleasantries: Her Majesty was not impressed with last night's performance. And, after seeing today's newspapers, she wishes to leave London as soon as possible to escape the scandal and speculation – and dodge a certain bothersome villain who remains at large.'

'Where will Her Majesty go and when?' Headmistress Thornton asked.

'She's still deciding, having mentioned Aix-en-Provence, but I should imagine it will be Sandringham, Balmoral or Osborne House.'

Celeste gasped. 'I do hope we are to be her companions for the journey. How I'd love to visit any of those destinations, but Balmoral in particular. Scotland would be lovely this time of year. Or the south of France!'

'I advise you to keep your expectations in check, Celeste.' Mrs Campbell sipped her coffee. 'Last night's events didn't allow the Queen to see you in a good light.'

Headmistress Thornton harumphed. 'An understatement.'

Mrs Campbell shrugged. 'I regret not staging a demonstration of your group prowess before launching you into a real mission. Something with fewer contingencies. The gift of the Fabergé egg surprised us and perhaps our villain too. It was the first of his exploits that involved a theft, despite having had opportunities in earlier venues.' She sat. 'My mother adores receiving gifts, the costlier the better. I feel certain if she hadn't suffered such a significant loss, she'd be more inclined to give you another chance.'

'What do we do with them now?' Headmistress gestured to the ladies seated around the table.

'We continue training them, of course! As soon as they have the chance to prove themselves useful, Mother will be eager to have pretty and protective young ladies at her beck and call.'

Winnie puffed out her relief. How could she ever give up her laboratory? She'd barely begun dreaming up big ideas and finding ways to use the array of materials at her disposal.

The electric lift door clattered. Mrs Campbell and Headmistress Thornton exchanged a puzzled look.

The Prince of Wales stalked in. Dark semicircles shadowed his puffy eyes, and grey whiskers bristled on his pudgy cheeks. Everyone in the room rose respectfully. Prince Bertie stopped by the sideboard to inspect the breakfast options and picked up a piece of bacon with one hand and toast with the other. 'Good morning, Loosy, Thornton, ladies. I do hope the coffee is hot. My head is *thumping*.' He nibbled the bacon.

Lines creased Headmistress's forehead. 'Good morning, Your Royal Highness. With all due respect, as spymaster, you should not come to the waxworks. It could appear irregular.'

'Bertie, dear, do sit down. It's not healthy to eat standing up.' Mrs Campbell gestured to the far head of the table. 'I'll bring you a plate.' Headmistress quickly set a place for him.

He took his seat and nodded, inviting the ladies to sit. He snatched the newspaper and began reading, shaking his head. 'This Magpie business has gone too far. He must be stopped!'

Princess Louise hovered behind him. 'Bertie, put the paper away. You'll upset your digestion.' He scowled and refolded it. She laid a plate piled with food in front of him. She cleared her throat and said cheerfully, 'Ponsonby sent word this morning that Mumsy wishes to engage the Admiralty for her getaway and is sulking over the loss of her Fabergé egg.'

He puffed. 'Forget the egg – it's a mere trinket in the grand scheme. There's far more at stake here. Mr Magpie's antics are growing more vexatious.' He stabbed his breakfast. 'It's fine for the Queen to run off on a remote holiday. After all, London is far nicer without the Royal Standard flying over Buckingham Palace.' He made a shooing gesture. 'But the rest is ridiculous. Involving the Admiralty and armed forces as escorts? For a puny pest like Mr Magpie who's motivated by revenge for petty trifles?'

Winnie cocked her head. She caught Celeste and Stella exchanging a questioning look. Indeed, this was the first they'd heard of motivations. Adelaide folded her arms and glared at her untouched breakfast. She obviously didn't like being kept in the dark. But why were they all silent? This was important information.

Prince Bertie smoothed a napkin on his lap. 'While you read your notes from Ponsonby, Loosy, this morning I ventured to Windsor to see Mumsy.'

'My! Aren't you brave!' Mrs Campbell shook her head. 'Well, how did it go?'

'Apart from the bellowing and hurling of objects, it went rather better than I'd expected.' He sipped his coffee and grimaced. 'Blech, it's cold. Where was I? Oh, yes. I want that fiend apprehended, and I want these ladies to do it. I managed to remind the Queen of the value of *her* League of Remarkable Young Ladies. She has agreed to permit them to act as her escort and bodyguards for the journey—'

Celeste squealed at this point, and even Headmistress looked relieved.

'—but if anything – *anything* – unfortunate happens on the way or at the destination, the League will be, as we say in German, *kaputt*. I'm afraid even I shan't be able to revive it.' Prince Bertie tucked into his eggs.

Winnie smiled at the others. Another chance to prove

their worth was welcome news.

'At least a week is needed to prepare for a royal journey,' he said, liberally salting his remaining food. 'Assume that we'll leave by royal train next Sunday morning the fifth of May.'

The fifth of May – the day she needed to be in Paris to meet Papa! Winnie sucked in a nervous breath, which earnt a concerned look from Stella. She lowered her gaze to her lap. Somehow, she had to convince Mrs Campbell to excuse her from the mission. How dangerous could a journey on the royal train be? Surely the protection of four remarkable young ladies would suffice.

'A week is barely enough, but it will have to do.' Headmistress Thornton gestured to Winnie. 'Miss Weatherby needs time to finish the customized chatelaines and other tools of espionage.'

Winnie tapped the table nervously. This was her chance to ask for leave. 'Your Highnesses, Headmistress and colleagues, I'm pleased to report the four new chatelaines are nearly complete. And the tiny pads of disappearing paper are ready to be added to the notebook equipage, so if I may—'

Mrs Campbell raised a finger. 'That reminds me. I want the chatelaines equipped with a vial to hold a dose of chloroform. Administering a sedative is far more effective and ladylike than clubbing someone unconscious with an umbrella, don't you think, Winifred?' She arched an elegant brow.

Was this a trick question? Winnie replied carefully. 'Not only an umbrella, ma'am. Stella and my Fan Fatale finished him off. Although the fan would have been more effective if DI Walker had been hatless—'

Effie snorted and dissolved into an exhausted giggling fit. All heads swung in her direction.

Stella blurted out a snigger. 'Whack! Ooh, I'm so sorry, sir! That was painful, I believe? I do beg your pardon,' she mimicked Winnie's voice.

Celeste exploded, spurting a mist of coffee. She patted her chest to catch her breath, and Stella wiped tears from her eyes with a lacy handkerchief.

The Prince clapped. 'Really? How amusing!' He slapped the table. 'I wish I'd seen it.'

Stella nodded, tears of laughter streaming. Everyone joined in, snorting, hiccupping and shaking with hilarity – including Winnie.

Adelaide reached across the table to give Winnie's hand a friendly squeeze.

Winnie pressed her lips together, fighting down a smile. Her cheeks burnt. 'If you're all quite finished having fun at my expense, I must say I agree. A vial of chloroform would be a welcome addition to the chatelaines. I'll get straight to work.'

And as soon as everything was ready, she'd present the chatelaines to the Spymistress and then secure her leave.

Paris, I'm on my way.

CHAPTER 24

*Wee hours between Monday night
and Tuesday morning*

Winnie's tiny lamp lit her way through the dark library. Her shoulders ached, her legs dragged, and her eyes ached with fatigue. It was well past time for bed.

She'd spent a most satisfying day in her magnificent Quartermistress's Laboratory, finishing the five ladies' chatelaines with custom equipages to hold chloroform. Each contained a specialized nostril-shaped wick for rendering targets unconscious. She'd moved on to other projects – reappearing-reorganizing ink, retractable daggers, lace gloves reinforced with chainmail, bullet-proof corsetry and Deterrent Vapour for Ladies made of oil infused with pepper and hot chillis delivered by perfume atomizer. (The final item held the most promise, but it needed much more development . . .)

The hours between eight in the morning and now, long past midnight, had slipped by in a blur of creative delight. If Effie hadn't brought her a tray with afternoon tea, Winnie would have gone on happily working until she collapsed from hunger or exhaustion. Now, with the Agency work completed, she could focus on the Telautograph designs and preparing for the Exposition Universelle. Tomorrow, when she showed the completed chatelaines to Mrs Campbell, she'd put forward her case for leave of absence for her trip to Paris to exhibit the Weatherby Telautograph Machine with Papa. And perhaps, with a stroke of luck, she might still find a way to enter her Boot-Button Butler . . .

She opened the door to the electric lift and stepped into the small cubicle. How inconvenient to have to operate the elevator while holding an oil lamp! The up-down lever was best worked with two hands. She gritted her teeth, shifted it to 'Up', and the lift lurched.

Despite the grinding gears, she heard something crunch under her foot, but the full fabric of her skirt blocked her view. When she reached the attic, she shifted the lever, stopping the carriage with a shudder. Once outside the lift she held up the lamp. On the floor of the elevator lay a squashed ball of paper. She dialled down the lamp's light and picked up the paper.

The door to the ladies' attic bedroom creaked open. Silvery bands of moonlight sliced through the shutters, casting a weird zebra pattern across the furniture.

Tiptoeing across the shadowy room, she set the lamp on the table and smoothed the crumpled page flat. It was a letter, and it was addressed to—

His Royal Highness the Prince of Wales?

Winnie squinted. Was she really looking at a letter addressed to Prince Bertie? Good golly! The crown prince? She rubbed her eyes and looked again.

And it was from . . . *a solicitor*?

Rubbing her temples, Winnie slid on to the creaky straight-backed chair. It would be undeniably wrong to read someone else's mail. And the fact that the 'someone' was the Prince of Wales – heir to the throne – made it worse. Didn't it? She bit her lip.

Breathing noises rose from the box-beds around the room, and outside the bells of a church far away chimed twice.

No one would know if she read it.

But it *was* a private letter . . .

26 April 1889
London

Your Royal Highness,

I write regarding the delicate matter we discussed on the First of April at the Carlton Club, which was reiterated in our demand letter sent on the Second of April 1889.

It has come to our attention that Sire has not yet responded to that letter, nor the subsequent three demand letters sent on our client's behalf.

We respectfully beseech Sire to heed this, the final invitation to meet privately and discreetly with our solicitors to arrange financial compensation, etc., for our client, as previously discussed . . .

We regret to inform you our client has flatly declined our counsel of patience and prudence. Instead, our client promises to, 'continue Harassment of the Royal Family'. (Nota Bene: We certainly do not understand what this refers to.) Furthermore, our client has overtly threatened to begin a campaign of 'Very Public Shaming' and 'Red-hot Retribution'.

Sire, we are duty-bound. Professionalism requires us to honour our client's wishes and privacy. On the other hand, we have an obligation as loyal subjects and faithful servants of Her Majesty the Queen to advise you of our grave concerns. We fear our client's growing agitation could precipitate unpredictable and unsavoury behaviour. The resulting damage to Your Royal Highness's public image and role as our future King could be detrimental, if not disastrous.

It is our sincerest desire to avoid such unpleasantries by meeting with Sire at our rooms as per our invitation. We look forward to your expedited reply.

As always, we remain,

Respectfully yours,
Oliver C Martin, Esq.
O C Martin & Associates
Solicitors at Law
London

Winnie's eyes boggled at the implications. Who was harassing the Royal Family? But Mr Magpie! These lawyers knew his identity! And if they knew, why couldn't the Prince of Wales use his clout to make them stop him? Surely he had tried . . .

Winnie reached for a non-existent plait. Drat – this was a plait-chewing conundrum if ever there was one. Should she show the letter to the others? They might think she was rude for reading the letter in the first place. She'd have to think.

She tiptoed to her trunk and took out her nightgown,

then she went to the modesty screen to undress and change. She wriggled out of her day clothes, savouring the release and yawning deeply. She ducked into her smocked flannel nightgown and stepped out from behind the modesty screen.

Pooled in the dim golden glow of the oil lamp was Celeste, wrapped in a blanket and bent over the table, reading the letter.

Winnie let out a gasp.

Celeste turned. 'Winnie! Where did you find this?' she hissed.

Oh, bother. Winnie put a finger to her lips. She darted back across the creaky floor. 'Shh. You'll wake the others.'

The curtains on the nearest box-bed slid open, and Stella peeped out. 'It's too late. Winnie is as silent as an approaching locomotive. What are you two doing?'

Celeste locked eyes with Winnie. 'This is supremely important.'

Winnie nodded. 'Stella, wake Effie and Adelaide. I have something to show you.'

Stella crawled out of her bed with a shiver. 'Brr. This room is so draughty. Effie, Adelaide!' She pulled back the curtains on Euphemia's bed. 'Get up.'

Adelaide's bed was empty. *Out riding her safety bicycle at this hour?* Winnie frowned.

Stella shook her head. 'How she thrives on so little

sleep I shall never know!'

Effie yawned. 'Perhaps she's using the privy. She took a dose of castor oil earlier.'

Celeste turned up the lamp. 'Look what Winnie found – a letter to Prince Bertie from a solicitor.'

Stella's eyes widened. 'Oh, dear! We really shouldn't.'

Celeste sniffed. 'We're spies. Peeking at correspondence is part of the job.' She shrugged. 'Besides, *they* trained us.'

All the young ladies nodded.

Celeste draped part of her blanket over Winnie's shoulders. 'This is very interesting. I suspect the "client" is Mr Magpie, but who is he? And how did the letter end up in the electric lift?'

Winnie rubbed her eyes. 'The most likely explanation is it fell out of His Highness's pocket before or after breakfast yesterday.'

Celeste shook the letter. 'I don't know about the rest of you, but ever since Prince Bertie mentioned motives, I've been seething. It seems he knows *why* Mr Magpie is doing what he's doing.'

Winnie nodded. 'I thought the same thing. Why not tell us? It could help us better defend Her Majesty.'

'Precisely.' Celeste scooted closer to the table and the others. 'According to this, Prince Bertie was thrice asked to reply to "the matter" but he instead chose to ignore it.

Hence, the activity of a certain magpie has escalated.' She tapped her chin. 'Why?'

Winnie leant back in her creaking chair, tucking her knees beneath her chin and covering her cold toes. 'How intriguing! All along, I'd assumed Mr Magpie was bothering the Queen, but this suggests His Royal Highness Prince Bertie is the target.'

Celeste nodded. 'Indeed.'

Effie and Stella shivered, and Celeste pulled her blanket tighter.

'I don't understand why we haven't been informed of Mr Magpie's motives if the Spymaster has known all along.'

Effie cocked her head. 'It's a secret, Winnie. It is possible even Mrs Campbell and Headmistress are in the dark.'

Celeste clicked her tongue. 'I reckon Mrs Campbell knows. She appears to have a close relationship with her older brother.'

Stella grimaced. 'I wonder what the secret is. It must be shameful.'

Effie's lips shifted. 'Perhaps he was unfaithful to his wife.'

Celeste puffed. 'Sadly, no one cares that he's a libertine. No, I think he's made some grand faux pas, a mistake with international consequences. Otherwise, why would they engage private spies?'

The door creaked open, and Adelaide tiptoed in. She froze. 'Gracious, how frightening you look, wrapped up like a congregation of mummies in the moonlight! What's this, then?'

Celeste held up the paper. 'Winnie found a letter. You should look at it.'

'Can it wait?' Adelaide groaned and batted her hand. 'All I want to look at is the inside of my eyelids.'

Celeste rose and snuffed the lamp. 'A wise idea. We shall take up the matter in the morning. Goodnight, ladies.'

One by one the five young ladies crawled into their box-beds.

Winnie wriggled under her warm woollen blanket and pulled the curtain shut. How pleasant to close her eyes, lie on her side, sink her cheek into a cool feather pillow and drift into silence . . . except for the tiniest, faintest sniffs . . .

CHAPTER 25

~THE QUARTERMISTRESS'S LABORATORY~

Tuesday afternoon, 30 April 1889

'And finally, as requested, this equipage appears to be a vinaigrette, but instead of smelling salts, it holds chloroform.' She cleared her throat. 'My purpose-built Nasal Wick, patent pending, allows the user to render the target unconscious without the use of brute force. The wick expands as it's withdrawn from the bottle, like this.' She demonstrated. 'One simply jams the wick up their opponent's nostrils, and in a moment or two, he's out cold.' She waved the apparatus under her nose and swayed dizzily.

After fumbling the wick back into the bottle, she stepped away from the waxen figure of Marie Antoinette. 'I hope you're pleased with the tools?' Her hands twined together nervously.

Her colleagues clapped daintily.

'Brava, Winifred,' Mrs Campbell said,

before expelling a stream of tobacco smoke.

Headmistress nodded. 'Yes, you've done exceedingly well. We are most pleased with your designs and with the speed of production.'

Mrs Campbell mashed her cigarette in a dish. 'That reminds me. I have some news for you. But first, you wanted to ask something of us, I believe?'

News? Of Papa? Her tummy twisted; her thoughts faltered. 'Um, er, yes. May we speak alone?'

Celeste cast a curious squint in Winnie's direction.

'Of course. Ladies, to the palaestra for some exercise.' Mrs Campbell gestured to the fireplace passage.

Winnie baulked at the explaining she'd have to do later, but she didn't need the presence of the others to influence this discussion. The truth was her request was selfish and unfair – and completely essential. Winnie swallowed. 'Because I've completed all the quartermistress's tasks, I wish to request a leave of absence to attend to my father's business. The fifth of May is—'

'The fifth of May is the date of Operation Migration, Miss Weatherby.' Headmistress squinted at her, as if defying her to continue.

With nails digging into her palms, Winnie smothered the angry eruption Headmistress always inspired. 'I'm aware of the conflict, but I was promised—'

Mrs Campbell sighed. 'You were promised help

finding your father *when* there's time to devote to it, which there is not. Winifred, you seem to forget the importance of this mission. We must be successful, or Her Majesty's League of Remarkable Young Ladies will be . . .' She rolled her hand.

'I believe His Royal Highness said *kaputt*,' Head-mistress offered.

Winnie gritted her teeth. *Successful – ha!* Beneath Mrs Campbell's words lay the truth: if they failed, Prince Bertie's dirty little secret – whatever it was – would be made public. Winnie braced herself against the barrage of words that exploded like fireworks in her chest – furious words about undisclosed motives and accusations about keeping her and the others in the dark like bleating sheep heading for the slaughter.

Pawns – she and the other four young ladies were expendable players in a game about royal privilege. Meanwhile, her father's livelihood – and possibly his life – were being dismissed as irrelevant. Not to mention a brilliant invention that could change human interactions for the better.

Winnie drew in a breath through her nose and gather-ed her wits. 'Ma'am, the future of the Weatherby Manufacturing Company is at stake. Papa is counting on me to deliver the Weatherby Telautograph Machine to the Exposition Universelle in time for the close of registration for the Grand Prix on the fifth of May. If *I* fail, we will be ruined – and worse, that horrible bully Peter Geier will swoop in for the kill! If Papa is forced to relinquish the rights to our most promising invention, I shall never be able to forgive myself . . .'

Mrs Campbell massaged her temples. 'Very well, Miss Weatherby. I think it best we grant you leave of absence. Your mind would be elsewhere and of no use to Her Majesty or your colleagues. I wish to register my sternest displeasure at having to make this concession. Your leave of absence begins on Friday at noon and not a moment earlier, and it ends on the following Wednesday at noon. Do you understand?'

The trip to France would be rushed, but it could be done. Winnie curtsied. 'Thank you, ma'am. If that's all . . .'

'I expect you'd like to hear the latest intelligence about your father?'

Winnie covered her mouth, bracing herself for anything.

'According to my sources, your father left the country yesterday. His name was registered on a passenger ship headed for Brussels.'

'Thank you, Mrs Campbell. He'll be making his way indirectly to Paris. It's good to know he's following the plan.' The room seemed to sway. This was good news, and yet every time Papa was mentioned, a sick feeling washed over Winnie.

Mrs Campbell's brow knitted. 'Except his name also turned up on the manifest of a ship heading to New York and again on a ship to Melbourne. It would appear he's indecisive.'

Winnie's eyes widened. 'I believe the term is "muddying his tracks".'

'Let's hope that's the case. That's all, I'm afraid.'

Winnie curtsied again. On her way along the corridor, she checked over her shoulder and veered off to the spiral staircase, which she scurried down. At the landing to the second floor, she pushed open the door and peeked into the Shakespeare Gallery, populated by utterly still figures. Shadows stretched across the clusters of wax effigies frozen in dramatic poses. Glass eyes stared; hands reached; and three hairy hags leered into their iron cauldron.

Winnie tiptoed across the room to the *Macbeth* display. A week had passed since she'd found Clancy here, but until Mrs Campbell mentioned Papa's unexpected evasive strategy, she hadn't thought to check for a message from him. 'Excuse me,' she said as she ducked under the gnarled hands of the waxen witch who appeared to be chanting, 'Double, double, toil and trouble.'

Winnie peered inside the cauldron's dark interior. Bother, she'd have to feel around. Squatting awkwardly, she reached to the bottom of the pot where there lay a surprising amount of rubbish. She clutched a handful to have a look.

Among the refuse was one crumpled envelope. The name and address had been completely blacked out except for two letters on different lines: 'W' and 'w'. *Winifred Weatherby.*

Winnie smiled at Clancy's clever trick. He'd make a rather good spy!

Miss,

I've called past your home twice. No sign of YF. The Liar left, but someone's watching for you. Don't worry about me. I use the <u>high road</u>.

Your faithful friend,

C

Sunday 28 April

P.S. The Bloody Chamber gave me nightmares. DO NOT ENTER.

Clancy's reconnaissance was timely and resourceful (*YF* was Your Father, *the Liar* was Geier, and *high road* meant cloudlarking), but his news was alarming. Who was watching the house? What if it was DI Walker? He'd told the news reporters he had no memory of the event, but a proud man like him would never admit the truth – that he'd been bashed unconscious by young ladies and stuffed among reeking barrels of nightsoil . . . If only she'd had chloroform and her Nasal Wick for that assignment.

Walker or not, she had to go home because, as Papa had informed her in his mirror-written letter, 'Franc is safe.' Cleverly concealed in the walls of Papa's bedroom was a safe, and in it there was an envelope of francs to cover her train fare to Paris and incidental expenses. Sneaking away from the waxworks without anyone knowing would be tricky enough, but she also had to break into her house without alerting whoever might be waiting there to nab her.

Winnie opened the notepad equipage on her chatelaine and removed the thin pencil from its holder. How could she tell him she was leaving for France and would put money for him in the chimney pot on the roof without revealing any of the secret details? It was unlikely anyone would intercept the message, but still. She tapped her chin, thinking.

Tuesday
C,
   You've been so helpful again. Before my ship departs, I shall return to the high road for goods. I will put your bees and honey in the top pot. Take care.

   Your fond friend,
   Miss

She chuckled at her code word for money. Even Susan, Papa's washerwoman, would be proud to know her lessons in Cockney rhyming slang had been helpful. He was clever enough to work out the 'top pot' was the chimney pot. Winnie tore the note from the pad and inserted it in the envelope Clancy had used. After removing all the rubbish from the cauldron, she dropped the note inside. With her business concluded, she opened the hidden door to the spiral staircase. As she pulled the door behind her, she froze, clutching the handful of rubbish to her chest.

A click echoed around the Shakespeare Gallery. Fear jolted down her limbs. Had someone seen her? She peeked through the gap back into the hall, but all was still and eerily quiet. Holding her breath, she gently, slowly, closed the door.

THE LONDON MORNING NEWS
Mr Magpie Takes Aim AGAIN —
HM Unscathed but 'Shaken'

The brazen fiend calling himself 'Mr Magpie' took aim at Her Majesty Queen Victoria in this his latest act of incivility. The Queen was reportedly 'deeply shaken' by a terrifying incident involving a misfired arrow at Windsor Castle's Great Park on Wednesday evening.

The errant archer, believed to be 'Mr Magpie', has not been apprehended.

The Palace is downplaying the event, saying it was not an attempt on the Queen's life, but rather 'only a bored little man seeking notoriety'.

In the official statement, private secretary Sir Henry Ponsonby said: 'At no time was Her Majesty's life at risk.'

The Queen was enjoying an evening ride in her pony chair when a stray arrow sliced through the air in front of the animal, landing shallowly in the bark of a nearby historic oak. The sudden movement and sound startled the royal pony Picco, who took flight despite his advanced age.

The Queen single-handedly regained control of Picco and returned unaided and unharmed to the rest of her party.

HRH the Prince of Wales remarked on his mother's skill. 'We can all be thankful Her Majesty knows how to handle horses.' He added, '(She's) quite capable of subduing even the most spirited of men and beasts.'

Accompanying the Queen on foot were several of her staff. None was injured.

Her groom Mr Hugh Brown leapt into action after estimating the approximate position of the archer. His search of the grounds was fruitless. After dislodging the arrow, he noticed its uncustomary fletching of *magpie* feathers, a clue to the archer's identity.

The identity of the perpetrator was further confirmed upon returning to the Royal Windsor Mews. 'Mr Magpie' had left his mark in Picco's stall using a second identical arrow to pin his calling card to the royal pony's bale of hay.

Miles Owen, an impish stableboy at the Royal Mews, claims the calling card accompanied a letter. 'I saw it! It were addressed to "Her Majesty the Queen" and sealed with a blob of wax with a small white feather pressed into it.'

As no such letter has been found, authorities have discounted the boy's account. Sir Francis Knollys, private secretary to HRH the Prince of Wales, issued a statement saying the claims are, '. . . the product of the mischievous imagination of an illiterate boy who deserves a proper and thorough telling-off.'

The Metropolitan Police are investigating the incident while increased security measures are being introduced at all royal residences and outings.

CHAPTER 26

~Waxworks Dining Room~

Noon on Thursday, 2 May 1889

The French doors banged open, making the five young ladies around the table jump. Headmistress Thornton stalked in. 'Luncheon is finished, ladies. There's been a change of plans, and you must pack your trunks immediately. Ensure that your chatelaines and other personal tools of espionage are kept on your person or stowed for easy access.' She slid the morning paper to the middle of the table, headline facing up.

The words *Mr Magpie* leapt off the page. Winnie grimaced at the others.

'You'll be fully briefed this afternoon, but for now the newspaper can inform you of Mr Magpie's latest attack. The Queen insists on leaving London immediately; however, given all a royal journey entails, the best we can do is depart tomorrow – and making *that* happen will be akin to moving the moon six inches to the left.'

What about Paris and her leave of absence? Winnie opened her mouth to protest.

Headmistress cut her off. 'Miss Weatherby, your leave of absence has been cancelled. Mr Magpie is no longer playing a game of pranks. His tactics have escalated to potential bodily harm. We need *every* young lady on duty and alert. We meet in the library at four.'

Winnie puffed her cheeks. Arguing was futile – that was obvious. 'If I am to come, the Weatherby Telautograph Machine comes too.'

'I forbid it.' Headmistress raised her chin.

Winnie folded her arms. 'Where I go, it goes. That cannot change. It was a condition of my acceptance.'

Headmistress Thornton closed her eyes. Her left lid twitched; her nostrils flared; her neck blazed crimson. Finally, she spoke. 'Very well, Miss Weatherby, but you will be responsible for getting it to the station and finding room to stow it on the royal freight train – not on the royal passenger train.'

She returned to the French doors. 'I have business to attend to at the Beacon Academy. Adelaide, I require your assistance.'

Adelaide stifled a sigh. Dark circles puffed under her eyes. 'Yes, Headmistress.'

'I beg your pardon, ma'am,' Celeste called out. 'Where

will we be going? Which of the Queen's preferred destinations?'

Headmistress tutted. 'That is the question of the hour. It is classified information – for now. All of London is wondering. According to my cabman this morning, bookmakers all around London are taking wagers, and Provence is the current favourite. Good day, ladies. Adelaide, don't be long.' The French doors swung closed.

Provence! Finally, some good news. Winnie crossed her fingers under the table. *Oh, please let's go to France.* Perhaps she could make something happen – slip off the train in Paris, call into the World Fair, and rendezvous with Papa. She could catch up with the royal train a day later.

Or not. What a fanciful dream! She shook her head. As if she'd be permitted to leave her post for personal business.

But if they were in France anyway . . .

A tiny spark of hope glimmered in her spirit. *Be positive and alert.* She'd prepare as if she were going to the Exposition Universelle, so when an opportunity presented itself, she could grab it.

Tonight was the night for her sneaky visit home. It was all the more important to retrieve essential funds.

Across the table, Adelaide growled and shook the newspaper. 'Those despicable, lying scoundrels!'

Stella put down her fork. 'What is it?'

'This!' Adelaide poked the paper. 'There was a letter from Mr Magpie to the Queen – or so it says, and they are acting as if no such letter existed.' She read aloud the relevant parts of the article. 'You see? They are twisting the facts to cover the truth.' Her voice was shrill and her face splotchy.

Winnie, Stella, Effie and Celeste stared wide-eyed at Adelaide, who rarely expressed such emotion. She was right, though – the very people they were supposed to be protecting *were* hiding the truth.

Winnie pushed away her plate. Her belly panged with worry for her friend. Ever since Adelaide had read the lawyer's letter, she hadn't been herself.

Winnie thought she understood why. To Adelaide, their work no longer felt principled and just – she didn't know what she was fighting for. Now, instead of being the first to rise and last to retire, Adelaide lingered in bed and moved as if she were walking through knee-deep mud. She'd hardly eaten for the past few days, and her usual rosy complexion had paled.

Celeste shrugged. 'Adelaide, if there was a letter, maybe its contents put the Queen at further risk.' She narrowed her eyes at her colleague. '*That* is our concern – Her Majesty's safety, not politics or fairness or anything else, virtuous or otherwise.'

Adelaide rolled her eyes. 'I know what our concern is. But I don't see how we can protect the Queen if we have piecemeal information. If that letter is important enough to be made to vanish, it contains something we need to know.'

Stella nodded. 'It's an excellent point. We must ask about the alleged letter at our briefing this afternoon.'

Adelaide rubbed her temples. 'Yes, yes. Indeed, we should. I will see all of you there. Duty calls at the Academy.' She rose with a frown.

'So you're not rushed this evening,' Winnie said, eager to ease her friend's burden, 'perhaps I could pack your trunk for you?'

'No!' Adelaide grimaced. 'That is, no, thank you. I appreciate your offer, but I'm particular about packing and people touching my things, as you know. Let us hope Headmistress's business at the Academy is brief. Good day.'

Winnie quickly finished her lunch. The sudden change of plans required a new agenda, and Step One was to set up an alibi for tonight. 'Apart from packing and the briefing, I shall spend the rest of the day in the Quartermistress's Laboratory. I fear my work will keep me there until the wee hours.'

Stella frowned. 'Oh, dear! We all have a big day tomorrow.'

Winnie shrugged sheepishly. 'So much to do, so little time.'

And Step Two was to arrange a favour . . .

*

Dearest Adelaide,

I'm writing to request a favour – another favour, that is. I fear it may be unreasonable to ask for your continued secret support when you are so busy and disillusioned, but I hope you'll extend your assistance one more time.

I shan't explain my mission fully, lest you try to deter me. What I must do relates to the future of my father's business and his safety, but first I need to collect the finances to carry it out.

If I succeed, I will carry on to the Queen's destination with the rest of you, meeting everyone at the train station before the royal train departs. If my separate arrival is noticed, I shall pretend my late arrival was necessitated by having to retrieve a forgotten item from the laboratory. Would you please go along with this excuse?

Should I not arrive at the train station, it means my father's foes have been successful. (Please don't worry – I intend to use everything the League has taught me about self-defence!)

I know this act of disobedience may cost me my prized position as the quartermistress of Her Majesty's League of Remarkable Young Ladies, and it will be a loss I shall feel sorely. In this unfortunate case, I ask you to pass on my sincerest apologies, especially to Mrs Campbell and the other ladies.

I thank you for all your help and belief in me, and I wish you well.

I remain,

Yours fondly,
Winnie

Winnie placed the sealed letter on Adelaide's pillow. Now for Step Three: to the laboratory to make some special *deluxe* adjustments to her own chatelaine before the briefing.

OPERATION MIGRATION

CLASSIFIED TOP SECRET CLASSIFIED

YOUR MISSION, part 1:

o Ensure uninterrupted travel and safe
  arrival of HM Queen Victoria (and her
  family and belongings) to her holiday
  home.

Royal Holiday Destination: Osborne House,
Isle of Wight

> Departure Date: Friday 3 May 1889
> Return Date: Following the Capture and
> Arrest of 'Mr Magpie'

> To avoid alerting Mr M, there will be no
> public announcement of HM's travel itiner-
> ary. Only necessary railway officials will
> be notified to facilitate planning for
> the considerable disruption to the British
> train schedule.

TRAVEL SCHEDULE:

Train Journey Details

> Three Trains: Pilot, The Royal Passenger
> Train, The Royal Freight Train
>> Pilot (10 minute gap) Royal Passenger Train

(10 minute gap) Royal Freight Train
*When not on duty, Her Majesty's Young Lady
Agents will ride in a compartment of the
carriage behind the Royal Saloon.*

Slough, departing 8.45 (Accompanying Agent:
Miss Lee). Godalming, arriving 10.15.
Refreshment Stop - 20 minutes
Godalming, departing 10.35 (Accompanying
Agent: Miss Davies). Gosport, arriving
11.50.

Godalming Refreshment Stop Details:
20 minutes exactly (or as required by HM)

> HM's Privy Guards: Miss Lemieux and Miss
> Davies. Platform Guards: Miss Weatherby
> and Miss Lee. Royal Family Detail: Miss
> Culpepper.

Solent Crossing Details
Vessel: HMY Alberta
Gosport, departing 12.30
Ryde, arriving 13.00

> Passengers: HM, Royal Family, Royal House-
> hold Staff and Her Majesty's League. Any
> others will cross with the freight. Freight
> will be loaded on a separate vessel.

Isle of Wight Travel
In order of departure

1. Express Carriage - Young Lady Agents (except
   Miss Lemieux) to Osborne House for a <u>secur-
   ity sweep</u> ahead of the Queen's arrival.

2. (Departing 10 minutes later) Royal Osborne
   Coach - HM and Royal Family (accompanied by
   Miss Lemieux).

3. Victoria Railway - Royal Household
   Staff, etc.

YOUR MISSION, part 2:

During the Queen's indefinite stay at
Osborne House:

o Ensure the safety of HM the Queen on the
  Isle of Wight.

o Monitor arrivals on the island to
  detect, identify and STOP Mr Magpie.

o Should Mr Magpie arrive on the
  island, ensure he does not enter
  Osborne House.

---

*AFTER COMMITTING TO MEMORY, DESTROY THIS
DOCUMENT WITH FIRE.*

HML

CHAPTER 27

~Tite Street, Chelsea~

Wee hours of Thursday night

An hour after sneaking out of Madame Tussauds, Winnie paused in a puddle of muted gaslight to catch her breath and collect her swirling thoughts. She'd successfully reached her neighbourhood in Chelsea, but somewhere south of Hyde Park her confidence had abandoned her. With every step, her doubt grew. Trekking across London in the middle of the night now seemed like a very bad, very dangerous idea. She shivered in her disguise and pulled up the collar of her men's jacket.

Drat and double drat. If only HM hadn't vetoed holidaying in France. They were going only as far south as the Isle of Wight. She'd be stuck there, minding a grumpy old woman while Papa's big debut at the Exposition Universelle flopped.

She wriggled her jaw to release the knot of tension. But just maybe . . .

One tiny spark of hope glimmered: as soon as the Queen was settled into Osborne House, perhaps they'd allow Winnie to carry on to France. The Isle of Wight was halfway to Paris, so she might still have time to meet Papa. Winnie squared her shoulders and bolstered herself with one of Headmistress's favourite sayings: *Opportunity favours those who are prepared.*

Now to retrieve the francs from Papa's safe.

It was well past midnight, and the deserted streets were quiet, save for yowls of alley cats, the clatter of rats scampering across dustbins, and the distant rumble of carriage wheels over the pavement.

Winnie walked down the street pushing the Portarobe, a recent invention consisting of luggage mounted on a wheeled chassis with a handle, an ingenious cross between a perambulator and a street vendor's cart. Inside its sturdy, mounted travel trunk, she'd stowed the Weatherby Telautograph Machine – WA-model. Her official blueprints were scrolled up inside the shaft of her umbrella.

Even with Headmistress's reluctant permission, precautions were needed to make sure these precious belongings weren't left behind when her colleagues departed for the station in a few hours. *Where I go, they go.* Papa was counting on her. He would need the plans and machine in Paris even if she arrived too late to enter the Grand Prix.

She sauntered along until she could glimpse her house along the row of nearly identical three-storey brick homes. How empty it looked! The colourful flowers that usually spilt from Mrs Pugh's window boxes were brown stalks. Still, the sight of the front door made Winnie's heart pang for the familiar comforts of home and the simple life of a young girl who created a fanciful device to make boot buttoning easier.

She stifled a laugh. Now she built devices to knock grown men senseless without the use of brute force! How had this metamorphosis occurred? Gone was the clever, studious girl who imagined other possibilities for a common kitchen whisk. In her place was a suddenly worldly young lady (dressed as a man) who was quarter-mistress-spy in the service of Her Majesty Queen Victoria. She had barely registered the change until she approached her home, a place that felt as if it belonged to another life – another person.

There was no sign of life within the house – thank goodness, because any movement would signal danger. Still, she'd take the cautious route and enter via 'the high road' as Clancy had done. At the end of the block, she slipped around the corner and behind the building belonging to the ancient spinster Miss Hortensia Make-peace, who, unless she slept with her ear trumpet engaged, wouldn't hear Winnie clambering across her roof.

In the back garden, Winnie darted between shadows to the privy and traced her path from the ground to the roof. She'd use the tree branches. She squeezed the Portarobe between some bushes and the privy, and hung the hook of her umbrella over the handle. She'd collect both after her mission was complete.

After ten minutes of grunting and straining, she'd made it up three storeys to Miss Makepeace's roof. She sat, panting, in the crook of a dormer window. Her throat clenched. *Don't look down!* She was fully equipped with her deluxe chatelaine (pinned to the inside of her coat), and her pocket held a nub of a candle. She puffed a breath. Time to go.

Carefully she shuffled along the edge of the roof, placing each step carefully. She moved from Miss Makepeace's building to the next and then the next and so on until she'd forgotten how many houses she'd crossed. Finally, she spotted a familiar sight – Admiral Higson, Papa's dearest (and oddest) friend and nearest neighbour, had a ship's figurehead mounted on the front of his house, a prancing unicorn bust. As soon as Winnie spotted the twisted horn (made from a real narwhal tusk) poking from under the eaves, she knew she was close to home. She hurried along the roofline to the half-moon window of the attic at number 34, jimmied it open and wriggled her way inside.

How peculiar to return home for the first time in six weeks without Papa to greet her. She dusted herself off, patted her pockets again, and crept down the attic stairs, skipping lightly over the squeaky tread, and carefully pushing open the door into the second-floor hall.

She listened. The grandfather clock downstairs ticked as steadily as a heartbeat, and the bones of the old house creaked as if welcoming her back into its embrace. Unable to resist the quickest peek into her bedroom, she turned the knob and pushed open the door. Familiar scents enveloped her – soap, ink and wood mingled with the faint ammonia smell from blueprint paper. Home – her heart ached.

She found a candle holder, stuck the candle nub in it and lit it. The golden glow revealed a room that reflected her former self – small and plain and far simpler. She frowned, feeling both erased and at odds with the space. How small the room seemed, as if, like Alice in the White Rabbit's hole, she no longer fitted and never would again. Was it possible to outgrow a place so quickly?

Against the wall was the narrow bed she'd slept in since she was small. Its faded coverlet had been lovingly stitched by her mother. The pull of it was like gravity, but she would surely fall asleep as soon as her cheek hit the pillow . . . Pinned to the walls were dozens of newspaper clippings about her hero Thomas Edison and the upcoming Exposition Universelle in Paris. Her drafting tools and pencil-mark calculations covered the surface of her sloped desk. Her brow creased.

Strewn at the base of the shelves was a messy pile of notebooks, paper and texts. Clancy had mentioned the home's disarray, but seeing proof of intrusion in her room sent a chill through her core.

Winnie blew out the candle and backed out of her room, shutting the door firmly but quietly. An ache throbbed in the hollow space between her collarbones as she padded to her father's bedroom. Opening the door, she tripped on a rumpled rug. She relit the candle and gasped. Good gracious, what a mess the thugs had made. The bed was partially stripped and, like her room, books and papers lay everywhere, but she had to focus. She opened Papa's roll-top desk. Inside was a faux set of drawers and pigeonholes, and behind them was the safe. Winding the hidden crank engaged a mechanism to lift the heavy wooden set of drawers away.

Slowly it rose on tiny hydraulic lifts, her invention, which she'd dubbed W.A. Weatherby Hydraulic Elbows (or Weatherby's Lifts). She'd designed and built them as a summer project, though Papa had declared her little lifts 'charming but completely impractical', forbidding her to apply for a patent. As usual, he cited the stigma of her mechanical-mindedness. Months had passed and still Papa's words and dismissal stung. The Weatherby Lifts were promising – no matter what he'd said.

Winnie dialled the combination to the safe, the sequence of numbers in her mother's birthdate. The lock released. The safe was tightly stuffed with papers, designs, notes and notebooks – much messier than usual. Papa must have been in a frightful hurry the last time he opened the safe. After struggling to prise out the wad of papers, Winnie finally reached the squat metal cashbox at the back. She lifted the lid.

A handful of copper-coloured coins lay in the bottom. The envelope of francs for the trip to the Exposition Universelle was gone. No! Had she misunderstood Papa's hints about money? Maybe he'd taken the money himself. She fingered the scant coins – and looked again. Each one had a hole in the centre.

These weren't coins. They were the Madame Tussauds Wax Museum tokens she'd given to Clancy.

CHAPTER 28

Thursday night, wee hours

How had Clancy's tokens ended up in here? It didn't make sense. She sucked in a breath – unless he'd been recaptured and (she gulped) compelled to reveal her secrets . . .

If only Papa had heeded her warning to make the combination harder to guess. Mamma's birthdate was engraved on her tombstone for anyone to discover.

'Looking for something?'

Winnie yelped and spun around to the doorway. There stood a stout, moustached man in a familiar suit and a slightly misshapen bowler hat. After leaning his umbrella with its creepy bat-shaped handle against the fireplace, he waggled an envelope – Papa's envelope with the francs.

Double drat. She swallowed. 'I beg your pardon, sir! You are trespassing in a private residence. I insist you leave at once or—'

'Or you'll call the police?' DI Walker scratched the whiskers at the side of his face with the envelope, making a grating rasp. 'If you don't mind me saying, "sir", you don't sound old enough or manly enough to insist on anything.' After stuffing the envelope in his breast pocket, he crossed the room slowly, like a lion preparing to pounce.

'Stop. Don't come any closer, or . . . or I shall—'

'Scream? Like a girl? You, Miss Weatherby, are not a very convincing man, but you *are* a very troublesome young lady.'

She lifted her chin. 'You're not the first to say so.' Her voice shook as she scanned the room. A weapon . . . what was there? The poker by the fireplace. She took a breath and lunged for it.

Walker caught her by the arm. 'Oh, no. There'll be none of that tonight, miss. You caught me off guard last time, but I won't underestimate you again.' He wrenched her arm behind her back, making her whimper with pain. 'You're coming with me.'

Winnie twisted and kicked and screamed.

He clapped his hand over her mouth. 'Make another sound like that and I will hurt you proper.' He twisted her arm harder as if to prove his intent. 'Move!' Walker shoved her along in front of him, downstairs to the dark parlour. 'You will sit here quietly until Mr Geier arrives.'

He pushed her on to the faded settee, bound her hands and feet and gagged her.

Familiar smells surrounded her – ash from the grate, oil from the lamp, hints of Papa's pipe smoke. But next to the fireplace was an oddly shaped mound, a new tea table? She groaned. *No.*

It was her Portarobe and draped over it were her blueprints removed from the umbrella. She squeezed her eyes shut. This was worse than she'd imagined. How foolish to think she could outfox a fox.

Winnie lay on her side on the faded settee, and while her capturer paced the parlour, she wriggled her hands in tiny movements, rolling the rope down her wrists in small increments. In the hallway, the grandfather clock ticked a steady beat.

When the front door creaked open, Winnie wriggled herself upright. Had minutes passed or hours? It was still dark.

A man in a smartly cut coat strode in. He removed his hat and gloves and placed them on a chair. The French-forked beard, the tortoiseshell monocle! It was him, the man who'd pretended to be Sir Phillip at the Beacon Academy and bumped into her at the soiree.

'Herr Geier.' DI Walker cleared his throat and rose wearily to his feet. 'Here's the girl you wanted.'

Winnie sat tall, trying to master her fear. So, finally she

was face to face with Peter Geier, the monstrous villain who'd loomed large in her nightmares.

Geier didn't look at her. He raised his chin towards the Portarobe. 'Is that the machine?'

Walker nodded. 'And the plans and the girl. I believe that concludes our business, which means you owe me—'

'Shh, shh, shh,' Mr Geier said coolly. 'I decide when our business is concluded, Detective Walker. Please, light the lamp so I may examine my invention.' He lifted the sheets of blueprints off the top of the trunk.

His invention! Winnie wriggled and grunted her dissent.

He gave the Portarobe a push back and forth. 'How ingenious! Luggage with wheels!' He unfastened the catch on the trunk and lifted the lid. 'What is this?' He pulled out and discarded Winnie's costume change, her day gown, a hat and a shawl. He frowned as he lifted her Boot-Button Butler. Unceremoniously, he shifted it to a table. 'Rubbish.'

The lamp flared, flooding the room with pale, flickering light. Spotting the Telautograph, he gasped and clutched his heart. 'Look what God hath wrought!'

Those words! Winnie shuddered at the memory of them appearing on the machine at the Academy.

Geier recoiled. '*Was ist das?* This machine has been altered! It no longer matches Professor Weatherby's transmitter.' Spinning on his heel, he turned to Winnie and yanked away the gag in her mouth. 'This is your handiwork, Fräulein, is it not?'

As if she'd engage with him! She turned her head away.

DI Walker huffed. 'Sir, respectfully, it's very late, and it's been a very long day – a long week, working to bring you these goods, which I have done. I should like to go to bed. So, if you'd kindly pay me for me labour, I shall take my leave.'

Geier ignored Walker. 'You foolish girl. I can't win with this . . . this . . . monstrosity! I would be laughed out of Paris.'

Monstrosity? Her WA-model? She blinked. But she had removed the temporary copper jelly moulds to make it look sleek and . . . *Monstrosity?* His brutal appraisal of her workmanship stung like a slap. Shame burnt up her neck and flamed across her cheeks. What if he was right, and her work was . . . *laughable*? She struggled to swallow.

'I require a working receiving machine to display in Paris. You, Fräulein, *will* restore it to its former state immediately.'

She glared. 'Over my dead body.'

Herr Geier slowly twined his fingers together, his jaw shifting. 'As you wish.' He turned to Walker. 'Dispatch the girl, and *then* we are finished.' He rolled up the plans and grasped the handle of the Portarobe.

Dispatch? Winnie's breath caught. Geier had just ordered her murder. Her ears rang.

Even Walker seemed to baulk at the order. 'But the deal was—'

'My man will deliver your fee plus extra for a *tidy-up*, but he'll require a token. A lock of her hair or . . . a dainty pinkie finger – no, both, to show her father. If he thinks I have her, he'll fix the machine for me.' Geier pulled on his gloves. 'See if you can do better than your bumbling assist-ants did with that irritating boy.'

He glanced at Winnie and bowed his head cordially. 'My dear Fräulein Winifred,' he said, as if he had never ordered her murder. 'I don't suppose you would have plans for this thing with you?' He pointed to the Portarobe.

Winnie snorted and refused to look at Herr Geier. She did in fact have plans with her – miniature images under Stanhope lenses on her chatelaine, but she would not be sharing them with him, *thank you all the same*.

He nodded agreeably while donning his hat. He gave the trunk containing the Telautograph an affectionate pat. 'To Paris we shall go. Nothing can stop me winning the Grand Prix. *Gute Nacht.*' With a bow, he turned the Portarobe around and pushed it through the doorway. After a moment of grunting, the front door banged shut behind him.

Papa's beautiful Weatherby Telautograph Machine! Her father's hard-earnt success was rolling down the street, along with her WA-model modifications and her designs *and* her family's future.

'No! Stop!' Winnie wriggled upright and struggled to her feet. Geier could not win! Feet and hands bound, she hop-charged towards the doorway.

'Sit down!' Walker knocked her back. 'I'm trying to think.'

Winnie thudded on to the settee again, releasing a moan of despair. There would be no Paris World Fair glory, no ecstatic meeting with Thomas Edison, no happy reunion with Papa. There would be no life at all! Unless she got out of this, she would never see the other ladies of the League again. 'Help!' she wailed long and loud.

Walker stuffed the gag over her mouth and roughly retied it.

Winnie wriggled and kicked, screaming into the cloth.

'Unbelievable . . .' DI Walker stood in the parlour doorway, shaking his head at Geier's departure. He chewed at the side of his thumb for a long moment. Finally, he turned to Winnie. 'Time to tidy up.' He dragged her to her feet. 'But I'll fetch my assistants to do the dirty work. Until then—'

Winnie lowered herself to a squat and propelled herself upwards under DI Walker's chin. The top of her forehead painfully smacked his jaw. His teeth clacked together, and white stars spangled her vision. Both of them fell through the parlour door, landing heavily on the floorboards of the hallway.

He lay groaning stupidly beside her on the wooden floor.

Untangling herself from his clutch, Winnie spotted the envelope of francs that had fallen from his coat pocket. She kicked it under the grandfather clock before worming herself away from him. She inched her way on to the first stair then the second.

Her coat constricted across her chest as Walker grasped the back of her collar. Buttons dug into her throat and hair pulled painfully in his indiscriminate grip. He dragged her to a door, threw it open, and the cellar's cool, dank smells enveloped her. He yanked her like a sack of rotten potatoes down the rough stairs.

Winnie twisted and bucked, writhed and grunted as the ominous coal bunker loomed closer. The door to the windowless, closet-sized room scraped open. Walker shoved her backwards into the black cave.

Her head smacked a hard surface. Rocky protrusions stabbed her back and buttocks. She'd landed on the coal heap. The door slammed shut and the bolt rasped into place.

'Moafp! Mowp meh!' Winnie screamed into her gag.

Her ears shrilled. Meanwhile, upwards, downwards and sideways twisted into a sickening, spinning knot.

She was drowning in a swirling pool of thick black ink.

CHAPTER 29

Time unknown

A noise scratched at the edge of Winnie's consciousness. It grew louder and clearer and nearer. She opened her eyes. Blackness and stabbing pain greeted her. Her head stung; her mouth was dry; her limbs ached.

Something – someone – nearby shifted and moaned.

What was that? Where was she? Winnie wriggled the muscles in her face. She shifted her body. Beneath her, hard lumps clinked, shifted, crushed.

Coal. The coal bunker at her home.

She struggled to sit up, and as she did, the taste of cloth registered in her mouth, the sting of her cuts, the thirst. Everything drifted into place in her memory. She whined behind her gag.

A whine responded.

There was another person – gagged too – in the coal bunker with her! Winnie crawled forward in the pitch-dark, grunting and feeling around. The other person was moving around too. Finally, following her ears, she collided with her co-captive. They worked their backs together so they could help each other with the bindings on their wrists. Eventually, Winnie's hands were loosed.

Hands free, she tore at her gag. 'Thank you!' she cried. Tears streamed warmly down her cheeks. 'Now yours.' She picked at the small person's gag.

'Oh, that's better!' gasped a familiar voice.

'Clancy?' Winnie gasped into the darkness. She picked the knots at his wrists free.

'Miss?' He threw his arms around her, awkwardly mashing his shoulder into her chin.

'Ow.' She hugged him. 'Oh, my! I have never been happier to find an old friend. How did *you* end up here?'

'Same as you, I imagine. That horrible detective. He's sending his thugs to deal with me – he told me so. We must find a way out before they arrive.'

'But how did he know to find you at my home?'

'Said he guessed I was the key to finding you, so he followed me – to the museum. I found your note, and I left a reply saying I'd meet you here.'

Winnie sighed. 'Clancy, I am sorry. We must find a way out of here.'

'Too right, miss! I hate the dark. If only we had a match.'

Winnie patted her coat. 'I have a match; too bad my candle is upstairs.' She felt for her buttons and reached inside her coat to the deluxe chatelaine pinned there. The metal tinderbox equipage felt unusually warm from being next to her chest. She felt her way to the matches, struck one, and it fizzed a flash of golden light. 'Look around while we have the light.'

Opposite the locked door was a coal chute that opened to the street. Clancy ran for the door and threw himself against it.

'It's no use. I heard Walker bolt it from the other side.' Winnie blew out the match before it burnt her fingers. She struck another. 'I don't suppose you could fit through the coal hole?'

'I could try!' Clancy clambered over the shifting, clinking mound of coal pieces to the bottom of the chute.

Winnie followed, carefully holding the match aloft. 'We have a short supply of matches, so be quick.'

'Not to worry.' Clancy reached into the chute. 'I can feel my way.' His voice muffled as his head rose into the narrow chute.

'Well?'

He dropped down beside her. 'I can't figure out how to open it. It's very heavy, and it seems stuck.'

The noise of carriage wheels and horse hooves clattered down the chute.

Winnie grabbed his arm. 'If we can hear street noises, perhaps someone will hear us.'

'Good plan!' He shouted up the chute, 'Oi! Down here! Help!' He stuck his head and shoulders back up the chute and yelled some more. 'Pass me a lump of coal.' He banged the iron lid of the coal hole and hollered until he was hoarse. He plopped down, panting, beside her. 'It's pointless. It's too early for people to be about.'

Winnie patted his arm. 'Well, let's save our strength. When we hear movement on the street, we can . . .' *Whistle!* Winnie clapped her hands together. 'I have just the thing.' She felt along the chatelaine's chains for her whistle equipage. 'Listen to this.' She stood and leant her head and shoulders into the chute opening. She took a breath and blew the metal Ladies' Personal Safety Whistle harder than she'd ever blown it before.

She pulled back, blinking at the excruciating shrill-ness. The closed bunker, the hill of coal and the shape and material of the chute all intensified its volume. Physics in operation – the room and the chute amplified sound in the way the horn of a phonograph did!

'Crikey! I reckon that'll be heard at Westminster!'

'Well, the cover is a problem, and it won't be as loud outside, but it will be heard. Cover your ears – ready?' Winnie plugged her fingers in her ears and continued blowing long whistle blasts up the chute until she was breathless and tiny dots of white danced around the corners of her vision.

Clancy shifted on the coal mound. 'Inside me head sounds like the bells in a church steeple. It's like an echo that won't stop.'

A whistle shrilled, tickling Winnie's ears. Inside her head or out? It was hard to tell. There it was again, coming from outside and growing in intensity. She stood unsteadily. 'Good golly! That's not an echo, Clancy.' She blew again, but this time she blew a series of long and short sounds: -.-. --.-

'Miss, this is no time to play a tune.'

Winnie chuckled. 'It's not music; it's a Morse code distress signal, "CQ", two letters that sound like the French word "*sécu*" for help.'

Someone outside whistled a reply: .... . .-.. .--. / .. ... / --- -. / - .... . / .-- .- -.--

Winnie squealed and then found Clancy in the dark and squeezed him tight. 'That was their reply. "Help is on the way".'

'I hope you didn't call the police.'

'No police. I gave all my friends a whistle just like this one, and they're not far away.'

A few minutes later, the bolt slid back, and the door to the coal bunker scraped open. Winnie squinted at the light from lamps carried by Stella and Effie. Celeste reached out her hand, and Winnie grasped it, allowing her friend to haul her to her feet. 'Just look at you! Please let that be coal dust on your face and not bruises.'

Winnie's hands touched her cheeks, which were gritty and dry. Her fingertips and cuticles looked like they belonged to a chimneysweep, not a proper young lady. 'How did you know where to find me?'

'Adelaide, silly! She worked out where you'd be from your letter – and knew you'd put yourself in danger if you showed up here,' said Stella. 'She's gone ahead of us to assure Headmistress we'll meet them at the station.'

Stella dabbed at Winnie's forehead. Celeste patted her hands and winced at the rope burns on her wrists. Effie twisted her hands and fretted about the time.

Clancy clambered out behind her. Winnie's eyes boggled at the sight of him. If her face looked like his, it was no wonder her friends were so scandalized.

'Aren't you going to introduce us?' Celeste said with a friendly tilt of her head. What a soothing sight she was.

Winnie nodded wearily. 'Ladies, I present Master Clancy, my guide and friend – and co-captive.'

Clancy blushed under Celeste's gaze.

Effie looked Winnie up and down. 'You must clean yourself up, Winifred, but quickly, if we're to join Her Majesty at the station. We haven't much time. It's well past dawn, and frankly I'm struggling with my nerves.'

Clancy spluttered in protest. 'Her Majesty? Do you know the Queen? You didn't tell me that, miss.' He threw Winnie a sulky scowl.

Winnie laid her hand on his shoulder. 'I haven't the time to explain now, but one day I will. Clancy, we have a very important appointment. Would you mind keeping watch while I scrub up and make myself presentable? If you see Geier, Walker or his thugs approaching, please sound the alarm.' She tossed him the whistle equipage.

He nodded gravely and gave a bow, deep and proper. Stella sniggered.

'Come with me,' Winnie said, scurrying up the cellar stairs. 'Before I wash, there's something I must fetch.' She slid to a stop at the grandfather clock and retrieved the envelope of francs. She might have lost the Telautograph, but last night's mission wasn't totally in vain.

CHAPTER 30

Eight thirty, Friday morning

Winnie, scrubbed clean and re-dressed as a proper young lady, with the Boot-Button Butler tucked under her arm in a carpetbag, gazed around the inside of a rattling carriage. She was wedged next to Stella and across from Effie. Outside on the driver's seat, Clancy was snuggled next to Celeste, the only one of the young ladies who knew how to drive a coach. 'I still do not understand how Celeste procured a carriage at the last moment.'

Effie stiffened.

'It's not important *how*,' Stella said, twiddling her thumbs. 'Rather, let's be thankful that she did. Riding is far easier than walking, wouldn't you agree?'

'In other words, you nicked the carriage.' Winnie's knees bounced nervously. They'd taken too many risks for her. 'And why Paddington Station?'

'Lucky for us, HRH Prince Bertie

complained Slough was inconvenient for him and insisted on being collected at Paddington.' Stella sighed. 'Adelaide has gone ahead to explain that we shall join Her Majesty's entourage there.'

Winnie moaned. They would all be in trouble, and it was her fault. 'I am so sorry. I had no intention of involving any of you in my affairs.'

Effie, nerves clearly frazzled, snarled, 'If we hadn't *involved ourselves*, you and your little street urchin *guide* would still be locked in a coal bunker.'

Stella hissed, 'Stop it, Effie!'

Winnie groaned and rubbed her temples. 'This is by far the worst mess of my life. Not only have I allowed my father's livelihood to slip through my fingers, but I've also embroiled innocent lives in danger, first Clancy, and now all of you! If only Adelaide had said nothing about the letter—'

Effie leant towards Winnie. 'As if she could keep silent! She cares for you – stupidly.' Her face blazed with frustration. 'You are the most selfish person I have ever met. We should be minding Her Majesty the Queen as we have been trained to do, but instead we are cleaning up your messes—'

Stella glared. 'Euphemia, *stop!*'

Effie huffed, folded her arms, and jolted back in the seat.

Stella's nostrils flared. 'That is enough. Winifred has apologized. We are in league, and that means what hurts one of us hurts us all. Can you not understand the gravity of what Winnie is experiencing? Her father is missing, and his livelihood and future have been stolen. Winifred herself was attacked and deprived of liberty. If we did not care for one another, our work, as important as it is, would mean nothing.'

Winnie's eyes stung. Fat, hot tears ran down her cheeks. *So tired.* 'I really am sorry. I am . . .'

Stella's hand slid under Winnie's and squeezed. A moment later, Effie's hand landed on Winnie's knee and gripped it.

Their support bolstered Winnie, allowing her finally to think clearly about the tasks ahead. Somehow, she had to telegraph the Hotel Terminus in Paris to advise Papa of their terrible loss. There was little point now in rushing to join him, even if it meant relinquishing her dream of meeting Mr Thomas Edison and showing her inventions to him . . .

The carriage had stalled, stuck in an early morning snarl of carts, wagons and hansom cabs. Men raised their fists, and street urchins ran between the carriages, begging and pestering.

Stella lifted the watch equipage of her chatelaine. 'It's fifteen minutes until nine. I'm beginning to fear we will miss the royal train.'

Effie clutched her belly. 'Oh, dear! Late for the Queen . . .'

Winnie peered out of the window at the backed-up vehicles. 'I have no doubt Celeste is a fine driver, but London traffic is a beast only locals understand.'

'This snarl would be the result of the royal train's new route. The country's trains will be halted for the Queen to pass. I daresay it's not the first delay we shall experience this morning.' Stella squinted through the windows. 'I wonder if we should walk from here.'

'Walking on legs is faster than standing still on wheels,' Winnie quipped. They were completely stopped, and the carriage hadn't moved forward an inch in nearly five minutes.

Effie looked through the rear window. 'But what do we do with the carriage? Its owner will surely have us arrested and—'

Stella cut her off. 'It will be fine. Celeste has made arrangements with Master Clancy for its return.'

Winnie fiddled with her chatelaine, considering the equipment at hand. Could she clear the road? 'I have an idea. Help me with the door.'

'But, Winifred—'

Winnie stood on the step and carefully pulled herself along the chassis to the front of the carriage. As she did, she studied the snarl ahead of them.

Having spied Winnie hanging off the side of the vehicle, Celeste gave a little yelp. 'Ooh, Winnie! Do take care!'

'Celeste, I've decided to take control of this situation.'

'What's the plan?' Celeste cocked her head quizzically.

Winnie hauled herself to the bench seat, dropping between Clancy and Celeste. 'Tell everyone to hold on.' She quickly assembled her slingshot equipage and loaded a plumb bob. 'I'm going to clear the way for you with this. Ready . . . here we go!' She fired the bob over the stationary hansom cab in front of them, pinging the old horse's hind quarters. It whinnied and snorted, edging forward. Around it, horses bristled.

'Good shot!' Clancy cheered.

The horse pulling their carriage buzzed awake. Her tail swished and her ears twisted.

Winnie fired another shot to the right, pinging another horse's haunches. 'Now, Celeste, this is the moment. Are you ready?'

Celeste's eyes widened. 'You've made me very nervous, Winnie, but yes, I'm ready.'

Winnie pulled out an equipage. 'Behold! Our newest defence. Every chatelaine comes equipped with this.' On her palm lay a tiny vial stuffed with a wad of white material. 'Guncotton.'

Celeste's eyes widened. 'Winifred Weatherby, you are a genius.'

Winnie wriggled her brows.

Clancy scratched his head. 'How is a wad of cotton going to help?'

'Not cotton, my friend. *Gun*cotton.'

Winnie set the equipages she needed in order on her lap: glass vial with guncotton, slingshot and tinderbox. 'Here we go!' She struck a match and blew it out. She loaded the open vial into the sling and held it in place with a finger. She inserted the still-smouldering match into the vial and fired it off, aiming a few feet in front of the carriage ahead of them.

POOF! A flash of white silently lit up the grey early morning sky. All around them, horses skittered and snorted. The horse in front of them reared and bolted sharply to the left. Other vehicles pulled out of the way. Wild-eyed horses skittered and twisted. And a pathway opened before them as wide and clear as the Red Sea parting.

Celeste gave a nod of utter admiration, and Clancy clapped.

'Hup!' Celeste flicked the reins and drove forward.

Fifteen minutes later, they pulled into Paddington Station where the harried stationmaster flapped around like a headless chicken. Crossing lights flashed. The royal train chugged slowly towards the platform, steaming and whistling.

'Perfect timing!' Clancy cheered.

Effie and Stella alighted from the carriage.

Celeste handed the reins over. 'Now, Clancy, you're sure you know how to drive?'

He nodded vigorously. 'I used to drive the wagon at the matchstick factory. You needn't worry.' He flashed a grin.

'Very well. You know where to go, Clancy. The owner will give you a nice fat reward for rescuing and returning his horse and carriage from the four *highwaymen* who nicked it.' She winked and climbed down. She whispered in Winnie's ear, 'The chloroform and Nasal Wick worked so well there was no need to use my customized knuckle-duster equipage.' She flexed her right fist and kissed it. 'Another time.'

Winnie's chin dropped. They knocked out the driver *and* stole the carriage? For her?

Celeste giggled at Winnie. 'Wave ta-ta to your friend.'

Winnie waved. 'Take care, Clancy. Thank you for everything. I shall see to that reward when I return.'

He nodded. 'Take care, miss. Thanks for the adventure. And don't do anything . . . you know, dangerous.' He tipped his hat. 'Hup!'

Winnie watched the carriage rattle into the clogged street.

'Excellent timing, Miss Lemieux,' Effie said, linking her elbow with Celeste's.

'I could not have done it without our genius quarter-mistress's help.' She linked arms with Winnie and Stella.

The four ladies reached the platform just as the train stopped. As they passed the Queen's carriage, Winnie peeked inside. Lush cornflower-blue silk and gold braiding covered every surface. Her Majesty sat on a tufted bench with her little pug next to her. Prince Bertie read a newspaper at the other end of the carriage. Princess Louise glanced out of the window at them, widening her eyes with disapproval. And in the far corner, near a closet of some sort, sat Adelaide. She opened her fan and waved a coded greeting.

Winnie and the others walked past the next carriage where the staff of the royal household were seated. The doors opened, and a familiar voice boomed out.

'There you are!' It was Headmistress Thornton. 'It's about time! It's only the *Queen of England* who's waiting on you four . . .'

The frazzled stationmaster directed them back to the last carriage, opened a compartment and gestured for them to board. Winnie moved to the end of their queue to get a good look at the entire train of separate carriages.

Keeping Her Majesty safe from a distance would be an interesting challenge. Only when the train stopped would they be able to enter the royal saloon.

She pondered the length of hitched carriages. Wouldn't it be clever if one could walk between the carriages *while the train was moving*? She reached for her notebook equipage on her chatelaine.

The stationmaster cleared his throat impatiently and held out a hand indicating she should board.

'Oh, I beg your pardon.' She'd save that inspired idea for the train ride. She laid a gloved hand in his and stepped up into their compartment. The door closed and his whistle shrilled. The train rolled slowly out of Paddington Station.

Seated close to the window, Winnie leant her cheek on the cool glass and watched the platform trundle past. Her last glimpse of the station made her look again.

On the corner of the station's roof sat a solitary black-and-white bird, stretching its wings and cawing sadly into the din. 'Hello, Mr Magpie,' she said with a wave, remembering Clancy's warning about lone magpies and bad luck. Such superstitious nonsense, but then *Mr Magpie* . . .

What was the rhyme? One for sorrow, two for joy, three . . .

There had been three magpie eggs in the Fabergé box.

Was the number significant? She shook her bleary head –
she was suddenly far too tired to remember the rest of the
rhyme anyway.

CHAPTER 31

~WATERLOO STATION~

Quarter past nine

A pat on her knee roused her. Winnie opened one eye.
Effie was standing in the train compartment. She
checked the watch on her chatelaine then looked out
the window again. 'The train has stopped. Why has it
stopped? The first scheduled refreshment break isn't until
we reach Godalming.'

'Ooh – trouble so soon?' Celeste leant forward. 'We've
not even left London! Where are we?'

Stella pointed to a sign on the platform. 'Waterloo
Station.'

Headmistress Thornton appeared outside the door to
the compartment, and a stationmaster opened it. She
clapped twice. 'Ladies, if you'll follow me. We have a
change of plan at Her Majesty's command.'

While the others alighted, Winnie took
down her carpetbag from the luggage

rack – she wasn't about to let any more inventions out of her sight. She repinned her hat and stepped out to the platform, walking quickly to catch up with the others. They were queueing outside the royal saloon. How odd. The mission brief for Operation Migration had specified one agent at a time in Her Majesty's carriage with a changeover at the scheduled refreshment stop. Winnie glanced up and down the platform, scanning faces and scrutinizing behaviours. Was this unscheduled stop an opportunity Mr Magpie could exploit?

Prince Bertie, newspaper shoved under his arm, stalked out of the royal saloon. He mashed his hat on his head and thrust an unlit cigar between his lips. The tight clench of his jaw and bright crimson of his cheeks suggested he'd just been in an argument with his mother – and lost.

Following him was a flustered-looking Mrs Campbell. She paused to adjust her elegant hat. 'Ladies, Her Majesty is in rare form this morning. Mumsy is displeased with everyone, especially Prince Bertie. She's dismissed him to the staff carriage, as she did when we were small and he was being unruly.' She breathed in through her nose.

Headmistress Thornton for once said nothing.

Princess Louise continued. 'To make her point all the more pointy, Mother has requested all of you as "preferred companions" for the journey. Don't think for a moment it is because she likes you, but rather, it is because she wishes to put Bertie in his place. I shall join him in solidarity – as we did as children.' She forced a smile.

The four young lady spies stood awkwardly outside the royal saloon, steam swirling overhead and clusters of onlookers gawping across the tracks. Winnie chewed her lower lip, trying to remember if the Beacon Academy's etiquette lessons had covered what to say – or not to say – when the Queen was grumpy.

Mrs Campbell added over her shoulder, 'Bon voyage, ladies. Good luck.'

The door to the saloon opened, and a tall turbaned attendant bowed his head and smiled gently. Winnie squeaked a gasp of recognition. He was the Munshi, or teacher, who famously taught the Queen Hindustani. 'If you'll please board, Her Majesty wishes to carry on.' He led them into the plush saloon. Blue tufted silk covered everything, even the ceiling.

Winnie pressed her arms against her sides, trying to take up less space, but her lumpy carpetbag stuck out. Drat. Perhaps she should have left her belongings in their previous carriage. She glanced around for a place to deposit the luggage, but every space seemed earmarked for royalty, every surface stamped with privilege. She winced at the raggedness of her nails, the scruffiness of her shoes. *Please don't ask me anything. I do not belong here.*

Winnie watched Celeste properly yet breezily engage with the Queen. And then Stella, with her slender neck and elegant, powdery voice, presented herself beautifully. Poor Effie curtsied just as the train lurched, throwing her ungracefully forward. She was so mortified that she seemed to forget her name until the Queen said something in Hindustani. Effie replied without a pause, and Her Majesty applauded, and the Munshi smiled in surprise.

Effie beamed and dropped a perfect curtsy.

Winnie stepped forward. Adelaide swooped past, silently taking the carpetbag out of the way. *God bless her.* 'Good morning, Your Majesty.'

The little pug lying next to the Queen popped its eyes open and wheeled them around to focus on Winnie. Fawn hair bristling, it bolted upright and yapped.

Winnie stepped back.

'Bosco! Hush!' the Queen scolded and gave him a scratch behind the ears. 'Ignore him. He is not fond of travel. I suspect the motion unsettles his little tum-tum.'

'Oh, dear.' Winnie glanced at Celeste. 'Miss Lemieux is experienced with animal medicine – mostly horses, but perhaps she knows a remedy.'

'Is that so?' The Queen began speaking to Celeste, who recommended rice boiled in an infusion of rosemary and camomile tea.

Winnie puffed out a breath. Thank goodness for

Celeste. The others had moved to the attendant's closet. Stella and Effie sat inside on the narrow bench with Winnie's carpetbag between them.

Adelaide stood in the doorway. 'Let's examine the maps of the Isle of Wight and the floorplans of Osborne House Effie brought. Since we're all together, we can use this time to strategize and coordinate our plans.'

'Where's that signal button, Munshi?' the Queen asked when he brought her tea. 'The one to wire the driver to slow down. Bertie usually does it.' Her hand hovered over a panel of knobs that Winnie had noticed earlier.

'I believe you mean that one, ma'am.' He pointed to the centre. 'Remember, His Royal Highness said the far-right button must never be pushed. It's only for dire emergencies.'

'Yes, yes. Bertie always tries to bamboozle me with technology.' She gave the middle button a firm push. 'There. Let's wait for a moment while the captain slows us down. Otherwise, I shall get indigestion. Thirty miles per hour is to be our maximum speed this time. Exceeding forty miles per hour deranges the brain and internal organs, you know.'

Sure enough, the train started to slow.

The Queen patted the dog. 'Ah, that's a more civilized speed.' She waved dainty silver tongs over a stand of small but perfect cakes, placing a cream sponge cake on her plate and two iced petits fours on another. 'The petits fours are *Bertie's* favourites.' She said the name with a frown. 'And he's not here, so you, darling Bosco, get two.' She sniffed them and wrinkled her nose. 'The crystallized violets are pretty but too perfumy for my liking – almost medicinal.' She stroked his wrinkly ruff before placing the plate in front of the pug.

Bosco launched himself at the tiny treats, gobbling up the petits fours before his mistress could pick up her fork.

Out of the corner of her eye, Winnie saw Celeste's expression twist.

Celeste lifted a map of the island in front of her face and whispered, 'I shall be surprised if he keeps them down. If only I had some camomile with me.'

As they studied the map of the Isle of Wight, Winnie patted her cheeks. She had to stay awake, but her eyes twitched with fatigue. Had it only been a day since she'd worked in her beautiful laboratory? So much had happened . . .

Adelaide squinted at Winnie, looking concerned. She pushed the carpetbag to the corner of the bench. 'Lay your head there. Don't worry. We have the second half of the journey to finalize our plans. I'll alert you if you're required by HM.'

Winnie flashed a grateful smile at her and leant into the lumpy carpetbag. It was so lovely to close her eyes . . .

CHAPTER 32

Later that morning

Winnie woke from her cat nap at the sound of a strange, guttural noise, like a distant roll of thunder. Not much had changed in the carriage, though Effie struggled to stifle yawns. Winnie moved her carpetbag and patted the bench seat so both Effie and Stella could rest.

Her Majesty played solitaire, and Bosco, eyes glazed, lay beside her footstool.

Celeste, who was sitting closest to the Queen, sniffed the air, her face contorting into a look of disgust.

'It's only Bosco,' the Queen said. 'His digestion is off. Perhaps a train speed slower than thirty miles per hour would have suited him better.'

Winnie steadied herself when the cloud of pungent gas reached her. Good golly! The gong barrels at Holland House had been less offensive.

The Queen wiggled her feet on the

footstool. 'Munshi, my feet are swelling again. I think I should like to change into my slippers sooner rather than later.'

'Perhaps for the sake of propriety, it would be best to allow Mrs MacDonald to help you change out of your boots, ma'am. It's only a quarter of an hour until the refreshment stop.'

The Queen frowned. 'Oh, bother. I am quite uncomfortable. It's the train's excessive speed that does it.' The Queen sighed and wriggled. She caught Adelaide's eye. 'Young lady, I shall need your assistance to remove my shoes.'

'Yes, ma'am.' Adelaide nodded and knelt beside the stool. Using the button hook on her chatelaine, she began working on the tiny jet buttons on the royal feet.

'Ouch! You're pinching me. And, Bosco! You're asphyxiating me! My gracious – it smells like the river-bank at low tide.'

Winnie's fingers fluttered. If ever there was a perfect moment for her Boot-Button Butler, it was now. She cleared her throat. 'Adelaide, if I may interrupt . . .'

Adelaide turned to look, and Winnie held up her carpetbag with a waggle of her brows.

'Oh, yes, of course. Er, Your Majesty, the quarter-mistress wishes to show you a clever contraption that may be of use.'

Winnie approached with a bow. 'Ma'am, may I present the Boot-Button Butler? A device I created to undo ten buttons at once. And it is as easy as inserting one's foot like this and depressing the mechanism with one's heel.' She demonstrated on her own foot, depressing the lever with a satisfying metallic *crunch*. '*Voilà!* All buttons are completely unhooked with one simple motion.'

The Queen scowled. Or perhaps it was a smile – it was hard to tell.

'Would ma'am like to try?'

'Are you suggesting I should unbutton my boots myself? It's been years since I've done so.' She looked utterly scandalized – and slightly excited.

Winnie shrugged. 'If one's feet are painfully swollen, one might appreciate not having to wait for assistance.'

'Indeed. Let's try it, shall we?'

Winnie set up the device on the footstool and helped the Queen aim her foot between the wires. Winnie manually depressed the heel mechanism for her. When the royal foot emerged, every button was unfastened.

'Why, that's remarkable! Let me try the other foot, but on the floor so I can operate it.' After her attendant had helped the Queen to her feet, she did it herself. 'Munshi, do you see this? You should have a go.'

He laughed. 'Oh, ma'am, thank you, but it would be most improper to remove my shoes now.'

'Yes, I suppose it would. Help me sit again. Would you fetch my slippers, young lady?'

Winnie looked to the left and the right. 'Me?'

'Yes, you. They're in the basket at the end of the bed.' She pointed down the carriage to the door to the sleeping compartment.

'One moment.' Winnie darted to the door. The sleeping compartment had two single beds covered in black counterpanes, each with a basket at the end. The silk slippers in both were identical, except for the monogram, A for Albert and V for Victoria. Winnie patted her chest. How heartbreaking to keep one's late husband's slippers for nearly thirty years.

There was another small closet in the chamber, and its door was ajar. It was a washroom, equipped with a basin and mirror for shaving, and lined with white tiles trimmed with the Order of Saint Patrick. The small space smelt manly, of shaving soap like the brand her father used.

She took the slippers out and helped the Queen into them. In close proximity to Bosco, the noxious cloud of doggy funk stung Winnie's eyes.

'That's much better,' the Queen said nasally, her nostrils pinched.

Bosco began walking in fitful circles, sniffing the floor and whimpering.

The attendant backed away, covering his mouth with his fingertips. 'Oh, dear. Ma'am, I suspect your doggy is going to do something unhappy . . .'

The Queen turned to look. 'Oh, no. Quickly, stop the train. Ladies! This is an emergency.' The Queen began randomly stabbing the buttons on the communication panel. 'Someone must pick up Bosco!'

Celeste swooped in, grabbed the farting dog and held it away from herself.

'Don't point him at me!' the Queen shrilled, indiscriminately poking at buttons.

The Munshi stopped the Queen. 'Ma'am, no, you mustn't push the buttons! You are confusing the message! You see? The train is going faster! And the far-right button is an emergency stop, which His Royal Highness Prince Bertie forbade you ever to touch!'

'But we must stop immediately!' Her finger hovered over the button.

Winnie stepped forward. 'Begging your pardon, ma'am. A train cannot stop immediately. Because of its huge mass and fast speed, it takes quite a distance to come to a complete stop. These are the laws of physics in action!'

'Well, those laws are a great bother, because Bosco is going to blow. Do something before he—'

A gigantic squelch gurgled from the small dog's belly.

'Quickly!' she screeched.

'Celeste, this way.' Winnie led her back to the royal washroom. 'Stick him in there.' She pulled the door closed. 'At least it's tiled. If he messes, it will be—'

Another horrible gurgle rumbled out of the washroom.

'—easier to clean up.' She grimaced.

An odour most foul seeped under the door. Both girls gagged.

Celeste pointed to the door. 'That is not normal.'

'You said the petits fours the Queen gave him an hour ago weren't a good idea.'

Celeste shook her head. She moved closer to Winnie and whispered. 'It's more than that. I think that little cake was poisoned – or laced with a laxative, like castor oil. The Queen complained it smelt "medicinal".'

Winnie gasped. 'She said the petits fours were Bertie's favourites. They were intended for *him*, not Bosco. It must be Mr Magpie!' She glanced around the sleeping quarters.

'Look for a calling card.' Celeste gingerly lifted the pillow, quietly slid open drawers, looked under the bed. 'I don't see one in here. Perhaps it's in there . . .' She pointed to the washroom with a shudder.

After poking around a bit more, Celeste stopped Winnie from leaving the sleeping compartment. 'Let's keep our suspicions among the ladies of the League. And be sure to remain inconspicuous while searching the rest of the carriage.'

Winnie bit her lower lip. 'Are you sure—'

The door to the sleeping compartment opened and Adelaide slipped in, finger to her lips. 'Ladies, we have a problem. Look what I found in the cake box.' She held up a small white card edged in blue.

Bon appétit
Mr Magpie

CHAPTER 33

~GODALMING TRAIN STATION~

Ten thirty-five, Friday morning

The scheduled twenty-minute refreshment stop at Godalming would not suffice for the monumental task of cleaning and deodorizing the royal saloon – the train would have to stop for an hour. Every train in the country and every passenger had to wait.

On the platform, Mrs Campbell handed a dog leash to Winnie. 'I suggest you keep Bosco moving until the train whistle blows. Then return immediately.'

Winnie took the leash. Bosco stood nearby, glassy-eyed and unsteady.

'Off you go. The walk will do him good,' Mrs Campbell said, glancing dubiously at the rain. 'I'm sure the station-master will lend you an umbrella.'

Winnie tried to clip the leash on, but Bosco flopped on his belly. 'Very well.' She looped the leash around her neck and picked him up. 'Goodness, you're heavy!'

Not far from the station, Winnie found a grassy spot near a hedge. Fumbling with the umbrella, she deposited Bosco on the wet ground. He sat bleary-eyed and listless. 'Come on, boy. Now's your chance to do doggy things . . .'

Before long, he took a tentative step and sniffed the grass while Winnie waited in the drizzle. Each drop of rain on his back made him wince as if being scalded. With a roll of her eyes, Winnie held the umbrella over the spoilt royal pug.

Sheltering under the hedge was a rather battle-scarred black-and-white cat who warily watched Bosco. 'Hello, puss,' Winnie said. 'It looks as if you're staying drier than I am.'

Bosco turned. Spotting the cat, his body went rigid, his hackles rose, and he growled like a cornered bear.

Ears flat, the cat hissed and skittered menacingly in place.

Bosco, miraculously healed, charged at the cat. Both animals disappeared into the hedge through the other side. In a twinkling of an eye, the Queen's dog vanished.

Winnie blinked at the vacant space at the bottom of the hedge. 'Drat.'

The whistle of the royal passenger train tootled from the station, signalling its imminent departure.

*

'Achoo-achoo-AH-choo!' Winnie sneezed and dabbed her itchy eyes.

'God bless you, miss,' a sturdy stableman said from the wooden bench across from Winnie. He wiped his nose with his grimy knuckles.

Hay dust and horse dander swirled through the air. Having missed the departure of the royal passenger train at Godalming, thanks to Bosco's wild cat chase, Winnie had had no other option than to join the groomsmen, stablemen and royal animals on the royal freight train. The plush comfort and rich blues of the Queen's saloon were only wisps of memory.

She tried to pet Bosco, but he turned away from her with a huff. Even he was disgusted at their change of fortune.

The train slowed as it pulled into Gosport Station, heaving its steamy breath at the end of the line. Winnie alighted with Bosco in tow. The outdoor servants jumped to work, leaving her standing on the platform amid the hubbub of unloading. No one had told her how she was to cross the Solent to the Isle of Wight, since the Queen and her party had already left on the royal yacht. She found a crate, perched Bosco on it, and sat down beside him. Perhaps she could join the horses. After an afternoon on a dusty, smelly freight train, a cargo barge couldn't be any worse.

'Mr Barker,' she called, spotting the groomsman. 'May I join you on the barge? Her Majesty is expecting me this afternoon.'

'Then you'd best find another way, miss. There's no room.'

She and Bosco left the station and walked across the road to an inn. Perhaps the innkeeper of Keppel's Head could direct her.

The cosy inn welcomed her with smells of savoury meals and comforting sounds – the clinking of cutlery and hearty chatter. As she crossed the foyer, she caught an unmistakable silhouette – the Prince of Wales, who was dining alone. She approached his table and dipped a bow.

'Miss Weatherby! I didn't expect to see you here.' He lowered his voice. 'Nasty business with the tainted petits fours . . .' He widened his eyes.

'Indeed,' she replied softly, twiddling her fingertips. So, he'd heard about Mr Magpie's latest strike. He didn't seem particularly perturbed.

'But what are you doing here? The *Alberta* left hours ago.' His gaze fell to Bosco, then to Winnie's muddied hem. 'Ah. I think I can guess what happened. A cat, per chance?' He chuckled. 'Bosco is determined to single-handedly drive them all out of the British Isles – or at least out of the royal residences.'

'The cat in question escaped this time, sire. I beg your

pardon, but I've currently no way to make the crossing to meet up with the others at Osborne House. Perhaps when Your Highness crosses to the island, I could join your party.' She grimaced. None of his staff were waiting on him. Maybe she shouldn't have entered the dining room.

He squeezed his chin. 'I would welcome you – if I were crossing to the island. But I've changed my plans. I should prefer to have my eyes pecked out by a mischief of magpies than holiday with Mumsy in her current tempestuous mood. She's a veritable battleaxe.' He sipped his wine.

Winnie gulped. *What does one say to that?* 'Ah, well. Never mind, then. I shall make enquiries about the departure of the next ferry.' She dropped a curtsy.

'No, please. Allow me. I shall send a telegram to Osborne House with a request that instructions be sent to you.'

Winnie raised Bosco's leash. 'Thank you; however, I'm eager to deliver Bosco to Her Majesty by day's end. I fear she's fretting for him.'

He batted his hand. 'She has a kennel full of them waiting at Osborne. I doubt she'll miss him, and besides, I'm sure Bosco is enjoying the better view.' He toasted her. 'After my pudding, I shall send that telegram.'

She bowed again. 'Bosco and I will wait near the fire.' She took her leave. At the back of her mind, thoughts of poisoned petits fours and mischievous magpies swirled.

*

Winnie sat on her own in another room at a table reserved for lone lady travellers. At eight o'clock, she and Bosco were still waiting for His Royal Highness to send the telegram. A group of naval officers from Royal Clarence Yard had joined him for cigars, cognac and merrymaking.

When finally he stepped out of the dining room, his nose was noticeably redder. 'Oh! My dear Miss Weatherby, there you are. I shan't be but a moment. I want to introduce Bosco to my pals.' He picked up the sleeping dog and tottered back to his table.

'Huzzah!' the group cheered. Silly toasts were made to 'Bosco the Brave, the Royal Taster' and the Queen.

The wife of the proprietor slid a huge steaming bowl of rabbit stew in front of Winnie. Her eyes boggled at the feast. She had very little money with her (other than the francs she'd tucked between her chemise and her corset). 'Oh, my! I beg your pardon!' she blurted. 'I didn't order this.'

'Eat up, missy. It's compliments of HRH Prince Bertie.' She placed a basket of golden bread rolls on the table. 'Wine or beer?'

'Neither, thank you. May I have a mug of milk?' Winnie devoured the meal and sopped up every drop of the savoury mustard gravy with the bread rolls. Headmistress Thornton would be appalled at her behaviour.

The sun had long set, a bread-and-butter pudding had been eaten, and Winnie's eyelids were drooping closed. Prince Bertie's unique laugh and voice rose above the music and chatter from the public bar.

Winnie jerked awake.

The lady who'd served her pulled her hand back. 'Oh, pardon, miss. Didn't mean to give you a fright. His Highness says I'm to tell you the *Alberta* shan't return tonight. Come along. I'll take you to your room.'

'But what about Bosco, er, the dog?'

'He said I'm to tell you the dog is having a marvellous time.'

CHAPTER 34

Saturday morning

Bands of morning sun streamed through the gap between the curtains, waking Winnie. She lay in bed listening to the almighty quiet of Gosport. Keppel's Head was so still, she could hear the creaking of the old hotel's timbers and beyond that the gentle lapping of waves against some unseen shoreline. She rose from bed and pulled open the curtains.

There was no sense marring a promising new day with yesterday's regrets. She'd wash her face, eat something, and see about sending a telegram to the Hotel Terminus in Paris to inform Papa about the theft of his Telautograph and her inability to join him immediately. She had the Queen to protect. She couldn't tell him that, of course, but if she were permitted, he would be proud . . . probably. Or perhaps not. Perhaps this, like her inventing aspirations, was another fault that would 'mar her chances on the marriage market'.

A sudden heaviness blanketed her fledgling optimism. A hole in her heart ached, the now empty space where her World Fair dream used to grow. Visiting Paris was pointless. Although Papa would no doubt enjoy her company, they had nothing to exhibit, not even her Boot-Button Butler. Who knew where it was now? With Adelaide, perhaps? She was a good friend, but she'd been so distant lately. The Queen had liked it, though . . . A satisfied grin curled at Winnie's lips.

Next year, she and Papa would find another way to exhibit his inventions – *if* they could survive Geier's machinations. In the meantime, she'd been hired to serve as the quartermistress of Her Majesty's League of Remarkable Young Ladies. Not only did she have a stupendous laboratory to work in, but she had also been tasked with the safekeeping of the Empire's most important woman.

Winnie followed the mouth-watering aroma of bacon to the dining room, where stale beer wafted from the floorboards and dust motes ambled through patches of sunlight. She sat down at a table, and a young lady brought her some bread and a soft-boiled egg. 'Are you Miss Weatherby?'

Winnie nodded.

The young lady pulled an envelope from her apron pocket. 'This arrived last night after you'd gone to bed, so His Highness instructed Mam to give it to you this morning.'

Winnie glanced at the envelope – a telegram. She ripped it open:

```
DEAR MISS WEATHERBY
HM HAS TERMINATED THE LEAGUE.
YOU MAY RETURN TO LONDON.
THANK YOU FOR YOUR SERVICE.
REGRETFULLY,
MRS CAMPBELL
```

Winnie read the message over several times. Her Majesty had terminated the League? No more League of Remarkable Young Ladies? No more Quartermistress's Laboratory or intriguing projects or camaraderie with her colleagues?

First the loss of Papa's invention, then her exhibition dreams, now this. It meant no more . . . anything.

She felt as if she were falling in a deep, dark hole. Breaths came in pants.

The Queen had dismissed her *after* she'd been forced to prioritize all this ahead of Papa and their future. A hurricane of emotions twisted through Winnie's core. It was insulting! It was degrading! It was . . . a disaster.

Tears welled in her eyes. Her throat tightened. Her hands shook.

His Royal Highness Prince Bertie had known about this decision last night, but he'd chosen to withhold it from her until today. How dare he not face her with this news! What kind of king would he be if he lacked the courage to face a young lady of fourteen years with unpleasant news?

She gripped her arms to stop their enraged trembling. This anger was like nothing she'd ever felt before – a volcano. If only she could kick something, hurt someone, scream it out . . .

What would she do? How would she return? Where would she go? The questions piled up so quickly she couldn't draw a breath. She stood and paced the length of the room. At the front window, she saw him – Prince Bertie, outside at the kerb, looking dapper in his spiffy shoes, tweed coat and smart bowler hat. He was climbing into a carriage – to flee.

Her feet knew what to do. She just followed them out of the door, down the steps and into the street.

Hands on her hips, she stood in front of the carriage.

'Out of the way, ya silly goose!' the driver scolded. 'Hup!' He tossed the reins.

Winnie grabbed the horse's bridle and looked the horse dead in the eye. 'HALT!'

The horse backed up, ears flattened.

'I say!' Prince Bertie poked his head out of the window. 'Why aren't we moving forward?'

'Not to worry, sire. There's a dimwit lass standing in the way. I'll make short work of her.' The driver pulled his long whip from the holder and flicked it.

'Whoa, whoa, wait! Is that . . . Miss Weatherby?' Prince Bertie yelled. 'Mr Todd, she's no dimwit! Leave her.' He quickly alighted. 'Why are you still here? Your ship has sailed. Mother's lady-in-waiting came to collect Bosco – and you with him.'

'Why am I still here? Why? As if you don't know,' Winnie exploded.

'But you're to join the others at Osborne House. Loosy's telegram . . . Didn't she advise you of the time of departure?'

'Mrs Campbell's telegram advised me to return to London, so I don't suppose it matters what hour I leave.'

'Return to London? But . . . we—'

Winnie thrust the telegram under his nose.

He read it. 'Mumsy *terminated* the League?' He pinched his forehead. 'Why, that's an outrage! This is the first I've heard of it.' He patted his breast pockets and withdrew a wad of envelopes. 'Of course . . . I didn't bother to read the last six telegrams Loosy sent to me. The first one was a mood dampener, and the next two gave me a frightful headache.' He stuffed Mrs Campbell's unopened telegrams back into the breast pocket.

Winnie stepped back. Was he sincere? Judging by the crimson shade of his neck, perhaps he was.

'Miss Weatherby, I'm aggrieved for you.' He waved the telegram. 'This is deplorable. But I'm afraid I can't help you.' His jaw shifted pensively. 'I have plans in France.'

Winnie's spinning mind seized upon one word. 'You're going to *France*?'

'Yes, indeed, to the Exposition Universelle. Tomorrow afternoon is the opening of the Royal Prince Albert Photographic Exhibition, a project to honour my late father's patronage of the art and science of photography, and I decided last night to accept the invitation to cut the ceremonial ribbon.'

Winnie blurted, 'My father is in Paris for the World Fair, and I need – that is, he'd be ever so delighted if I met him there. Perhaps the vessel you're sailing on has room for one young lady . . .' *So brazen! Who have you become, Winifred Alice Weatherby?*

Prince Bertie grumbled and blustered.

She wasn't giving up yet. She pulled a pitiful pout like the ones the silly Beacon Academy girls used when twisting the arms of their rich fathers. 'Having been dumped so unceremoniously from Her Majesty's League of Remarkable Young Ladies, I have *nowhere to go*.' She whimpered the final words for dramatic effect and polished off the performance à la Celeste – with two dainty sniffs.

Blech – such manipulative behaviour made her feel queasy!

Prince Bertie squeaked a tiny moan of concession. 'Oh . . . very well, then. I'm sure my Navy chums won't mind squeezing together to fit you aboard their "little" sailboat.' He gave the carriage a good-natured thump. 'Another traveller to Paris, Mr Todd. To the pier!'

As a doorman handed Winnie into the carriage, she suppressed a smug smile. Some young ladies are born lucky. Others *make* their good fortune.

CHAPTER 35

~Paris, Hotel Terminus~

Sunday morning

Winnie pointed to the guest register on the front desk of the Hotel Terminus. 'Would monsieur please look once again for a Professor Archibald Weatherby? He should have arrived yesterday.'

The man behind the desk blinked at her and glanced towards the open register on the lectern. 'Mademoiselle, the Hotel Terminus is newly opened, so there's only one page, and I have read through every name. Such a guest does not exist, and we have no vacancy, so I cannot help you.'

Over the concierge's shoulder, in a huge mirror, Winnie locked eyes with herself. She'd spotted something helpful, namely the reflection of the receptionist's back – and, more expediently, the guest register. Standing on tiptoe and leaning in, she could just make out the mirror image of the entries. With a little luck, she might spot the name her father had used to register. She had to distract the receptionist.

'Please, monsieur, perhaps you could help me find a place . . .' She spread out a map of the Exposition Universelle site. 'My father is expecting me at the Galerie des Machines, but I'm rather lost.'

She ignored his detailed description of the route, instead squinting at the mirror and skimming the column of guests' surnames: Cox, Swanson, Byrnes, Deverall, Severgnini, Burton, Sheraton, Gervay, Halpin, Munson, Fox, Gibbs, Catalano, Bates, Dunn, *Skerryvore . . . Voilà!* That was the lighthouse that Papa had used in the mirror-written telautogram all those weeks ago.

When the man finished the directions, he folded his hands. 'Clear, mademoiselle?'

'Very clear! *Merci*, monsieur. And happily, I just remembered the professor is staying elsewhere. Would you kindly check your register for my father, A.A. Skerryvore?'

The receptionist's brows rose. He ran a finger down the list of names and checked the key box associated with the room number. 'Here it is. Welcome to the Hotel Terminus, mademoiselle. Monsieur has not yet arrived, but you may go in ahead of him. For you.' He handed her the room key and a letter.

'*Merci.*' Winnie clutched the letter to her chest. It was addressed in Papa's scrawly handwriting to 'Miss W. Skerry-vore'. *Finally, proof Papa was alive.* The relief made her so giddy she dashed up to their accommodation on the third floor, forgetting ladylike deportment while ascending stairs. Although their rooms were delightfully French – from the elegant furnishings to the huge vases of magenta peonies – it would have been far nicer if Papa had been here to greet her.

She sat down to read his letter.

Winifred,

How I have missed you, my dear girl! Soon we shall be together. I imagine you will reach the hotel first, as I've had to take a rather roundabout route to avoid that rascal, Peter Geier. I do hope all my tricks kept him busy enough to leave you alone. The thought that he would track you down has been a terrible worry to me.

Never mind that. We have a Grand Prix to win, and my A.A. Weatherby Telautograph Machine has an excellent chance despite stiff competition from America. I managed to bring the receiver, and I've no doubt you understood my instructions to bring the transmitter and the designs.

I have a meeting with a very important backer who may be able to dig us out of the hole Geier has tried to dump us in. Let's meet in the grand vestibule of the Galerie des Machines at half past twelve. That will give us enough time to register and set up before the entry to the competition closes at three p.m. Let us hope the wondrous Telautograph will be enough to win the judges' approval!

Until then, I remain,

Your loving Papa

Winnie folded the letter, slid it into the envelope, and crumpled into a sobbing mess. Poor Papa! He was so full of hope and so blissfully unaware of how far they'd sunk. His receiver was only half a Telautograph machine. Without the other half – the transmitter – there would be no demonstration, and without a demonstration, it would not win the Grand Prix.

The thought of that thief basking in Papa's glory made her sick. All the years of development had been for naught. Weatherby Manufacturing would go bankrupt, and it would be her fault. Unless they did something – but what?

The clock on the mantel struck noon, startling her into

action. There was no time for feeling sorry for herself. She had to freshen up and find her way across Paris and the Seine to the site of the Exposition Universelle.

Thanks to the concierge's excellent directions and the doorman's loan of a parasol, Winnie had managed to navigate her way to the site of the exposition. She boarded the miniature Decauville Railway, which ran along the exposition's perimeter and offered good views of most of the attractions. Good golly, there was so much to see. The international pavilions, the Palaces of Fine Arts and Liberal Arts, and of course the Eiffel Tower, which she'd spotted from a distance earlier, but now, its magnitude and modernity took her breath away.

With all these people it might be hard to find her father. Today the site was busy, but tomorrow when the Exposition Universelle threw open its gates to the public, there would be a stampede. If only she could be among the celebrity visitors who got to tour today . . .

Prince Bertie was one of them – and he had invited her and Papa to his ribbon cutting at three at the Palace of Liberal Arts. The Prince of Wales had been a jolly travel companion and attentive, fatherly escort on their journey from Gosport over the Channel and on to Paris. He drew people in, shared food, drinks and laughter . . . It was little wonder he had so many friends.

But clearly, he had enemies too. Why would someone target His Royal Highness? Mr Magpie clearly had personal motives – highly personal. At least here in Paris, Prince Bertie would be safe from Mr Magpie's evil intent.

Or would he? She wriggled in her seat. His Royal Highness had made no attempt to cover his trail to Paris. On the contrary, he'd announced it to the driver at the inn in Gosport as if he'd wanted everyone to hear. Her jaw shifted. Perhaps the petits fours were the last straw, and he had decided to divert Mr Magpie away from the Queen. But why here? Why not go to the lawyers' rooms in London and deal with the threat discreetly and completely?

Avoiding Mr Magpie's reach had been hard enough in a familiar landscape. Anything could happen in these crowded buildings. Winnie gripped her parasol. Very well, then. She would have to be on spy duty – unofficially – while she was in His Royal Highness's company. If only she had Stella's measured aggression, Effie's eagle-like senses, Celeste's charm and Adelaide's hunger for justice, she'd be a League of One.

The miniature train jerked to a halt not far from the grand entrance to the Galerie des Machines, and Winnie alighted. It was a good day to be a spy in Paris.

CHAPTER 36

~GRAND ENTRANCE OF THE
GALERIE DES MACHINES~

While the busy world eddied around her, Winnie waited for her father in an alcove beside the grand staircase of the Galerie des Machines. The clock had long struck one o'clock, but she wasn't worried yet: tardiness was her father's strongest and most consistent trait. Her notepad equipage lay open on her lap, and she tapped her chin with the tip of the pencil. Her recent line of thought had brought on a sudden fit of sleuthing.

Mr Magpie had provided some clues they all had failed to examine. 'One for sorrow, two for joy . . .' She whispered the folk poem to herself, now remembering it in full, writing it out on her tiny sheet of paper.

On Easter Monday, the flock of trapped magpies had swooped out of the Queen's closet. There was no telling how many there had been, so that event didn't fit the poem. However, a group of magpies is referred to as 'a mischief', which may have signified Mr Magpie's intent to *annoy* rather than *harm*.

There had been the seven dead magpies on the Queen's dessert platter. 'Seven for a secret never to be told,' Winnie whispered. Perhaps this might link to the lawyer's letter, which referred to a 'delicate matter' and 'financial compensation'. Money was not a problem with this Royal Family. So, more than anything, His Royal Highness did not want that secret revealed.

The most recent event with the misfired arrow had included a single feather pressed into the wax seal, which might signify *one* magpie. *One for sorrow.* Clancy's warning about the bad luck of lone magpies rang in her ears. There may have been a letter to the Queen – a sorrowful letter?

The petits fours incident on the train was troubling. It seemed so personalized to His Royal Highness. But how? The train schedule hadn't been announced. The sweets had been provided by the kitchen at Windsor . . . hadn't they? This incident narrowed down the possible pool of suspects to staff, the royal household, the Munshi, the Royal Family, the railway workers, the ladies of the League . . . Could the petits fours hold a meaning? 'Petit *four*,' Winnie whispered. 'Four for a boy?' She supposed that could refer to the Prince himself. She wrote it down but struck it out immediately, remembering her very basic French. This *four* wasn't a number, but rather the French word for oven.

What else was there? Holland House – the nest and eggs. Winnie drew a nest of sticks, thinking as she filled it with small eggs . . . three small eggs. 'Three for a girl.' So, it was: Mischief. A secret. A sorrow. A girl . . . She sketched a girl from head to foot. While drawing the figure's shoes, the pieces of the puzzle clicked together. She shot to her feet: the velvet-covered heel!

'Good golly! I've got it!' Her voice echoed around the vast, ornate entry.

'Miss Weatherby?' a voice called out from the staircase above her. 'Winifred, is that you?'

Winnie stepped out of the alcove to look up to the stair landing. 'Stella?'

Stella clapped her hands. 'As soon as I heard "good golly" ring in the air, I knew we'd found you. Wait right there.'

A moment later, Stella and Effie were hugging her.

'We'd guessed you would be in the Galerie des Machines, and we were right,' said Stella. 'But I'm surprised you're not examining the machinery in there. It seems appealing – to your tastes.' She pointed dubiously into the enormous steel-and-glass exhibition hall.

Effie laughed. 'And I'm surprised you haven't figured

out a way to operate the electric rolling bridge. I should like a ride on it!'

Winnie blinked at them. 'I can't imagine how you knew I'd be in Paris, nor can I believe you're here!'

Effie interlaced her arm in Winnie's. 'We have *so much* to tell you and very little time.'

Stella steered Winnie back to the alcove, where they huddled together on the bench. 'We arrived at Osborne House all right – but the tainted petits fours had given Her Majesty such a terrible fright she was having palpitations. I'm sure it's occurred to you that the petits fours can only have originated within the royal household.'

'Indeed.' Winnie nodded gravely. 'I'm surprised any of you were still in the vicinity of Osborne House, for *I* had been dismissed and told to return to London.'

Effie nodded. 'Oh, we all were dismissed later that evening – Her Majesty didn't feel she could trust us any longer. But Mrs Campbell put us in the guest house until she could determine your whereabouts. She was concerned she hadn't heard from you since the whole . . .'

'Pug cat-astrophe,' Winnie supplied.

Stella chuckled and continued. 'That's when she learnt that you were with Prince Bertie. Only then did Mrs Campbell relax. We were all set to return to London.'

'Until?' Winnie coaxed. She wriggled at the dread creeping up her spine.

Effie squinted suspiciously at Winnie. '*Until* yesterday evening's supper at Osborne House. We weren't invited, of course, but according to Mrs Campbell, it was lovely until the Queen retired to bed—'

Winnie interrupted, '—and found a calling card from Mr Magpie in her bedroom.'

'Yes! However did you guess?' Effie said. 'Except it was her sitting room – where she'd set up your Boot-Button Butler, Winnie! She's ever so pleased to be able to remove her own shoes!'

Winnie clasped her hands at her heart. 'Oh, how lovely!'

'And when Her Majesty read the message on the calling card, she nearly fainted!' Stella added. 'This was no "compliments of" card. Rather, Mr Magpie threatened to humiliate and harm the Prince of Wales *in Paris*!'

Effie stomped her foot and pulled a dour Queen expression. '*If that Magpie man so much as looks at my son, he'll soon know what my wrath feels like.*' She mimicked the Queen's distinctive accent perfectly. 'That was decreed after she stopped hyperventilating, but before the doctor was called.'

'Good heavens!' Winnie gripped her belly.

Stella nodded solemnly. 'It's true. She is a mother bear where her children's safety is concerned – even to the black sheep, Prince Bertie.'

Effie grimaced. '*Especially* to him, it would seem. The prickly banter between mother and son hides a deep and complex love.'

Hmm. 'All of this is very interesting.' Winnie held up her notepad equipage. 'You see, I've been playing detective, and I've deduced some important connections. The others are here, of course?'

Effie nodded. 'Adelaide and Celeste are searching for His Royal Highness. Mrs Campbell has gone to Prince Bertie's hotel in case he's there.'

Winnie shook her head. 'They won't find him. He's dining at a favourite restaurant "for nostalgic reasons", he told me.'

Stella stood. 'Oh, dear! Do you know where it is? We must go immediately to warn His Royal Highness of the grave danger he's in!'

CHAPTER 37

~CAFÉ DE FLORE~

On the tram to ride to the Café de Flore, Winnie, Stella and Effie huddled together.

Stella frowned. 'I only wish we'd managed to find Adelaide and Celeste before we'd left the Galerie des Machines. They were supposedly searching the Palace of Liberal Arts for Prince Bertie, but I didn't see them anywhere.'

'We'll find them when we return.' Effie rubbed her hands. 'Well, Winifred? You haven't told us what you've deduced about Mr Magpie.'

Winnie twisted her fingers together, sick with worry. 'I wouldn't want to seem overconfident . . . but based on clues that have been in front of us all along, I think I've guessed who it is and what's about to happen at the café.'

'Clues? Like a riddle? You're saying

Mr Magpie *wants* us to guess his identity?' Effie wrinkled her nose. 'In my mind, he's always been a troublesome pest with far too much leisure time.'

Winnie shook her head. 'Think: why did he call himself Mr Magpie? Superstitious people believe a solitary magpie is unlucky – *unless* you greet him, right? Acknowledging him wards off the misfortune. Using the old rhyme about magpies, I've drawn some conclusions.' She explained her theory about the numbers in the rhyme and the link to the lawyer's letter.

'I suppose it's plausible,' Stella said. 'But cakes laced with castor oil don't relate to the birds.' She squinted at Winnie. 'Do they?'

'Actually, even the violet petits fours were a clue – a very specific signal for Prince Bertie about the Café de Flore. They are the café's house speciality – I saw it on an advertisement at the train station. But I don't know what other significance they hold. It must be something special for Prince Bertie to change his plans and come to Paris.' The tram reached their destination. 'Here's our stop.'

'Goodness! So this is quite a mystery.' Stella's brow furrowed. 'Well, who do you think Mr Magpie is?'

Winnie hesitated. If she was wrong, they'd never forgive her . . . 'The thing is, I believe His Royal Highness recognized the signal of the petits fours, and he's come with his own plans to carry out a dramatic finale, probably with help from the Paris police or private detectives.' She gulped. 'Ladies, no matter what, we must not let things go that far.'

Stella scowled. 'Winnie, we don't have time for riddles. The Prince of Wales's life is in danger.'

Winnie nodded gravely. 'Look for back and side exits to the restaurant, waiting carriages and back alleys. Watch for people in unconvincing disguises or anyone who's observing or communicating with the Prince of Wales. Be careful.' She gulped. 'Firearms may be involved.'

Effie widened her eyes. 'Winnie! If that's true, we should run and tell His Royal Highness to escape while he can. If anything happens to him, it will be on our heads!'

Winnie wrung her hands. It was true, but . . . 'I'm afraid if we make our presence known, Mr Magpie will strike and run, and His Highness's men will counter . . . with disastrous results. Please trust me – I can't reveal more for fear of unleashing a disaster.' Winnie glanced around at the patrons seated at tables on the terrace outside Café de Flore.

'I'll feel more comfortable when I've seen inside and around the café.' Winnie gazed up at the roofline for entry points and escapes. Who knew? Perhaps Parisian buildings had highroads for cloudlarking too.

'Let's be quick.' Stella's forehead crinkled.

Effie studied an approaching gentleman over Winnie's

shoulder. 'What if the Prince's hotel directs Mrs Campbell here? She could walk straight into danger.'

Stella shuddered. 'All the more reason to do this swiftly. Four minutes of surveillance and return here.'

Four minutes later, the three young ladies reassembled.

Effie reported first. 'His Royal Highness is seated at the back at the table with a candle, and he's just ordered the *plat du jour*, which is *Filet de Bœuf*, and a glass of red wine.'

Stella nodded towards the terrace. 'There's something odd about the two men who were just seated at the table outside on the right. I suspect they are studying the crowd, just as we are. Perhaps they're working for Prince Bertie.'

Drat. Winnie pointed. 'Let's take separate tables, spread apart. I'll go in closest – but not too close.'

Stella blew out a calming breath. 'Effie, if there's danger, you're to lead Prince Bertie outside to a tram and flee to safety. Winnie, you and I will stop Mr Magpie – assuming he arrives. Good luck.' She started to step away but stopped. 'Be careful.' She stepped off the kerb and crossed the street.

Separately, all three ladies were seated by the maître d'hôtel, and so the waiting game began. At least it was a charming spot with smartly dressed patrons and several amusing dogs. Winnie shoved the *carte du jour* aside, earning a pronounced frown from her waiter. 'A mug of milk, *s'il vous plaît*.' His expression of horror shamed her. 'Make that an *éclair au chocolat*.'

Heads turned around the room. Winnie leant forward to see what everyone was looking at. An elegant lady in a spectacular hat had arrived – it was Mrs Campbell. Winnie groaned. Their task had just doubled in complexity as well as risk.

Mrs Campbell nodded to her brother and made her way across the restaurant. When she passed Effie, she cocked a brow and stopped to look around the room. Her gaze landed on Winnie.

Winnie touched her forehead with two fingers – a hand signal meaning, *Possible Sighting*. It wasn't accurate, but it would have to do, as they had no signal for: *You're Ruining Our Mission, Go Away.*

Prince Bertie waved his sister over. Mrs Campbell gave a helpless shrug of the shoulder at Winnie and joined her brother at his table at the back.

Wonderful. Now there were multiple important people to keep alive and well. Winnie rubbed her temples. *Please let this end without bloodshed or shame.*

A thin waiter with unevenly waxed moustaches approached the royal table and bowed. He deposited a small plate on the table between Prince Bertie and Mrs Campbell. He bowed again and stepped back, linen towel draped over his arm.

Prince Bertie scowled. 'I say, *garçon*. I ordered the *plat du jour*, not a plate of petits fours.'

Winnie leapt to her feet, knocking her chair back with a crash. The waiter turned to face her.

It was Mr Magpie, and he glared at her. Winnie's heart lurched.

In two bats of an eyelid, Stella was beside Winnie; two more and Effie had joined her.

Around the restaurant, people stared and whispered.

Prince Bertie hissed at his sister, 'What's this? Why are the young lady spies here? I thought the League was *kaputt*. Did you organize this, Loosy? I must say, your timing is awful.'

Mrs Campbell's mouth moved, but no words came out. Her astonished gaze was fixed on Mr Magpie's face.

The waiter laughed. 'Allow me to pull up some chairs for this little reunion.' The voice was familiar. It belonged to Adelaide Culpepper. She yanked off the moustache and her men's wig, spilling her long, dark hair down her back.

Effie squeaked, and Stella gasped.

'Good golly.' Winnie shook her head. The satisfaction of deducing correctly was ruined by grave fears for her friend.

Prince Bertie raised a finger – he clearly hadn't caught on to what was happening. 'This has gone far enough,' said the Prince. 'I don't know what you girls are playing at, but you're tarnishing my reputation. I demand you all return to your lodging at once. You've completely disrupted my plans for this afternoon. I intend to trap a magpie.' His gaze dropped to the two petits fours iced with pale lavender ganache, each topped with a crystallized violet. Tucked under them was a calling card:

Just dessert
Mr Magpie

He shoved his trembling hands under the table.

'Young ladies, *Adelaide*, what is going on?' Mrs Campbell was using her Displeased Spymistress voice. Even when directed at someone else, it made Winnie wince.

Adelaide sneered at the Prince of Wales. 'Do you wish to tell her our secret, *Papa*?'

CHAPTER 38

~CAFÉ DE FLORE~

Prince Bertie's face blanched. 'You,' he gasped.

'Indeed, it is I, your long-forgotten, thoroughly unwanted, utterly rejected daughter.' She turned to Mrs Campbell. 'This place was a secret rendezvous for my mother and . . . *him*. The violet petits fours were her favourite.'

Winnie and Stella exchanged wide-eyed glances.

Prince Bertie scoffed. 'There is nothing you can say or do to prove your claims. I, for one, am not certain your mother was sincere. Lady Susan, may she rest in peace, was lovely, but untrustworthy and prone to bouts of hysteria.' He folded his arms. 'Traits that you've clearly inherited.'

Mrs Campbell clicked her tongue. 'Bertie! Don't be horrid.'

'She's a snake in the grass!' he thundered, shaking his head.

Winnie followed the line of Adelaide's profile. Her nose, complexion and cheekbones clearly hinted at royal Saxe-Coburg and Gotha blood. It was preposterous she hadn't noticed the family resemblance before.

Adelaide recoiled at his words. 'You see? This is why we are where we are. I do not wish to be "hysterical" or greedy—'

'You've pursued this wicked end for years – I see it now! I trusted you with my daughter!' He snorted. 'Well, dismissing you from your tennis instructor position was *one* thing Mumsy got right!' He thumped the table with his fist. 'And you stole my mother's priceless Fabergé egg!'

'Only as insurance, and besides, it's a worthless trinket compared to what I need and want. I need you to acknowledge me – to *see* me, your daughter, your flesh and blood. And I want you to know my mother died, broken-hearted and destitute, with no help from you, nothing to reduce her suffering—'

'You are mistaken!' Prince Bertie's face was ashen. 'I tried to help Susie. You have no idea, young lady, how the *busybodies* surrounding me organize and constrain my life – and how my overbearing mother meddles in my affairs and thwarts my intentions!'

Adelaide shook her head, refusing to hear him. 'Because of your inaction, my mother gave birth to me *alone* and left me with a lonely woman who turned out to have more affection for the gin bottle than she had for me. She died, but her enormous debts remain. When I turn eighteen next month, they will be transferred to me. And as I have no means to pay her debts, even factoring in my income from the Beacon Academy and Her Majesty's League, I could go to debtors' prison.'

Stella covered her mouth.

Shame swallowed Winnie. How had she not understood the enormity of her friend's suffering?

Adelaide turned to the Spymistress. 'I have tried for months, Mrs Campbell, using discreet, legal avenues, to obtain His Royal Highness's acknowledgement of my parentage and a modest annual income for my silence. He has inexplicably ignored my solicitors' repeated requests to draw up such an agreement. Because I could no longer afford my lawyer, I changed tack, resorting to Mr Magpie's rather unorthodox methods of persuasion. As I'm sure you know, a solitary magpie is an ominous and insistent creature . . .'

Bertie rose to his feet, grunting at the effort. 'I shan't endure another moment of this very public harassment and humiliation. I have a ribbon to cut. Louise, we're leaving.' He thumped the table three times.

'We are not, Bertie. Sit down.' Princess Louise folded her arms.

The three knocks rang oddly in Winnie's ears. It meant

something. She scanned the crowded restaurant. When her gaze returned to Adelaide, Winnie jumped.

Adelaide had pointed a small silver pistol, lady-sized and shiny, at Prince Bertie. 'Please return to your seat, Papa.'

The audacity of this young lady! It was . . . inspirational. And how apt was the dainty but 'deadly' handgun! Winnie had admired and feared it on that first day in the testing area of the Quartermistress's Laboratory. (Later, she learnt the bullets it fired could barely penetrate a lump of cold lard.)

'You see?' Prince Bertie said, sitting down. 'Untrustworthy and hysterical, as I predicted.' He thumped his table again a little less heartily. 'I beg you to stop this at once, young lady.'

'Use my name, Papa!' Adelaide screamed, thrusting the gun in his direction. 'Have you not even bothered yourself with my name?' Tears brimmed in her eyes.

An ache for her friend panged in Winnie's core. So much sorrow for one young lady to bear alone . . .

The maître d'hôtel, having seen the gun and heard the commotion, began scurrying around the front of the restaurant, driving patrons outside to safety. Chairs scraped, the pitch of chatter rose, the restaurant cleared in the blink of an eye.

'If you please, ladies, and Mrs Campbell, stand over

there, keeping your hands visible. A little further. There. Stop. I didn't want to have to use this, but His Royal Highness leaves me no choice.' Without removing her eyes or gun from Prince Bertie, she picked up the end of a long, thin piece of white cotton cord from the floor. 'This is a fuse that leads to a bomb stowed under His Royal Highness's chair.'

Prince Bertie's knees shot up, banging the table. He looked under it and scooted away. 'Great Scott, girl! Are you mad?' Beads of sweat glistened on his brow.

'Sit still!' Adelaide hissed. 'Thrashing about could set it off.'

Winnie reeled. 'A bomb! Really, Adelaide? Isn't that rather extreme?' Her legs began shaking. Nothing on her chatelaine could match a bomb. 'How ever did you procure explosives?'

Adelaide snorted. 'I helped myself to the supplies in your laboratory. Professor Dudley had all sorts of things lying about along with the most convenient notes on assemblage. No offence, Winifred, but her inventions were far deadlier than anything you've made.'

'No offence taken.' Winnie's gaze followed the fuse from Adelaide's hand down to the floor where it connected to something inside a wooden box placed under the prince's seat. She blinked – that box! 'You built the bomb in my Boot-Button Butler? Adelaide! How could you?'

Adelaide waved a hand impatiently. 'You're a genius. You'll make another.'

'*Zut alors!*' Prince Bertie boomed. 'Where are my asinine detectives? Punch and Judy would have been more organized.' He picked up a fork and gave his wine glass three clangs.

His detectives? Winnie gritted her teeth. She'd guessed correctly: he'd come to the café so his Paris police chums could make an arrest away from the scrutiny of his family and the London newspapermen.

Adelaide lit the fuse over the flame of the candle on the table, setting a spark sizzling steadily down the cord and racing towards the boxed explosives. Her voice cracked, and her hands shook. 'Promise me in front of these witnesses, *Papa*, you will acknowledge me as your daughter and supply me an annual income – nothing more. I'll go away. If you promise me now, I'll stop the bomb from exploding.'

Through the side door, two men barrelled, yelling in French.

'That one! Grab her!' The Prince of Wales pointed to Adelaide.

Winnie screamed. If they arrested Adelaide, who knew what would happen to her – jail or an asylum or . . . She had to block them. Winnie shunted a chair in front of one of the men, tripping him. The other fell over him, landing in a writhing heap. Winnie gave Adelaide a shove towards the kitchen door. 'Run! Along the rooftop! Go! Go!'

Adelaide's face twisted. She dropped the burning fuse, pulled a white wad from her pocket, and chucked it into the flickering candle flame.

POOF! White light flashed silently, sending Winnie and every other person screaming and ducking to save their lives.

Winnie slowly uncovered her face and patted her arms. Although her vision was dazzled, she was alive and whole. The room was intact. Voices around her murmured. And Adelaide had vanished. What an exit! She had created a superb distraction by igniting a hunk of guncotton.

'Don't just stand there – smother the fuse!' Mrs Campbell yelled, throwing her brother's glass of wine at the sparks and missing.

Stella leapt forward, stamping on the burning fuse, and Effie severed it from the box with a decisive snip of her scissor equipage.

Prince Bertie launched out of his chair, dragging his sister by the hand towards the door. 'Good god, do something with that thing before it explodes and kills us all!'

Winnie felt all eyes land on her. 'Me? But I've barely dabbled in explosives!' She gripped the sides of her head. It certainly didn't appear dangerous. And if Adelaide had assembled it herself, how hard could it be to disassemble? Winnie drew in a breath, grabbed a patron's umbrella, and gingerly poked the Boot-Button Butler to turn it around. She peered into the opening, trying to remember the chemicals and parts of a bomb.

Winnie dropped to her knees beside the Boot-Button Butler and peered inside. 'Oh, bother,' she moaned.

'What's wrong?' Stella asked, peeking over Winnie's shoulder. She gasped. 'No! Is that the—'

'Confound it!' His Royal Highness roared from outside the door. 'What is it?'

There was no bomb. Winnie reached into the box, untied the other end of the severed fuse, and withdrew a magnificent enamelled golden egg encrusted with rubies and seed pearls. She opened the Fabergé egg's hinged lid, releasing a familiar calling card:

Adieu
With great sorrow
Adelaide Culpepper

CHAPTER 39

~Galerie des Machines~

Two-fifty, Sunday afternoon

Winnie was two hours late for her rendezvous with Papa. She bustled into the grand entry of the Galerie des Machines and slid to a stop, gobsmacked by the sunlit stained glass, mosaic tiles and modern vaulted ceilings. Good golly! This vestibule was magnificent – all to pay homage to the spirit of innovation. The space could inspire awe and pride, worship and praise in the most scientifically minded of men – and women. How had she missed the splendour when she waited here earlier?

'Winifred! There you are, my dear girl!' Her father's voice echoed around the lofty interior.

Winnie turned in a full circle, seeking the source. 'Papa?'

Professor Weatherby, standing on the grand staircase, raised his closed umbrella like a baton to draw her attention. Winnie ran up the stairs to him. 'Darling! It's so good to see you. I suspect I've arrived behind schedule. Have you been waiting long?' He squeezed her hands and studied her face and dress. 'Something's different about you.'

Winnie stifled a chuckle. Well, for starters, her plaits were gone, and her hair was coiffed – more or less. Her hat was stylish, and her gown now reached the floor. Her padded corset gave her curves that weren't there before, and the heels of her boots were almost an inch higher. And those were only the *outward* changes.

He nodded. 'A-ha! I've spotted it. You've added something new to your mother's chatelaine. Quite fetching, my dear, though it surprises me you wish to wear something so domestic.'

'As observant as ever, Papa,' Winnie said, giggling as she laced her arm through his.

'Shall we? We don't have long before registrations close.' He steered her back out of the entrance and started briskly down the concourse.

Winnie gulped. It would be best to admit it all now. 'Papa, I have a confession. Regretfully, despite my most earnest efforts, the Telautograph was stolen from me.' She watched him out of the corner of her eye.

Papa's bushy eyebrows rose. 'Oh, dear.' His pace slowed.

'You see, Mr Geier took it. He . . . he's not a good sort.' Drat! Her voice betrayed her with a quaver.

Her father glanced at her. Colour drained from his cheeks. 'If that villain hurt you, I will not stop until he hangs. Never mind the financial ruin he's brought upon us—'

Winnie waved it off. 'I'm here safely, and we're together at last. I only wish I'd been able to bring the transmitter as you'd requested. I'd even invented – er, *devised* – a method of transporting it conveniently. It's a promising concept, Papa! Imagine a steamer trunk with wheels and a handle. It looks rather like a cross between a perambulator and . . .' She squinted across the Champ de Mars at a quickly moving woman. She stopped and pointed. 'Much like that contraption over there, the one that's rolling in this direction at great speed.'

Her father looked and grimaced. 'I say. It's quite unseemly for a lady to run in public. However, it appears there's a chap chasing her.' He sniffed and stamped his umbrella. 'Some men can be quite beastly.'

Winnie cocked a brow. The colour of the lady's dress was familiar, and its smart cut was unmistakably Monsieur Moineau. The contraption she pushed was decidedly *not* a perambulator. It was Celeste, and she was pushing Winnie's Portarobe! And if she had the Portarobe, she must also have the Telautograph! Good golly – what a stroke of luck!

But why was she running? Charming Lady Celeste

Lemieux would *never* condescend to unseemly behaviour in public. Unless that man chasing her . . .

Good golly.

Winnie ran her fingers through the chains of her chatelaine, selecting the newest equipage she was developing, an Emergency Skirt-Raiser. After clipping it to the front of her gown, she grasped the ripcord, ready to activate. 'Darling Papa, would you excuse me for one teensy moment? I believe I've spotted a dear friend. If you would kindly wait right here without moving and hold this.' She handed him the Boot-Button Butler.

'But, Winifred, my dear—'

Winnie yanked the cord and, like the rising curtain at the Theatre Royal, the skirt of her gown rose to her knees, freeing her feet from encumbrances. (Of course, showing one's calves was immodest, but tripping over one's petticoat and tumbling on the ground was decidedly worse.) She took off, racing diagonally across the Champ de Mars, hurtling over low hedges, ducking under sculpted lemon topiaries, dodging water features and trampling beds of spring flowers. With one eye on Miss Lemieux's speedy progress, Winnie calculated the approximate trajectory that would cause her to catch up between her friend and the assailant.

'That lady has stolen my machine!' the pursuer shouted. 'Stop that thief!'

Winnie pumped her arms and legs harder. Sailing over a fragrant hedge of lavender, she landed on the pavement just as Celeste and the Portarobe squeaked past.

'Winifred!' Celeste screamed into her slipstream. 'Be careful . . .' She said something about arms.

Confused, Winnie eyed the pursuer who was charging straight for her – without any sign of slowing. It was Peter Geier – no surprise there, but his drawn pistol *was* a shock, and it was pointed straight at her.

Ah – *those* kind of arms. Winnie froze.

'Out of the way, you stupid goose!' He didn't alter his course. He was almost on her.

From the left, a lean figure lunged from the branch of an ornamental tree, catching Mr Geier by the shoulders and twisting him sideways. His pistol discharged, its *BANG* echoing around the Champ de Mars and its many steel and glass structures.

Winnie dived sideways, somersaulting to the ground, round and round and round. Pain seared in her shoulder. Flitting stars and other celestial bodies orbited her line of vision. Nearby, footsteps slapped, and voices rang out with fuzzy-edged words and hints of familiar tunes.

And a blizzard of silent white blinded her.

Burning vapours assaulted Winnie's nasal passages. She opened her eyes, shunting away from the fumes.

Ow . . .

Someone stroked Winnie's hair. Her head lay in a pale-yellow lap. She looked up and met Stella's sweet face. Effie was patting her hand, and her warm tears spilt on to Winnie's skin. Celeste knelt in front of her, vinaigrette of smelling salts from her chatelaine at the ready.

Winnie recoiled from the equipage. 'I'm fine. No more of that, thank you very much.'

Celeste flashed a brief smile. 'Very well.' She cocked her head. 'Does anything hurt?' Her voice was hoarse.

Winnie puffed a breath. 'Erm, yes.' Her left shoulder ached, shooting pain down her arm and back. She squeezed her eyes shut. 'Was I shot?'

Celeste clicked her tongue. 'Oh, heavens, no, not you. It was the tumble. It's either a bad bruise or a fracture to your collarbone. Your father has gone to fetch a doctor. He shan't be long . . .'

Winnie groaned. 'Oh, no! Celeste, I tried to—'

'Shh.' Celeste rubbed Winnie's hand. 'Thank you for your valiant effort! It was most impressive! Winifred, you should be extremely proud of your progress in physical prowess.'

Stella nodded. 'I agree. Well done, Winnie. You raced through those gardens like a cheetah.' She sniffed and dabbed at her eyes. 'I was very impressed.'

Winnie tried to smile through the searing pain. 'It

must be due to the excellent company I keep.' She shifted. Everyone seemed tense and frightened, so she joked, 'Now that it's clear I will live, you must tell me what just happened. Celeste, was that my Portarobe you were pushing?'

'It was indeed. Imagine my surprise when I spotted your invention here, in Paris.' Celeste grimaced. 'I'm sorry, Winnie. I think I pushed it faster than it was designed to endure.' She cleared her throat. 'And I hit a kerb. The whole vehicle broke into pieces. The Telautograph . . . smashed to bits.'

'Oh, bother.' Winnie squeezed Celeste's hand. 'Never mind. We can rebuild it.'

'I shall never forget your father's expression when he saw the destruction.' Celeste's face twisted.

A wave of nauseating pain rolled over Winnie as she remembered the contorted face of that man. 'And Mr Geier? Was he captured?'

Stella shook her head. 'He jumped aboard a crowded tram and disappeared.'

Winnie winced at the pain. 'Someone leapt out of a tree. Or perhaps I dreamt that . . .'

There was no reply from her friends. Winnie twisted her neck to look. All three of them had tears streaming down their faces. She grunted herself upright. 'What is it?' she gasped.

The sight beyond them was horrific – a tragic trio.

On his knees on the pavement was the Prince of Wales, face wet, shoulders racking, and in his embrace lay a limp young woman, dressed in men's clothes – Adelaide. A huge crimson stain had spilt down her neck and spread across the front of her white waiter's shirt. Mrs Campbell stroked her brother's arm and wept.

'NO!' Winnie howled. Despite the searing pain, she crawled to them. 'No . . .' she sobbed.

Mrs Campbell shook her head. 'I'm sorry, Winifred. Adelaide saved you. She cracked her head when she fell, but it looks as though she was shot in the torso. She's still breathing, but it appears dire . . .'

Winnie gulped. 'Oh, it's too awful.' She moved forward on her knees. Poor Adelaide.

'Loosy, hold Adelaide while I attend to my nose.' Prince Bertie retrieved a handkerchief from his breast pocket and blew. 'I am the world's greatest scoundrel. I should have agreed to her wishes then and there. Who knows? If I had, this might not have happened.' He honked into the hankie again.

Mrs Campbell gently passed Adelaide's head and shoulders back into her brother's arms. 'Here come Professor Weatherby and the physician, Bertie. Pull yourself together.'

The doctor knelt and felt for Adelaide's pulse. He

checked her pupils and examined all around her head and under her hair. When he felt under Adelaide's shirt, Prince Bertie averted his eyes. The doctor sat back on his haunches and gave his bristly moustache a thorough massage. 'Most unusual.' He turned to Prince Bertie and Princess Louise. 'I was told there was a gunshot wound to the abdomen.'

'Yes,' Mrs Campbell said, pointing to the bloodstained shirt. 'Do you see the bullet hole there?'

The doctor examined the cloth, poking his finger through the singed fabric. 'That is indeed a bullet hole, but the bloodstain has flowed from the wound to her head. The bump knocked her unconscious. You see, the head bleeds profusely, often making a wound appear more serious than it is. There is no bullet wound on her torso. It appears the bullet miraculously deflected off her.'

Winnie gasped, then flinched from the pain caused by the deep breath. 'Good golly! My prototype! Adelaide must have helped herself to another project in the laboratory.' With her good arm, she rapped on Adelaide's abdomen. It clonked like a muffled gong. 'Yes, indeed, she's wearing the prototype of my Bulletproof Corset.'

Adelaide moaned. 'My head . . .'

'Adelaide!' Winnie squeezed her hand. Tears of relief spilt down her cheeks.

Stella, Effie and Celeste squealed and gathered around

their fallen colleague. After a few moments of mutual encouragement, Winnie leant back on her haunches.

Papa, still carrying the Boot-Button Butler, caught her eye and helped her to her feet.

'My dear! What a fright you gave me. I must say I'm dumbfounded by your, your . . .'

'Shenanigans?' Winnie offered.

He stared at her quizzically. 'Why, no. You've always carried on like a chimpanzee. I'm amazed by your circle of acquaintances. The Prince of Wales? Winifred, what have you been up to over the past two months?'

Oh, Papa, if you only knew . . . 'It's quite an adventure story, Papa. Perhaps I can tell you over supper.'

Papa shook his head most vigorously. 'I beg you, no, *not* at supper. We've been invited to dine with someone important tonight, someone who's interested in partnering with us on the future of the Weatherby Telautograph Machine, so you must be on your best and most ladylike behaviour. Absolutely no wild adventure stories. Rather, you can display everything you've learnt over the past months at the Beacon Academy for Poised and Polished Young Ladies. I'm sure your splendid deportment will impress Mr Edison.'

Winnie's chin dropped. 'Mr Thomas Edison? We're dining with Mr Edison, my hero?'

Papa smiled. 'I knew you'd be pleased. His new wife

and his daughter will be there, so you ladies can talk about whatever it is ladies discuss – millinery and embroidery and . . . recipes, I expect.'

Stella, who was eavesdropping, snorted. Effie and Celeste bellowed with fits of giggles. Adelaide, between gasps, begged them to stop. And finally, Winnie broke down, laughing, hiccupping, and holding her sore shoulder.

'I say. What's so funny?' Papa scowled.

Mrs Campbell waited until the laughter had died down. 'Professor Weatherby, it would please my mother immensely if she could purchase that contraption you're holding.'

Papa bowed. He glanced at the Boot-Button Butler he'd been lugging around, and his eyes boggled. 'What, this? This peculiar wooden box filled with what appear to be broken springs and repurposed kitchen whisks?'

'I believe your daughter's remarkable invention is called a Boot-Button Butler. Mumsy was smitten with it. In fact, when Her Majesty discovered it had been removed from her room, she was most aggrieved. Several telegrams were waiting for both His Royal Highness the Prince of Wales and me, with dire instructions to "Fetch it back *or else*."'

Papa's incredulous expression deepened into bewilderment. '*This*?' He held it up.

Mrs Campbell nodded. 'I expect Her Majesty will grant a royal warrant to the Boot-Button Butler, and perhaps to Weatherby and Weatherby Manufacturing Company for further innovations.'

Papa nodded. 'Jolly good.' He looked as if a wad of guncotton had ignited between his ears. 'Er, perhaps I shall take this *astonishing contraption* to dinner with us tonight, then return it to Her Majesty thereafter? I daresay Mr Edison will be fascinated by this story.' Eyes shining with emotion, he clutched the Boot-Button Butler to his chest.

Mrs Campbell smiled. 'Of course, as you wish.'

The pride rising in Winnie's chest nearly lifted her off her feet.

A gaggle of officials from the exhibition fluttered about the Prince, helping him up and presenting a telegram. After he'd dusted himself off, he opened and read the message. 'How delightful! Listen, Loosy. Monsieur Eiffel has invited us to visit his apartment at the top of the tower.'

'Spiffing! What a treat.' Mrs Campbell clapped her gloved hands. 'Might I suggest we invite Headmistress Thornton and Her Majesty's League of Remarkable Young Ladies to join us?'

'Agreed; however, it's only fair that we should wait until my . . . daughter is able to join us too.' He glanced back at doctor and patient. 'Miss Culpepper – Adelaide, would you kindly keep us informed of your recovery?'

She nodded tearfully at her father. 'I shall.'

His Royal Highness cleared his throat and twiddled his fingers under his chin. 'Adelaide, as your father, I am obliged to denounce your dangerous actions towards Her Majesty the Queen – and er, *me* – as reprehensible and completely unacceptable.'

Adelaide lowered her eyes and swallowed. 'I didn't want—'

He held up a hand to stop her. 'However, I acknowledge my considerable part in driving you to such desperation and shall confess it all to Mumsy. At first, I was appalled that we had inadvertently enlisted in Her Majesty's League the very villain we were hunting, but in retrospect, I must say this fact makes it much . . . tidier.' He widened his eyes, patted her hand and gestured to the officials waiting a few feet away. 'Carry on – and take special care of her. She's . . . precious.'

They shifted Adelaide to a stretcher and carried her to a medical carriage.

Adelaide called Winnie over. 'I'm ever so proud of you. Earning a royal warrant is far better than winning the piddly Petit Prix, Winnie.' Tears pooled in her eyes. 'You do realize it was your Bulletproof Corset that saved my life?'

Humbled, Winnie gave a nod. 'And your actions saved mine. Thank you.'

'Thank *you*,' Adelaide called as the carriage pulled away.

'Well done, Winifred.' Papa held out his elbow, and Winifred linked her good arm through it. He patted her hand. 'I expect you'd like to rest your injury and refresh yourself before our supper engagement with Mr Edison.'

Winnie cocked her head. 'Actually, what I'd like most is a large notebook.'

He squinted at her. 'You're in Paris for the first time, about to meet your lifelong hero, and what you'd like most is stationery?'

Winnie nodded emphatically. 'Yes, you see, Papa, I've had a brilliant idea for my unfinished mechanical sling-shot, and I want to sketch it before I forget what I was thinking.'

Her father paused, scratched his cheek, and glanced at the contraption under his arm. 'Remarkable . . .'

Masses of curious spectators have converged on Paris for the opening of the 1889 Paris World Fair to behold its symbol of modernity, a colossal iron spike known as the Eiffel Tower. While most overseas visitors approve of the structure, Parisians are scandalized, calling the tower a 'monstrosity and an eyesore'.

The nearby Gallery of Machines, an equally hideous hall of iron and glass, houses a head-spinning array of machinery, large and small, all testament to the genius of the world's engineers and inventors.

It is here, among the inventions competing for international prestige, that the exposition's controversy has reached a head. Accusations of fraud, theft, and even kidnapping and armed violence have marred the usual decorum of the Grand Prix announcement.

The Grand Prix winning invention of the 1889 Exposition Universelle is the Telautograph Transmitter, which enables

the sending of exact copies of signatures, handwriting and line drawings
across telegraph wires.

The Telautograph's inventor, patent
holder and now Grand Prix winner is
Mr Elisha Gray, who hails from the
American state of Ohio. Mr Gray
believes the machine will be ready for
public use in as little as two years.

Its inventor holds high hopes for his
machine. 'The Telautograph has the
potential to change human communication for the better. I'm certain people
will prefer it to the telephone.'

Gray is no stranger to competition
and controversy. His telephone invention
was pipped by minutes at the US Patent
Office by Alexander Graham Bell. A
lengthy lawsuit ensued. When asked
about similar dastardly competition in
the Telautograph market, Mr Gray
replied, 'The only Telautograph that
matters is my Telautograph.'

London-based inventor Professor
Archibald Weatherby begs to differ.
His competing Weatherby Telautograph

Machine was allegedly stolen and destroyed last week in a dramatic chase near the Eiffel Tower involving HRH the Prince of Wales. Although shots were fired, neither the Prince nor Professor Weatherby was injured. The alleged thief has not been apprehended.

Mr Gray, who was in no way involved, expressed dismay. 'Violence is the primary tool of cowards and idiots.'

Professor Weatherby congratulated Mr Gray on winning the Grand Prix. 'I salute his success. In the world of technological innovation, healthy competition is constructive, while criminal attacks such as the defamation, theft and violence I've recently experienced are not.'

Reports suggest the Weatherby Telautograph was superior to Gray's machine. 'The market will decide,' Professor Weatherby promised. 'The future belongs to the Telautograph.'

Regarding the speculation about HRH the Prince of Wales backing Weatherby's innovations, the inventor replied, 'No comment.'

VR

10 May 1889
Osborne House, Isle of Wight

My Dearest Loosy,
   Now that the Magpie business has
been put to rest, you and Bertie mustn't
dally in Paris. Osborne House is empty
and dreadfully dull. Even dear little
Bosco hasn't been himself. It seems he
was smitten with that disastrous young
lady who walked him — the inventress.
   While I look forward to finally
beholding my Fabergé egg, it is the
return of my Boot-Button Butler I'm
most eager for. I suppose you may as
well bring back the inventress and her
colleagues too. The five of them are a
bumbling lot, but their company was
agreeable.
   Don't be long . . .

   Fondly,
   Mumsy

Dear Father,

Thank you for your recent letter. I cannot express how much your correspondence means to me. I've enjoyed reading your witty reports from Venice.

With regard to Her Majesty's most benevolent offer of an honorific title, I must respectfully decline. Obtaining rank has never been my aim. I only wanted a father and security for my future, both of which you have fulfilled.

I am grateful for the stipend and for your gracious permission to continue as a spy. What a relief Her Majesty's League of Remarkable Young Ladies is not kaput!

You'll be pleased to learn we recently

outsmarted a bloodthirsty interloper who'd locked himself in Her Majesty's wardrobe aboard the royal train. We forced him out with Winifred's new Keyhole Blowing Machine. The pepper powder worked brilliantly, but HM and Bosco couldn't stop sneezing!

Until next time we meet.

Your (new) daughter,

Adelaide

Dear Reader,

Sir Bosco here, the (*ahem*) much-maligned royal pug. Having taken umbrage to the author's liberal interpretation of my character, I contacted Mr Barry Cunningham, the publisher, to request the opportunity to set the record straight. He has graciously permitted me, in my capacity as Chief Canine Companion to Queen Victoria, to write the endmatter.

Firstly and most importantly, let's be clear: I am a *dignified* dog of *noble* blood. While the 'gas' part of Ms Stegert's story *may* have some basis, the rest of her depiction of me is complete fabrication. I would *never* foul inside. Over my dead, adorable, roly-poly body!

With that travesty rectified, let us move on to the less important characters in this book: Her Majesty Queen Victoria is real, while Winifred Weatherby is made-up. It's historical *fiction*, so all events of this story, along with the people – historical and invented, goodies and baddies, the League itself – are products of the author's research and imagination (both of which could be described as *playful*).

You've probably encountered statues of Queen Victoria,

but I promise you, marble and bronze cannot convey what Her Majesty was like in real life. As her (self-proclaimed) favourite dog, I can confirm no other lap compared to the divinely squishy comfort of the Royal Lap! Her Majesty's proportions and sour expression are famous, but what many people don't know is for many years of her later life she suffered an uncomfortable medical condition, probably the result of giving birth to nine babies in her earlier life. If you've ever wondered why she rarely smiled, now you know.

Speaking of her children, two of them feature in the story. The Queen's oldest son was 'Bertie', as he was called by his family, but officially, he was Prince Albert Edward. (He had terrible taste in dogs – terriers. *Shudder*) He and his mother had a hard time getting along, mainly because she blamed Bertie and his bad behaviour for causing the death of her husband – his father – Prince Albert. When Queen Victoria died in 1901, Bertie became King Edward VII. He and his wife, Alexandra of Denmark, had five children. Contrary to the storyline, he had no (known) offspring outside his marriage, but he had many well-known affairs, including one with a Lady Susan.

Princess Louise, the Queen's sixth child, really used the alias Mrs Campbell, not because she was a spymistress but rather because she liked to travel incognito. She was a sculptor, but the Queen discouraged her in this art form, declaring it unsuitable for a princess. The statue of Queen Victoria at Kensington Palace is one of Princess Louise's works.

Stella Davies is another character who steps out of the past on to the page. While the historical record reveals little about Stella, her mother's story is becoming more well known. Her mother was an enslaved Yoruba girl named Aina, who eventually became Queen Victoria's African goddaughter. Aina's captor, King Ghezo of Dahomey (modern-day Benin), made her 'a gift' to Queen Victoria. The British Captain Frederick E. Forbes, who was there to negotiate with the King against his involvement in slave trade, accepted the gift of Aina because he thought her life was at risk. He renamed her Sarah (sometimes written as Sara) Forbes Bonetta and presented her to the Queen, who placed her in the care of guardians and paid for her education. After nearly 170 years, Aina's sad and truly exceptional story is finally finding its well-deserved place in history. Her youngest daughter, Stella Davies, was the ancestor of many remarkable people, including present-day politicians, doctors and scientists.

Hafiz Mohammed Abdul Karim was an Indian attendant to Queen Victoria. He entered her service as a table servant in 1887 for the Golden Jubilee as a display of

British control of India at the time. While the other Indian servants stayed in the background, Abdul Karim shone, quickly claiming the rank of *Munshi* (teacher or clerk) for teaching Queen Victoria to read, write and speak Hindustani. Even his authentic curry recipe pleased Her Majesty, earning a regular spot on the royal luncheon menu.

The queen's lavish favour and motherly affection for the Munshi caused friction with her staff and her family. When Bertie became king, he immediately sent Abdul Karim back to India and ordered the destruction of correspondence and photos, effectively erasing him from royal history. The Munshi's unique and controversial relationship with Queen Victoria was mostly forgotten until 2010, when his descendants in Pakistan released his hidden diaries to the public.

Winnie and her colleagues received training in self-defence from Danish-born instructor Colonel Thomas H. Monstery, author of *Self-Defence for Gentlemen and Ladies: a Nineteenth-century Treatise on Boxing, Kicking, Grappling, and Fencing with the Cane and Quarterstaff.*

Aside from me, the Royal Lapdog and Picco the pony, there ends the list of historical characters.

Many locations in the story are based on real places. Although Madame Tussauds Wax Museum seems modern, it was established in London in the 1830s.

However, it was not a nineteenth-century headquarters for spies – a prime example of the government's woeful lack of imagination. One of its most popular attractions was, and still is, the Chamber of Horrors. It just goes to show humans have strange fascinations. (And to think we pugs are bad-mouthed for sniffing bottoms . . .) The author suspects there were no electric safety lifts and water closets until a few decades later.

Holland House in its heyday was a glittering hub of high society, though not so much in 1889. Sadly, it was mostly destroyed during World War II, but parts of it and its gardens remain.

The Royal Saloons of 1869 and 1874, Queen Victoria's palaces on wheels, are displayed at the National Railway Museum in York. Her Majesty preferred a maximum speed of forty miles per hour, and a signal was fitted so her attendant could communicate with the engine driver. However, the author embellished its capabilities for added humour – at my expense, I might add! (For the record, I enjoy speed – zoomies are my jam, particularly if a lap-nap follows.) Ms Stegert also fudged the train timetables and Channel crossing durations for the sake of the story.

Keppel's Head in Portsmouth has been around since 1779 and continues to this day as a lovely historic hotel. Regarding the tale of my doggy misadventures with His

Royal Highness Prince Bertie and the jolly chaps from the Royal Naval Yard, I am not at liberty to comment. (What happened in the dining room stays in the dining room. I will say we had a *grand* time!)

In 1889 the Eiffel Tower was new – and intended to be temporary! Parisians hated it, demanding its demolition. The apartment atop the tower is real, but back then it was private. (No dogs allowed, *hmph*!) Monsieur Eiffel took only special visitors up there, notably Mr Thomas Edison, whose visit to the Exposition was not in May but rather in August. Café de Flore has been serving people and their dogs since the 1880s, but today's menu may not include petits fours with crystallized violets.

And finally, the inventions. In today's world with mobile phones and the internet, it is hard to appreciate how wondrous the telautograph truly was. While the Weatherby Telautograph Machine is imaginary, the Telautograph of American Elisha Gray is real. According to one historical source, he won the Grand Prix at the 1889 Exposition Universelle with it. Sadly for Gray, telautographs weren't as life-changing as telephones. Nevertheless, until the 1970s they served an important function in banks, hospitals, hotels – and perhaps even kennels and veterinary clinics, who knows?

At the author's request, I conclude with her note that history needn't be stodgy and dull. It can be as fun as a giant board game (or walkies!), as intriguing as a puzzle and as cosy (or chewable!) as favourite slippers. While Ms Stegert admits to occasionally massaging the facts for the purposes of the story, she intends no disrespect to historical persons or dogs. Rather, she hopes her playful approach to history will whet her readers' appetites to dig deeper and discover more . . .

Respectfully and regally,
His Royal Dogginess

Sir Bosco

Knight of the Dog Dish
Chief Canine Companion to Queen Victoria

Acknowledgements

If following my writerly dreams were a board game, I'd probably still be stuck in jail, trying to roll doubles to release myself and inch closer to publication.

Heartfelt thanks to my publisher and the Institution of Engineering and Technology who awarded me the most remarkable Get Out of Jail Free card in the form of the 2021 *Times*/Chicken House/IET 150 Prize. It has been a game changer – if I may extend the pun to its limit. Thank you to the judges: Barry Cunningham, Christopher Edge and Professor Danielle George for seeing the potential in my story.

The whole gang at Chicken House is wonderful. Special thanks to Kesia Lupo and Laura Myers, my editors. Thank you to Jazz, Liv, Laura, Rachel, Emily, Elinor, Esther, Rachel and Barry.

And special thanks to: Lucy Irvine, my agent and champion; historian Hannah Cusworth for the authenticity reading of the manuscript; and designer Micaela Alcaino. How about that magnificent cover?

As the lucky recipient of three mentorships, I'd like to thank: the Australian Society of Authors (ASA) and its Emerging Writers' Mentorship (2017) for pairing me with Catherine Bateson; the Sunshine Coast Council's Regional Arts Development Grant (RADF, 2019) for the mentorship with Dee White; and the 2020 Elizabeth Corbett Mentorship sponsored by the Historical Novel Society Australasia (HNSA), which matched me with Dr Wendy Dunn. These talented authors continue to inspire me.

A shout-out to the librarians in my life, particularly Lara Cain Gray, who unearthed a most helpful resource for me. After months of research and wrestling to pick a suitable nineteenth-century invention for Professor Weatherby, I finally settled on the Telautograph. Unfortunately, I couldn't understand how the thing worked. I tweeted an SOS, and Lara responded with a link to a document that had eluded me. Not only did it clarify the Telautograph's functions, but also one of the footnotes mentioned that Elisha Gray's Telautograph won the Grand Prix at the 1889 Paris Universal Exposition. Somehow, I'd picked the winner! I still get goosebumps at the serendipity. Thanks, Lara. You deserve a cape.

Similar help came from Mandy Downing, secondary teacher and engineer, who checked the STEM elements in an early draft of the story. Any errors that remain are mine.

Thanks to the readers any of my drafts: Natalie, Alison, Lesley and others. My book-buddy Elizabeth Swanson deserves a special mention, as does Rebecca Sheraton and my critique group friends from Brisbane

Write Links. A heartfelt thank you to Susanne Gervay, Jacqui Halpin and all friends in SCBWI Australia East. Lots of love to my darling buddies in the Sunny Coast Writers' Roundtable.

I'm thankful for the support of my mother, three remarkable daughters and my husband. Paul has unflinchingly traipsed through dusty bookstores, crumbling graveyards and historical fashion museums; he's suffered through Victorian documentaries, period dramas and musical theatre; hardest of all, the poor guy regularly tolerates lonely periods of one-sided conversations while I'm hyper-focused and locked in the zone. I hit the jackpot with him.

Call it luck or call it blessing – whatever it is, I'm grateful.